The Woman Outside the Walls

BOOKS BY SUZANNE GOLDRING

My Name is Eva

Burning Island

The Girl Without a Name

The Shut-Away Sisters

The Girl with the Scarlet Ribbon

SUZANNE GOLDRING

The Woman Outside the Walls

bookouture

Published by Bookouture in 2022

An imprint of Storyfire Ltd.
Carmelite House
50 Victoria Embankment
London EC4Y 0DZ

www.bookouture.com

ISBN: 978-1-80314-396-5
eBook ISBN: 978-1-80314-395-8

This book is dedicated to the survivors and the victims of the horrors.
May the truth always survive to be told.

Consider your origins: you were not made
to live as brutes, but to follow virtue and knowledge.

DANTE ALIGHIERI, *DIVINA COMMEDIA*
CANTO 26

Let no guilty man escape if it can be avoided...
No personal consideration should stand in
the way of performing a public duty.

ULYSSES S. GRANT, (E.P. OBERHOLTZER,
*HISTORY OF THE UNITED STATES SINCE
THE CIVIL WAR*)

ONE

Early every morning, for so many years she can't remember, after plumping her pillows and smoothing the ironed edge of the crisp white sheet that folds over her blankets, Anna lowers herself to her knees beside her bed, not for morning prayers, but to check that all is in order. It is harder now than when she first acquired the habit; her joints creak and it is an effort both to dip down to the bedside rug and then to stand up again. If it weren't for her routine of daily exercise, drilled into her from an early age, she wouldn't be able to do it at all. How she'd hated it at first when she was young, all of them with arms wheeling, jumping on the spot in unison; but now she recognises it has kept her body supple, helped her aging muscles stay strong and ready for any eventuality. Mama always said it was her duty to be fit and healthy and now she is glad she listened to her.

Anna steadies herself with one hand on the bedside cabinet and one on the edge of the mattress, then bends down to reach for the small suitcase hidden beneath her bed. At first, her dear, departed husband, Reg, had joked with her about her need to check every single day and indeed even to have it there at all. 'You're safe now, Margie,' he used to say. 'You don't need to worry now.' Then he'd shake his head and smile, saying, 'But if it makes you feel better, it doesn't bother me. You go right ahead.'

And it does make her feel better, safer, in the knowledge that if she suddenly had to leave her home, as she had done before, long, long ago, she'd be ready. The name she acquired when she married Reg has protected her thus far, but she knows that records will exist somewhere in her efficient, highly documented past.

As Anna reaches for the case, she notices the light catching the threads of a cobweb, which she wipes away with the tissue from her cardigan pocket. Reg had always teased her about her obsession with cleanliness. 'That little speck of dust's not going to harm anyone, Margie,' he'd say, laughing. And she would laugh along with him, sharing his amusement at her need for order, yet thinking, *but when you have seen the filth and ordure I have seen, it seems the only way to stem the tide of dirt and disease.* And then he would notice her scratching nervously at the pink scar on her arm, long healed, and he would kiss her on the top of her head and tell her not to fret so.

She opens the small, blue case, a replacement for the scuffed cardboard case she'd brought with her years before. It's not large enough for all her clothes, but just the right size for an unexpected, hasty departure. A vanity case, some would call it, little bigger than a shopping bag, but it can hold all she would need for the moment: her passport, in her married name, a change of underwear, a small towel, a toothbrush, a clean handkerchief, a comb, some folded newspaper cuttings, a notepad and a ballpoint pen. At first, she had kept a small amount of cash in there as well, but currencies have changed so much over the years that it has become pointless. Besides, she still cashes her pension at the post office every week and keeps a small portion in her handbag. She used to keep back a little of the

Family Allowance for such an emergency too, but Reg didn't need to know that.

Every day until now she has looked at the contents of the case and then slid it back under the bed. But not today. It's time, she thinks. Time to leave. For years she has wondered when it would happen. Known that one day They would come. One by one those like her have been found and now They are coming for the rest, including her and the man in yesterday's newspaper. He thought he was doing his duty and so did she. She recognised the young face in the photograph, and the uniform is all too familiar. Flicking open the clasps, Anna adds the latest newspaper cutting to her little collection, then clicks it shut.

She lifts the case onto the bed with shaking hands, to unburden herself so her old, her very old, knees will allow her to stand. There is no reason to wait any longer. The house is spotlessly clean, there are no cats, dogs or budgies to care for. Her dear, departed husband is long dead and her children are on the other side of the world.

A glimmer of dawn is breaking low over the rooftops through the grey clouds and birds are waking. If she goes now, it is unlikely anyone will notice. The milkman perhaps, or the paper boy, maybe an early-morning commuter, but they will be concentrating on the drudgery of their daily routine, not a spry, elderly lady tripping along the pavement to catch a bus or pop to the station.

Downstairs, she enters the kitchen and checks that the kettle is switched off at the socket and she hasn't left a ring burning on the stove after her morning porridge. She learnt to make it the English way for Reg when they first married, although she had tried to persuade him to sample her Bircher muesli with grated apple. She dries her breakfast bowl and teacup and puts them away in the cupboard. All is presentable, all is in order. There is nothing more for her to do. The clock is ticking loudly, telling her she must go now: it's time, it's time, it insists.

She hesitates by the hallstand, wondering for a moment which coat she should wear. It will be cold at this time of the year, so early in the morning, but she rejects her thick green raglan-sleeved loden coat in favour of the reversible hooded raincoat, khaki outside, black inside. She learnt long ago how easy it was to throw someone off the scent with a subtle change of clothes. And instead of a woollen hat, she wraps herself in a large headsquare that can hide her hair or her face or tuck round her neck. Satisfied that she will simply slip away into the grey morning, she steps outside the front door and sniffs the air. The milkman hasn't called yet; the empties are still on the doorstep, and anyway, she would have smelt his cigarette smoke lingering if he had just been.

As she closes and locks the door behind her, a blackbird begins trilling in the privet and her neighbour's ginger cat stares at her, then creeps beneath the hedge. She flips the latch on the garden gate and slips out into the street in her sensible rubber-grip shoes, as silently as the tomcat. Here and there, neighbours are waking; slivers of gold peep between drawn curtains, there is the clink of empty bottles set out on doorsteps, the bark of a dog released into a back garden. But no one sees her go, no one asks where she is going, no one wonders why an old lady is striding purposefully down the street so early this morning.

TWO

LONDON, NOVEMBER 2016

It is nearly lunchtime when Lauren notices the milk bottles. It's not like her, she thinks. She always takes them in first thing. She might be old, but she's still an early bird. But this thought flits out of her mind as she walks past Mrs Wilson's front garden and into her own house, desperate for the loo and thinking of the sandwich she's going to make for her lunch after her long morning at Tumbly Tots Nursery. One day, when Freddie has done his A-levels and set off for university like his big sister, Amy, she'll think about returning to teaching at the infant school, but for now she is satisfied with helping little ones scribble with crayons and learn to share toys.

Scraping fragments of chicken off the bird she had roasted the day before, she finds enough to make a couple of mouthfuls with lettuce and mayonnaise on the remaining slice of brown bread. At least I didn't have to use the crust this time, she thinks, checking her watch to see how long it will be before her weekly supermarket delivery arrives. And at that moment Mrs Wilson pops into her head again. Lauren always adds heavy items to her order for her elderly neighbour, to save her struggling back from the convenience store nearby. 'My dear, are you sure?' Mrs Wilson always says, whenever Lauren knocks and asks her if she needs anything that week. 'It is such a help, potatoes are so heavy. I don't want to trouble you and I vill still make a point of fetching my bread and paper every day. The exercise vill do me good.' Usually, she asks for more sugar and flour, because she is always baking, her tiny frame bustling in her tidy kitchen to produce delicious cakes.

I must stop calling her Mrs Wilson, Lauren tells herself. After all, I've known her for years now, ever since the kids were tiny, and she told me to call her Margie – short for Margarete, she said. She's never explained, but that name sounds foreign and she still has a bit of an accent. Came over here after the war, she said, when she married her husband after he came out the army. I asked her once if she'd ever been back to her home country, thinking she might say something about where she'd come from, but she just said, 'My dear, I came here to start a new life. I don't like to think about the time before I met my husband. My Reg helped me make a new start.'

And I've never been able to push her to say any more than that. I suppose wherever she came from, she must have had a terrible time during the war. It could be Germany or Poland, or even one of those countries further east, definitely not Italy or France though. I can tell that from her accent, even though she's been here for years and her English is very good.

She said her husband was very brave and had fought for his country, so they must have met just as the war ended. Thinking about it, she may have seen some dreadful things, much more dreadful than we've experienced since then. She's said he was her saviour, so I wonder what he saved her from. And now she's all alone, like me, both of us widows. Her husband dead from old age, my Colin taken far too young with cancer. Us widows must stick together, mustn't we.

Lauren bends down to open the washing machine and pulls out T-shirts, pants and socks, all black, all in need of matching partners. There are fewer socks now Colin's gone. Three years next summer and still she misses him, thinks he might text her any moment what he'd like for tea or to say he'll be late home. Maybe that's what did it, she thinks, those long stressful hours as a detective inspector, skipping lunch, snacking on crisps and cola. Couldn't have been good for him. But he loved his job, though he spent far too much time being thorough. 'Can't get caught out not following procedure,' he'd always say to her. 'If we want to nail the felons with a watertight case, we've got to get the paperwork right.'

She throws the underwear into the tumble dryer and pegs the rest out on the line, wondering whether she should bother, as the day looms grey. And then she remembers the milk bottles and decides she shouldn't wait until the grocery delivery arrives. She should check on her very elderly neighbour right away.

Usually, she puts Mrs Wilson's share of the order in a basket and takes it straight round to her, knocking on the back door before letting herself into the kitchen. If she doesn't have to rush back to get the kids' meal, she sometimes stays for a cup of tea with one of Mrs Wilson's cakes or biscuits. She is such a good cook and often says, 'Without your visits, I vouldn't make *käsekuchen*.'

'Oh, you shouldn't make that just for me,' Lauren says, enjoying the baked cheesecake. 'It's far too extravagant.' But she shovels a forkful into her mouth, while Margie only eats a crumbled morsel. Pecks at her food like a little bird, she does. Tiny like a bird, too.

'My Reg, he always said it was his favourite. "Make *käsekuchen* for me, Margie," he was always saying.'

It was unlike any cheesecake Lauren had ever had bought from Tesco or eaten in a coffee shop. There was no sweet, crumbly digestive-biscuit base, just firm but creamy sweetened cheese baked to a pale biscuity colour, with plump golden sultanas hidden in its depths.

'This is delicious,' she'd said the first time she tasted it, the cake melting in her mouth. 'Is it very complicated to make?'

'Not at all. A child could make this. It has simple ingredients: curd cheese, yogurt, sugar, eggs, lemon and vanilla. I learnt it from my mother. My grandmother taught me many recipes too and I also learnt from my best friend Etta's mother. I think of them all when I cook.'

And since then, there had been various kinds of delicious offerings that were wholly new to Lauren: lebkuchen, springerle and stollen. All served on gilt-edged china plates decked with a paper doily, such a contrast to Lauren's collection of chipped, mismatched mugs decorated with cartoon characters, 'Best Mum' and jokey quotes such as 'I'd Rather be Drinking Champagne'.

But as Lauren approaches the house, noticing again that day's delivery of one pint of milk and a large tub of yogurt on the doorstep, she feels apprehensive. The house is always quiet, but today it seems quieter than usual and as she slips round the side path to the kitchen, she wonders what she might be about to find.

The back door is locked and she raps her knuckles on the glass, hoping she might soon see a little figure shuffling through in slippers to let her in. All is still. She peers through the window. The kitchen is tidy, as always, the rug is straight, there are no cups on the draining board, no crumbs on the worktops. She can see through to the front door and breathes a sigh of relief that there isn't a body lying prone in the hallway, at the bottom of the stairs. But what if Mrs Wilson – no, Margie – has fallen in the bathroom? What if she has drowned in the bath, if she still takes baths? Or maybe she has slipped away in her sleep and is even now lying at peace tucked up in her own bed upstairs.

Oh, why am I responsible for this, Lauren frets. But with no nearby relatives, grown-up children on the other side of the world, she knows what she has to do. She races back to her house to find the spare key her neighbour gave her. Ages ago it had been. 'Just in case,' Margie had said. 'For my peace of mind. You may never have to use it.'

Minutes later, rummaging in the kitchen drawer, Lauren curses. 'Where is the bloody thing?' She pushes aside dusty elastic bands, coiled pieces of string, bottle-stoppers and novelty corncob skewers, along with rusty peelers, an apple corer and a meat thermometer she never uses. At last she finds it, a Yale key identified by a curled and slightly torn label marked 'Wilson'. She checks her watch and sighs. Twenty minutes till her delivery is due to arrive. She must hurry.

Before unlocking her neighbour's front door, Lauren knocks and waits. Then she bends down and calls out through the letter box: 'Mrs Wilson? Margie? Are you there? Are you all right?'

The house is quiet, holding its breath, so she inserts the key and opens the door. Calling again, she hovers on the doormat, wiping her feet before stepping inside this perfectly clean home, where every surface gleams, dust-free, scented with polish and bleach. No pills of fluff under furniture here, no cobwebs in corners, no grubby windows. Margie still does all her own housework, though she has a man to help in the garden, cutting grass and trimming hedges. Someone Reg found down the pub, she once said.

Lauren peers into the sitting room at the front of the house. The cushions on the three-piece suite are plumped, crease-free, the clock on the mantelpiece ticks and the mirror over the fireplace reflects the lowering light outside. Better hurry, Lauren thinks. The groceries will be here soon.

She runs up the stairs, calling out as she goes. 'Are you all right, Margie? Is something wrong?' The bathroom sparkles with cleanliness, the two smallest bedrooms display folded bedding on the clean, protected mattresses and the master bedroom with its bay window is empty. The double bed is neatly made, the pillow slips and top sheet wrinkle-free, unlike Lauren's, which have never seen a steam iron. The polished dressing table with its three-panelled mirror reflects her crumpled sweatshirt and faded jeans.

Frowning with concern, she runs back downstairs and looks again in the kitchen. She knows Margie isn't lying with her head in the gas oven – she had a clear view of the room through the back door – but she feels she has to check all the same. Anyway, everyone knows you can't gas yourself these days. And she can't resist opening a couple of the cupboards for clues. But the shelves are so well stocked with groceries, she thinks her neighbour is better prepared for flood and famine than she'll ever be. This is silly, she tells herself. She may be old, but that doesn't mean to say she can't go out on her own if she wants to. Why on earth am I getting in such a state?

But Margie never goes anywhere other than the church and the corner shop. Since she lost her husband, who was somewhat older than her, her life has been largely reduced to these two destinations. Maybe she had to see the doctor? But she must have been out all day. Hospital then, that must be it. Everyone knows how long that can take.

Lauren leaves the house and looks down at the milk still on the doorstep. Should she take it in? No, the day is cold enough. It will be fine till Margie returns.

THREE

HAMBURG, APRIL 1945

As Anna surveyed the crushed, blackened landscape of the once-proud city, she knew it hadn't been wise to return to the place of her birth. It was as if the ogres of childhood folk tales and nightmares had roasted the entire structure over a crackling fire then eaten each and every one of its residents as far as the eye could see. Why hadn't the horrors she had endured on her long walk from the East prepared her for this terrible, hopeless sight?

She had guessed all along that Hamburg would be unrecognisable after the onslaught from British planes nearly two years before. Even though the government and the German press had downplayed earlier bombing raids on other cities, the terrible destruction of her home town and the flood of refugees had reached her ears, even so far to the east. So, what possible chance was there that anyone she knew might still be alive? She hadn't heard a word from her parents since before that time of devastation and knew she should expect the worst.

And even now, although many had already left the ruins soon after the fires, despondent Hamburg citizens were still leaving their once-thriving, industrious city. As Anna tramped towards her family home, others were trudging along the road too, their weary, hollow faces streaked with soot, their backs bent under what little they had managed to salvage.

She noticed very few young, able men among the stream of hunched and ragged refugees. Most were tired women, traumatised children, frail crones and stooped grandfathers. They looked less well fed than the villagers she had seen on her trek through the countryside, where old men and women ploughed the fields with the help of a cow in place of the horse that had long been taken to feed the troops. She had begged for bread for her journey and was nearly persuaded to stay where there was food to spare, but she had to know, she had to see for herself and find out whether her parents were still alive.

Anna stopped on the road to rest for a moment and gazed upon the flattened city, where skeletal walls jutting here and there were the only clues to the once-prosperous businesses and bustling streets. She was as footsore as the other travellers on the road. She was tired and hungry and her blistered arm throbbed and she longed to plunge it into cool water and drink her fill.

'There's no point in going any further,' said a mother with a fractious baby on her hip, glancing at this young woman with nothing but the shabby clothes she was wearing. 'Everyone's leaving, apart from the dead. Hundreds of them still buried under the ruins after all this time. It's a city of rats and flies now.'

An elderly man joined in her weary moan, saying, 'Those arrogant pigs, it's all their fault. Damn Nazis. I don't care who hears me. They started this. We never wanted another war, we never asked for our lives and homes to be destroyed.'

But even as she encountered the sad, slow-moving trail of broken homeless and heard of their sorrows, Anna knew she had to press on. She felt she had to find out if there was a slight chance Mama had survived and was still at home, stirring her potato soup with chunks of succulent sausage on the stove, while Papa was salvaging firewood from the streets. Two years before, straight after Easter, she had been so glad to leave them, longing for independence, an income and accommodation of her own, desperate to escape their restrictions and admonitions, but now she wished she could see them again.

And maybe she could still hope, she thought. Maybe she would find their apartment was untouched, her bed still made, waiting for her to climb beneath the quilt Mutti had stitched for her. And on her pillow, she'd find her precious doll, Claudia, in her blue dirndl dress, with her porcelain face cracked but smiling. Then Papa would wind up the tin horse and cart he had bought for her one Christmas when she was small and they'd have games on the threadbare rug, while Mama told them to stop behaving like children, even as she smiled and laughed with them.

But as she grew closer and could see the extent of the destruction, Anna began to despair. Although she could see the towering spire of the renowned Nikolaikirche, the tallest structure in the whole of Hamburg, little else remained of the once-grand church. Twisted girders and the fingers of solitary chimneys traced that devastating flight path of the British bombers, metal radiators dangled from walls and hinted at what had previously housed families and businesses in warmth and safety.

Women, older children and a few men barely gave her a glance as they worked in the ruins, stacking bricks, in a hopeful sign that rebuilding could begin once the war was definitely over. But the streets were barely recognisable, and when she did finally discover a familiar stretch, she gulped back tears as she realised this had been the site of the well-stocked Karst department store, where Mama had bought threads, ribbons and fabric for her dressmaking business, which supplemented the family's income.

Here and there grey spirals of smoke curled up from below the ground, making her think at first that the city was still smouldering from the inferno caused by the rainstorm of incendiary bombs, but then she realised that this was a sign of life. The survivors of the Hamburg hell had retreated underground and were warming themselves, boiling water and attempting to cook on stoves and fires in cellars beneath the streets. But she couldn't detect any tempting aromas of wholesome soups and stews, just the overpowering stench of death, decomposition, damp and choking smoke.

At nearly every turn in the ruined streets, Anna saw pitiful but optimistic messages chalked on ruined walls, pleas for loved ones to return, to find their families, words of hope that they would be reunited. 'Tante Hilde has taken the children to Blankenese' and 'Where are you, Inge? We are in Flottbek'. And everywhere, the hopeful proclamation written in chalk on the remains of bombed-out homes, 'Wir leben', a message to anyone who might come searching that the former occupants had survived and were still living somewhere in this rubble-filled city.

But had they ever found each other again? Those poignant messages, written within days of the bombing in the summer of 1943, still stood as a painful reminder of how many families had been destroyed, never to meet again.

Eventually, by following a trail of shattered landmarks, Anna came to what she thought must be the street where she had last visited her parents, where she had grown up. That was so long ago, before everything changed, before she went away at the age of eighteen in the early spring of 1943. If she had stayed until the summer, she too might have perished in the raging fire-balls and the horror.

But hard as she looked at the street, trying to find a doorstep, a lintel or a wall that she recognised, it was not the same. All was broken, all was crushed. And there wasn't even a tell-tale plume of smoke to hint that life still existed here.

She was standing in the rubble-strewn street, wondering where to go next, thinking there must be a chance that her parents might have escaped on that terrible night, when she heard a voice. 'You won't find anyone here still; if they didn't escape, they burned to death.'

Anna turned to see a thin teenage girl, a little shorter than her, hair hidden beneath a tightly wrapped black scarf, in a grey coat several sizes too large for her that reached down to her bare ankles. 'Everyone in this street died. They're all gone.'

'But you're still here. Are you on your own?'

The girl took a moment to reply; her eyes showed how wary she was of strangers. 'No, there's a few of us. We can manage, just about, but the little ones aren't much help.'

Anna studied this survivor with interest. Perhaps the girl could help her. 'I came here hoping I might find my parents, but it looks fruitless.'

The girl shrugged, the coat nearly falling from her thin shoulders, the cuffs slipping down over her grubby hands. 'No one's left round here. Only the ones who ran to the parks and the canals made it. And afterwards many were taken away to other towns that hadn't been bombed.'

Anna shook her head and said, 'Then I don't know what I'm going to do. I have no money, no food and nowhere to go.'

'What's your name?'

'Why do you want to know?' Anna was hesitant. Could she trust this waif?

'I'm Ursula. Come with me and I'll take you to meet the rest of us.'

Anna felt wary, but what choice did she have? She didn't want to retrace her steps and with unsettled refugees roaming the countryside, along with vengeful former prisoners and soldiers, how could she find anywhere safe? And although it was spring, the nights were still cold. Perhaps she would be better off finding out how this girl was managing to survive.

Should she give her real name or was this her chance to start again? She didn't have any papers to identify her, so she grasped the opportunity. The name of her childhood friend came to mind. 'My name is Margarete,' she said, offering her equally grubby hand. 'You can call me Etta.' There was no need for a last name this time, she thought. She wouldn't be completing any documents to prove her identity.

As they walked through the crumbling streets of the city, she listened to Ursula telling her of the 'night of hell' as she called it. 'We were sheltering in the basement of our house in Hammerbrook. We heard the sirens howling and then the planes came over and dropped the bombs. The ceiling was shaking and then our mother said we had to get out right away, as the house was on fire. We all rushed out and every house in the street was filled with flames. Mama made us stand in the middle of the road while she rushed back to fetch her sewing machine, because that was how she made a living. But then there was a sudden ball of fire and in seconds she was gone.'

At that point, Ursula wiped her cheek with her sleeve, then continued, 'Most of our neighbours died that night too. It was just me, my younger brother Hermann and my little sister Ingrid. We were the only ones left.'

'What about others in the city?'

Ursula waved the long coat sleeves, dangling down to her fingertips, to show their escape route. 'Some of us ran to the parks and open spaces. You had to get away really fast. Windows exploded, flames were racing along the streets. The tar on the roads melted. We saw people dying all around us, burned to death. But we didn't know who to trust. It was safer not to. We can look after ourselves.'

Anna looked at this confident girl, her head held high, though her clothes were ill-fitting and the shoes on her bare feet were scuffed and worn. 'There must have been some help for orphans. Didn't anyone try to take care of you?'

'We aren't orphans,' Ursula said in a fierce tone. 'We are the Ausgebombten Gang and I am in charge of all of them. The authorities tried to send us out into the country and separated us, but we ran away because we have to be together. Anyway, we are staying here. We are waiting for our father. We know he will come back to us just as soon as he can.'

'All of them? I thought you said it was just you, with your brother and sister?'

'You'll see. We're nearly there now. Maybe the others have been lucky today. If not, we'll have to see what we can scrounge tonight.'

Ursula stopped by a broken wall where some steps had been cleared, leading to a dark opening, beyond which smoke spiralled up and out into the fresh air. She looked back at Anna, eyeing her up in a knowing way. 'You're really quite pretty. You could be useful. They might like you.'

FOUR

HAMBURG, 1929

Once upon a time, Anna had had a best friend. Her name was Margarete Löwenthal, but her family and friends always called her Etta, just as Anna's name was also shortened from Annaliese. Since they were only four years old, the two girls had played with their dolls in the courtyard of their building when the weather was fine and on the floor in Etta's apartment when it was raining or cold. They continued to play together every day when they weren't in school, but never at the end of the week, as Etta's family were always busy on a Friday and Saturday and Anna had to attend church with her parents on Sunday. That only left four days in the week for playing.

They lay on the threadbare carpet, its pattern of faded blue, red and orange triangles still visible, forming a dance floor for their twirling dolls. 'Klara wants to dance the mazurka,' Etta said, making her figure leap with outspread legs.

'That's silly,' said Anna, making her doll stand on one leg on tippy-toe and pirouette. 'Claudia is doing ballet, look.'

The girls moved on from animating their dolls to imagining that they too were dancing on the worn carpet, each trying to outdo the other with energetic moves, their jumps thumping on the floor and rattling the good china stacked in the glazed cabinet until Etta's mother would call to them, 'Girls, girls, the rug is worn enough already. Sit down and play quietly and I'll give you each a piece of challah.' Anna loved the soft white bread, so sweet and chewy and so different to the black bread her own mother favoured. When Anna asked why they couldn't have this plaited bread at home, Mama's mouth turned down in disapproval and she said, 'We don't eat that kind of bread.'

When Etta turned eight, about two months before Anna, she had a party for five of her friends. Anna knew all the girls invited, but had not seen them in school for quite some time. 'Don't you go to school any more?' she asked. 'Don't you have to do your lessons?' The little girls answered, 'Yes, we do, but we have our own school now. Your school doesn't want us to go there nowadays and we don't like it when the boys call us names.'

But Anna didn't worry for long about whether they were or weren't still being taught, as the highlight of the party was a special cake in the shape of a hedgehog. She'd never seen an *Igel* cake before. The sponge and cream were flavoured with coffee and chocolate and the cake was studded with slivers of almonds. All the girls pretended that the nuts were sharp spikes like a real hedgehog, before the cake was cut and served on Mrs Löwenthal's best porcelain plates with green and gold frilled rims.

'Please can I have a birthday party?' Anna asked her mother. 'And can I have an *Igel* cake too, like Etta?'

Mama was not sympathetic. 'We haven't got money to waste on parties. You'll have to make do with my *käsekuchen*. It's much better for you than all that sweet stuff. I'm surprised that family can afford to throw parties these days, the way things are. You'd have thought they'd have other matters to worry about. Anyway, this year your birthday is on a Saturday and you know Etta is never allowed out on a Saturday.'

Etta's father was a watchmaker – or had been. Now he

mostly just mended watches and clocks. And Anna's father mended shoes in a dusty workshop, patching and soling from a pile all day long. They were both the same, the fathers, mending the broken and the tired, weren't they?

Papa was more willing to listen to Anna's pleas, saying, 'If it was up to me, *Liebchen*, you could have lots of parties and all the cakes you desire, but your mama is in charge here, like I'm in charge of my workshop. She manages the house very well on the little I bring home and I'm not going to interfere with her house-keeping.' He gave her a bristly kiss and said he would try to bring his little Schatz a special gift on her birthday.

'Will you go to the school your other friends go to now?' Anna asked Etta soon after the party.

The little girl shook her glossy brown hair, only a little darker than Anna's. 'No, my parents want me to stay at your school.'

'That's good, then we can still walk there together and sit beside each other.' But none of the other children wanted to sit with Etta or play with her and Anna gradually became aware that her best friend was being shunned by her schoolmates. The other girls mostly ignored her, but some of the boys, including a strong, bold boy called Günther, teased Etta and shouted at her.

One day, Anna found her crying, her knees grazed, the strap of her schoolbag broken. She put her arm round her friend and a boy walking past shouted, 'Jew lover!' Anna was shocked. This was her friend, who she'd known since she was a small child; she was Etta, her best friend.

'They'll hurt you too if you're friends with me,' Etta said in a trembling voice. 'You should be careful.'

'I don't care,' Anna said, continuing to hug her. But maybe inside she did, for slowly, oh so slowly, she realised she was becoming aware of the whispering behind her back that grew louder until they were open taunts thrown whenever she was near Etta. They continued to meet in the seclusion of Etta's home, no longer accompanied by dolls but by card games and books. Anna loved the traditional tales of the Brothers Grimm and they both agreed that the best one was Hansel and Gretel. They giggled with horrified laughter at the moment when the witch in the gingerbread house is pushed into the oven where she had planned to cook the two children, once she had fattened them up for her table.

By the time they were both thirteen, Anna no longer sat next to her friend in class or allowed herself to be seen walking with her in the street. They still laughed together in private, but never in public. Then, that November, Anna's mother made it clear that she didn't want her daughter to visit Etta at home either. 'They're trouble, that family so you're to stay away from them, do you hear me?'

Anna couldn't understand why they had to stop being friends completely. Even if everyone else at school didn't like Etta, Anna still did. But Papa tried to explain a little to her the night Etta's father staggered back to the apartment block out of breath, bloodied and bruised, his clothes torn. '*Liebchen*, their kind is very unpopular in these times. No one will buy from them or trade with them.'

The next day she found Etta sitting on the stairs outside her front door, crying. 'Papa's shop has been smashed,' she said. 'And others have been set on fire. His business is ruined.'

Anna was alarmed. Where would people go now if they had watches and clocks in need of repair? And would her father's business be destroyed too? But Papa put her straight, saying, 'We won't get in trouble as long as we do what the Party asks of us. We'll keep quiet and hope this unrest will soon pass.'

But it didn't, did it? The violence of Kristallnacht grew like a virus, spreading from city to city, town to town. And one day a week later Etta didn't attend school. Anna knocked on her door at the end of the day and there was no answer. She went back several times that evening and again over the next few days until finally a neighbour poked her head out of the apartment across the landing, saying, 'You can stop all your banging. There's no point in knocking for them at all hours. They've all gone.'

Gone? Without even saying goodbye? Etta, her friend of ten years, gone without saying why? 'Where have they gone? Did they say?'

The neighbour pulled a face. 'Paris, the parents said. All right for some, isn't it? Well, that type's always got an eye for the high life and the money, I say.'

Anna's despondent steps echoed in the stairwell as she trudged down to her parents' apartment. Etta's family hadn't seemed rich to her. Her clothes weren't extravagant and there was that threadbare carpet, for a start. She was sad to have lost her best friend, but maybe now the other girls in her class would like her more and Günther and his gang of boys wouldn't call her names.

DIE ZWEI REISENDEN

THE TWO TRAVELLERS

The shoemaker said, 'I'll give you
a piece of bread, but in payment,
I will have to cut out one of your eyes.'

FIVE

HAMBURG, APRIL 1945

Anna followed Ursula down the steps and ducked beneath a low, charred lintel into a dingy, dark cellar. The combined smell of smoke and unwashed bodies was not as bad as she had experienced before in that place where The Others suffered.

As her eyes grew accustomed to the hazy dimness, lit only by the glow of a stove and a broken upper window, she saw an older girl lying on one of the stained mattresses. Her arms cradled a bulging belly beneath her partially unbuttoned dress and she'd flung a coat over her legs in place of a blanket. Was this why Ursula thought she might be helpful? Anna knew only too well what it meant to give birth, but she had also seen too much of the terror and horror of it in recent years. She tried to shut away those images of tiny wizened beings slithering out of bodies that could not sustain them or be allowed to care for them. Some lived for moments, others were taken away and, it was rumoured, met their ends soon after their first days on Earth.

And then she realised the cellar was also home to two other children, a boy and a girl of six or seven, huddled by the glowing stove. They sprang to their feet and rushed to hug Ursula, shouting, 'Mama, Mama, we're hungry. What have you got for us?' It was clear that an attempt had been made to keep them fairly clean and well-dressed. Their knees and hands were grubby, but the girl's hair had been combed and twisted into pigtails tied with scraps of ribbon and the boy wore a long sweater over his shorts, the sleeves folded back so his hands could just be seen.

'Stefan, Therese, wait a moment, you must be polite and say hello to Etta. She is our guest and may come to live with us, if you are well-behaved.' Ursula dug deep in her pockets and gave them each a knob of sugar. 'More later,' she said. 'Now go outside and play.'

As they ran off, she bent down to the pregnant girl and kissed her on the forehead. 'I've brought a new friend for us, Gertrud. Etta will help us until you are able to work again.'

Gertrud turned her head to look at the newcomer and gave a faint smile. 'I was only resting for a moment. I can do the cooking again tonight.'

'If we have anything to cook,' Ursula said. 'I haven't had any luck so far. Have Hermann and Ingrid not come back yet? I hope they are being careful.'

'Why don't you take your new friend Etta out with you? She'll need to eat if she's to start work soon.' Gertrud heaved herself to her knees, then grabbed Ursula's hand to get to her feet. 'I can manage to fetch water from the street standpipe and look out for the children. You get off and see what you can find for us.'

'Where are we going?' Anna asked, as she followed Ursula back up the steps.

'Down to the south. As far away from the harbour as possible. We might have more luck, but there will be others sniffing around as well.'

And it dawned on Anna that they were all scavengers, city rats, surviving on whatever the bombs and the fires hadn't destroyed. It wasn't looting as such, it was sheer desperation that was driving them and everyone else in the city to crawl through the shells of buildings, homes and shops, risking their lives in the broken ruins for scraps of food, clothing and fuel that might be buried alongside the remaining decomposed bodies.

'Haven't the city authorities managed to organise supplies for everyone? They used to be so efficient.' Anna remembered the regimented systems in place earlier in the war, before she left Hamburg.

'Huh, they're no help,' Ursula said with a dismissive shake of her head. 'They just want us to leave the city and go to an orphanage or foster homes. And there's no way we're doing that. How would our father find us then?'

And Anna felt a twinge of admiration for this plucky girl, faced with choosing between regular meals if she and her siblings succumbed to civic administration, or staying where their remaining parent might one day find them. She could not have been much more than sixteen at the most, only four years younger than Anna.

'The other day I found herrings, salted in a barrel. We ate those with pickled gherkins. Gertrud said it gave her stomach ache and she complained it was going to make the baby come too soon, but she was all right the next day.' Ursula gave a whoop of laughter and said, 'That baby had better hurry up and come. We won't get any cigarettes or chocolate when the Allies arrive, as long as she's lounging around in bed and not working.'

Anna was puzzling over this remark when Ursula suddenly dived into a derelict shop, shouting, 'In here, Etta. It used to be a grocers.' Following her, she found the interior littered with debris and broken glass, the shelves and counters smashed. Ursula kicked the mess on the floor aside as she made her way through to the back of the abandoned shop. 'There should be a storeroom here somewhere. Through a door perhaps.' She examined all the walls, hung with posters and crippled shelves, then she cleared a space in the litter on the floorboards and pointed down to a trapdoor. 'This looks promising. Give me a hand.'

Together they bent over the heavy, boarded flap, searching for a way to open it. Anna brushed splinters and fragments of glass aside with the cuff of her coat, uncovering a large iron handle set into the wood. They both slipped their fingers into the heavy ring and heaved, and as it opened they could see a short flight of wooden steps down into a black basement.

'You wait up here and I'll see what's down there, then pass stuff up to you,' Ursula said once the door was open. 'Keep a lookout and don't let anyone else in.' She slipped down the narrow steps and into the dark void, then gave a triumphant shout. 'There's loads of things down here. We'll take what we can carry for now.'

She passed a series of canned goods up to Anna and after a few minutes, they had a small pile of tins and a bag of rice. 'Hide the cans in your pockets, Etta,' Ursula said, stuffing her finds inside her voluminous, long coat. 'You don't want anyone else knowing we've found a great stack of supplies.'

Anna filled her pockets too, while Ursula kicked debris back over the trapdoor till it was hidden and tucked the bag of rice inside her coat, under her armpit, hugging it tight to her skinny frame. 'If we can get some meat, we'll be able to have *eintopf* tonight.'

Anna hadn't heard that word for a long time, but the mention of that dish immediately reminded her of her mother's efforts to make a nourishing brothy stew out of scraps and root vegetables on *Eintopfsonntag*. Every family in the country was encouraged to give the money they saved by sacrificing their Sunday roast dinners to the Winterhilfswerk charity, to help feed and clothe veterans and the poor through the winter months. How Mama had hated that pious campaign, created by the so-called noble Party. It was not so much the limitations imposed on her cooking she minded as the demands on her housekeeping purse when she was required to hand over her donation.

'But where will we find some meat for the stew? Surely there aren't any butchers' shops still open here, are there?'

'Don't ask,' Ursula said, laughing. 'As long as it fills our stomachs, who cares what it is or where it came from?'

'So shall we come back here tomorrow and collect more of the goods from the basement?' Anna glanced around the damaged street as they left the shop, wondering if they'd been spotted by scavengers hiding in the ruins nearby, ready to dive into the cellar as soon as they left with their plunder.

'Maybe, if it's quiet. We need to keep this to ourselves and not draw attention to it. If we come here too often we might be noticed and people will soon find out we've discovered a secret supply. Best to keep quiet about it. There's enough down there to keep us going for quite a bit if we're careful.'

'Could you see anything else worth taking, down there in the cellar?'

'It was hard to tell in the dark. I'll bring a lamp next time. But I think there could be cooking oil, which we could really do with.'

They began trudging back towards the other side of town, to their cellar, where the ill-assorted family had gathered around the stove and Gertrud was stirring a large pan, her free hand rubbing her aching back. Steam carried the smell of savoury cooking into the air and Anna began to feel very hungry after her day of walking around the city. The crust she'd had for breakfast, saved from the little she'd bought the previous day, seemed a long time ago, but she knew she'd fared better than many that day.

She wondered if she would be allowed to share in their supper as she had not yet contributed anything to the meal, but

Ursula was already ahead of her, calling out to her brother and sister, 'This is Etta. She's joining us for dinner.' She produced the bag of rice with a flourish and began emptying her pockets, so Anna did the same. 'We were in luck today and with the help of our new friend we have been able to bring all of this back.' She stacked the cans of vegetables on a brick shelf near the stove.

'Welcome, Etta. I'm Hermann and this is my younger sister Ingrid.' A gangly teenage boy, his thin cheeks scarred with angry red pockmarks, stood and offered his hand. 'We did well today too. We found another mattress and we brought back meat for the *eintopf* tonight.'

'But we still couldn't find any potatoes,' Ingrid said with a frown. 'We haven't had any for ever so long.'

'Never mind, we'll still eat well tonight,' Gertrud said, opening the bag of rice and throwing a couple of handfuls in the pot. 'This will fill us up and give us the strength to face another day tomorrow.'

SIX

LONDON, NOVEMBER 2016

Not far from home, just round the corner near the bus stop, Anna falls. She has stepped to one side to avoid the twiggy, unpruned growth of a privet when a cyclist hurtles past her along the road in the just-before-morning gloom. She doesn't see or hear him approaching and although his wheel only catches the edge of her little case, it is enough to tip her off-balance.

He screeches to a halt. 'Oh, bloody hell! Are you okay?' He throws his bike down and bends down to help her up. 'I'm so sorry, I simply didn't see you there.'

I should have turned the raincoat the other way round, Anna thinks. Black, how stupid of me. Of course he couldn't see me. She gives him her hands and he pulls her to her feet. She is shaken, but she doesn't seem to be badly hurt. She landed on her case, luckily, so she didn't hit the stone kerb with her hip.

'Would you like me to take you somewhere? Call an ambulance? I've got a phone, I can call your family, or a neighbour?'

He has taken off his helmet, so she can see his face, see how distressed he is by the accident. 'I don't think I'm hurt. I'm just a little shaken. Please don't vorry yourself. Maybe I should just sit down for a little while. I'm sure I'll feel better in a minute.'

'Here, let me help you to the seat in the bus stop. Are you sure you don't want me to call you an ambulance?'

He escorts her in slow steps to the bench, one arm round her shoulders, the other carrying her case. He helps her to sit, places the case beside her, and she clasps the handle. Thank goodness it didn't spill open, throwing her underwear into the road. She feels her knee stinging and looks down. Her stocking is torn and her skin is grazed, but it isn't trickling blood, it isn't broken; she knows she will live, unlike The Others. They are all long gone, while she is forced to face her memories every day. 'I'll be fine now,' she says. 'I'll wait here for the bus.'

'If you're really certain. And again, I'm so sorry I made you fall.' He stands back, looking at her, and she knows he is keen to escape, to get to his workplace, before she changes her mind. Then he walks backwards a few steps, observing her, before running to his bike and speeding away, the red light on the back wheel flickering.

Anna closes her eyes and prepares to wait. She knows the buses are quite frequent and that soon that day's school-children, commuters and shoppers will begin to queue at the stop, will jostle her on the bench, will notice her sitting there with her case on her knees. Just wait a little longer, she tells herself. Wait till your heart is steadier, till it's fully daylight, so your black coat won't hide you in the dark, then you can go. But go where? The station? And beyond that?

After half an hour, maybe more, she decides to leave the safety of the bus shelter. She walks less steadily than when she had first set out, but she knows she isn't injured, just a little shaken. She wants to walk to the station, where she can take a train to Waterloo. And from there she could go anywhere she liked. Down to the coast perhaps, or deep into Dorset. Or Kent maybe and then a ferry to the continent, far away, where no one will find her.

But she can't manage to walk that far and after a few uncertain, shaky yards, she stops to rest on a picnic table bench outside The Crown, where Reg once liked to sup a pint and gossip with old chums, long departed. I'll just stop here for a while, she decides. Until the morning rush is over, then I'll go back and wait for a bus. She hopes that Bob, who mows her lawn and trims her hedges, will be gardening elsewhere and not calling in for an early drink.

Much, much later, Anna is still waiting at the bus stop. How long she's been here, she cannot tell, but the sun has set and bright neon flares from the street lamps. Which bus is she meant to take? Does she want to go to the station or further? She thinks she knew where she wanted to go when she left the house earlier that day, but now she can't remember. She's sure she knew at first, but she's been sitting here so long, she no longer knows. Why did she want to leave home anyway? What made her come out of the house today? People come and go, hopping on and off buses, laden with shopping bags, struggling with toddlers and buggies. They all know where they are going and rush past her, barely noticing the old lady on the bench clutching a case on her knees.

You don't have to be here, it is not so bad at home, Anna tells herself. You are warm, safe and well fed. Think of all those times when you had none of those things. All those years ago in the terrible years, when you had no one. When one by one they all disappeared. Think what your mama would have said, 'Be a good Deutscher Mädel. Be strong.' Or as Reg said many times, 'Come on, old girl, buck up. You've got me to look after you now, Margie.'

That framed photograph of him in his uniform comes to mind. He was much older than most of the recruits; that was why he was so ready to marry and settle down once it was all over. 'I've seen enough of the world to last me a lifetime,

Margie,' he would say. 'Now all I want is to settle down and make a home and a family.' And he'd squeeze her tight, hugging her tiny waist; so small she was, he could pick her up in his arms and carry her over the threshold.

He did that every time they moved, swooping her up as if she was a new bride, even when they finally moved into the semi-detached, pebble-dashed house in Barnes where she still lives. They only had a couple of rented rooms to start with, in a dirty part of London near the smut and smog of Paddington station. When she first arrived after the war, she'd thought it was wonderful, compared to the conditions she'd endured in the Hamburg ruins, but the shared bathroom was never clean; their rooms had a hissing gas ring and a tiny sink, which she preferred using to wash her body as well as her pants and stockings. When the launderette opened in Queensway, she was one of the first there, desperate to wash the smell of other tenants' fried onions and boiled cabbage out of her bedding and clothes.

'Why are you always washing and scrubbing, Margie?' Reg used to say. 'I like a clean house, you know I do, but you don't have to go mad, my dear.'

But what did he know? What did he really know about the filth, the stench that permeated every pore? He'd seen it of course, they all had. Some of them had been taken there in the early days, others had seen the newsreels. No amount of soap and water could ever cleanse those memories. That's why even now, even though she is in her early nineties, she has to scrub her nails clean, polish every stick of furniture, sweep every inch of floor and constantly wash clothes and linen. You could never be too clean, but being dirty is another matter. Disease and death are the consequence of dirt.

Anna shakes herself. Too much thinking. Too much dwelling on the past. Whenever she did this while Reg was still alive, he'd say, 'Snap out of it, old girl. You're at it again. The potatoes are going to boil dry if you carry on like this.' And she'd pull herself together, grab the kettle and top up the water in the pan, or lay down the spoon that had endlessly stirred the soup as if she was back there in the cellar, and then she'd try to laugh to convince him she was happy with him.

But now he is no longer here. Fifteen years she's been alone. She always knew she would be, him being so much older than her. But all the same it feels as if he went far too soon. Such a gentle, kind man, the kindest man she'd ever known. Every Friday when he was still teaching at the boys' school, he'd bring her a bunch of flowers from the stall near Hammersmith tube station. And when he'd retired, he still often used to give her flowers or sometimes a box of chocolates. 'Cos I treasure you, my little Margie, plucked from the ruins, just for me.'

He was a good father too, always ready to play with the children while she fretted over another smear of mud or sprinkling of dust. Perhaps that's why they left in the end, she thought. Peter and Susan both went far away, seeking the warmth of another climate, warmer than she could give them. A climate where they could make their own rules and not see her frown over a crumpled wet towel, an unmade bed or a stained tablecloth. She just couldn't help herself; the need to constantly clean and tidy was ingrained.

She could remember the first time she'd ever seen Reg. It was the autumn of 1945 and life was so hard then. But those soldiers out in Bahrenfeld didn't know how lucky they were in their warm NAAFI canteen, supping pints of cheap beer as they celebrated their victory and their imminent return to their homeland. And the lines of hungry lost people of all nations, but mostly Poles, queued for the magic cards that began the restoration of their identity and their health and promised them shelter and food.

Reg wasn't one of the clerks registering the queues of displaced people, he was supervising the process of registration, there to ensure there was no trouble, but he told her he saw the haunted eyes and the numbers inked onto their wasted arms. She remembered what he told her about the process of registering. 'The official procedure required them to give their name and home address, but do you know, sometimes when the officer asked them, they couldn't remember. I saw one woman start to cry. She said she'd been a number for so long she no longer knew who she was or where she'd lived. I can tell you, Margie, that pained me and that's why I will never ask you questions about your past. If you ever want to tell me anything, I'll listen with an open mind. But I will never insist.'

Anna can imagine he really did feel the pain of the displaced refugees. He was soft like that. She opens her eyes to see the number 533 leaving the stop. Is that the bus she needs? She doesn't know. Maybe if she waits a little longer she'll be able to remember.

SEVEN

HAMBURG, APRIL 1945

Little was said while the Ausgebombten Gang ate their one-pot meal. The only sounds were the scraping of spoons on the metal bowls and hungry slurps as they supped the golden broth. Anna recognised beans, onion and rice, but the pale shreds of meat, though tasty, were not recognisable. When they had finished every morsel, Ingrid took the two younger children outside to rinse the bowls and spoons with water fetched from the street pump.

Gertrud saw Anna looking and said, 'We have to stay healthy and clean, Etta. It is not easy with so little water but our greatest fear is typhus. It spreads so quickly.'

Anna felt a thump in her stomach. Not from the food she had just consumed, but from the memory that lurched into her mind, taking her back to that awful place. She could hear the weakening coughs, see the purple rashes that signalled the imminent approach of death. 'You are right to be cautious,' she said. 'I have seen the speed of its path of destruction.' She tried to will herself to blot out the humiliating sight of uncontrollable human waste fouling clothes and dripping from the tiers of bunks.

'Etta? Where were you before you came here?' Hermann was staring at her curiously.

Anna hesitated, placing a protective hand over her sore arm. Should she say? Or was it too early? She didn't know where their loyalties lay. Perhaps it was better not to tell them yet. Or maybe never. 'Much further east,' she said.

'Oh, one of those places,' he said. 'Then you're lucky to be alive at all. After the bombing, they sent prisoners from the Neuengamme camp not far from here to help clear up the streets. They looked so desperate and hungry. I saw one take his chance to escape. He stole some clothes from a bombed-out house to cover his striped uniform, then he slipped away from the lazy guards.'

Good for him, Anna thought. He might not have got far, but at least he tried, and maybe that's one more that's still alive.

'But the prisoners weren't much use cleaning up the streets,' Gertrud said. 'They could barely lift a shovel, let alone heavy rubble.'

'Because they weren't strong,' Ursula said. 'They were dreadfully thin and probably brought typhus with them as well.'

Anna knew exactly who they meant. She could picture men like The Others, wasted figures in their dirty striped uniforms, being hustled onto the streets to do a job even strong men would find arduous and repellent. 'Were they made to remove the bodies as well as the rubble?'

'Probably, but there weren't many whole bodies to find.' Hermann frowned as he recalled the horror after the flames had died down. 'It was awful. I went around trying to see if anyone else we knew was still alive. But the dead were shrivelled to the size of children by the fire, or they'd been burned to ash inside the buildings. You've no idea how dreadful it all was, Etta. You had to be here to really understand. It was like a blazing storm, balls of fire racing through the houses. After a few days, the smell was terrible. In the end they sent in men with flamethrowers to clear up the corpses and the maggots bred by all the flies.'

'They cordoned off the worst part in the east of the city,' Ursula said. 'There were too many bodies there. But we don't want to keep talking about those times. We must make a plan for tomorrow. Me and Etta found a great hoard of groceries today and I want to collect as much of it as possible before anyone else stumbles upon it. But carrying bags or baskets will look too obvious. We'd be raided before we could get back here.'

'Ingrid and I should come with both of you,' Hermann said. 'We can take it in turns to be lookout and form a chain to pass stuff out more quickly.'

'But how are you going to get it all back and will it then be safe here?' Anna could appreciate just how important this find really was and how much it was going to help this little ragbag group of young people and children survive.

'Take the Kinderwagen,' Gertrud said, waving towards the corner of the cellar. 'You'll be able to get loads of tins in that.' The pram was battered and scratched, but still had its wheels and looked sturdy enough to transport a large quantity of goods.

'It's a good idea, but if we pack everything into the pram and it gets stolen, we'll lose the whole lot,' Hermann said.

'Then still fill your pockets and maybe a couple of sacks, but make out there's a sick baby in the pram,' Anna said. 'Say it has typhus.'

They all screeched with laughter at this suggestion. Ingrid, returning with the dishes and the younger children, looked bewildered by their merriment. 'Who's got typhus?' she asked.

'The baby,' Ursula shrieked, helpless with laughter, while Hermann explained their plan for the next day.

'And when you all come back with the goods,' Gertrud said, 'we must store them safely, maybe bury some in case looters discover our stores. And we must think of a way to protect the food from the rats. Anything that isn't in a tin or jar they'll have in no time.'

Anna thought for a moment she was referring to the residents of the city, scavenging the nearby streets, but when she saw Hermann grinning, she realised she meant real rats.

'I'm doing my best to deal with them,' he said. 'But I'll dig a couple of chambers in the floor and line them with bricks. That should keep some of them out.'

'And once we've done that,' Ursula said, 'we might think about paying another visit to one of the communal kitchens again. It should be safe if we send Etta. She's older than us, she doesn't look like an orphan.'

Anna couldn't really understand what all this meant and she wasn't keen to be questioned or registered by any of the city's authorities, but the group was distracted by the younger children, who were tired and needed cuddles and stories to calm them for sleep. Gertrud and Ursula tucked Therese and Stefan under a ragged quilt on a mattress and Ingrid lay down too. Hermann placed a plank along some bricks to make a bench near the stove and invited Anna to sit beside him. The evening was cool and the only light was the glow of the fire, which warmed the space filled with their bodies.

'You enjoyed our *eintopf* tonight?'

'I did,' she said. 'I was very grateful for it, thank you. I hadn't had a hot meal for a few days. Do you always make it like that?'

'It depends.' He grinned. 'We make it with whatever we're lucky enough to find.'

'And tonight? What was the meat?' And she almost wished she hadn't asked.

'How do you think I deal with the rats?' Then he laughed. 'We don't have much choice, Etta. Haven't you noticed? The city is empty of cats and dogs.'

EIGHT

Groceries delivered and unpacked, Lauren puts her neighbour's order in her basket and steps outside once more. Over the hedge she can see the milk is still on the doorstep. She wonders whether to knock on the door again, then decides to make a pot of tea and wait a little longer. She can't be at the hospital all day, surely, she thinks, as she switches on the light in the kitchen. The day is fading and it will soon be dark.

She stirs the teabags in the pot and allows herself a toasted teacake, thick with butter, then peers out of her back door, thinking she might see Margie switching on her kitchen lights too. But the house next door is still in darkness.

I'll take my mind off it, she decides. Watch *Location, Location, Location* for a minute. Freddie should be home soon and then there'll be no peace. But why do I feel so responsible, she asks herself as she tries to settle her mind. We're not related, we're just neighbours. But we're good neighbours, never intruding, but there to help when needed. She was so kind when Colin died. Brought us a treat every day for a couple of weeks. I can't say I did as much for her when she lost her husband years back, but Amy was a demanding three-year-old then and I was pregnant again.

Ever since we moved here, nearly twenty years ago, Margie's been the perfect neighbour. She's quiet, private and keeps the house and garden beautifully. When the children were little, she babysat for me and the kids have always thought of her more or less as a surrogate grandmother so they'd be just as concerned as me, if they thought she was in trouble.

Lauren sips her tea, nibbles her teacake and tries to watch the programme on TV. But her mind won't stop thinking that something is wrong. Going to the hospital is such an awkward journey. She'd have had to take a bus and then walk quite a way, or take two buses. A woman in her nineties shouldn't have to do that. If only she'd asked me to give her a lift. But then I couldn't have stayed there with her all day till she'd been seen.

And then she hears Freddie's key in the door and the thump as he throws his rucksack down in the hall. 'Mum, where are you?'

Now what, she thinks. Not another problem. 'You've not been in trouble at school, I hope?'

'No, Mum. It's not me. It's Mrs Wilson.'

'Oh, is she home at last? Then you can take her shopping round to her.'

He appears in the doorway, leaning on the frame, still wearing his padded jacket. 'No, I can't do that. She's sitting on the seats at the bus stop. She wouldn't come with me. I tried to persuade her, but what she said didn't make any sense. Can you come and help me?'

Lauren gets up and grabs the coat she threw over the banister earlier. 'What's she doing there? Did she say she was waiting for a bus?'

'I don't know, do I? I'd just got off the bus and crossed the road and she was sitting there. I asked her if she was waiting for another bus but I couldn't understand what she was saying.'

'She must have been out all day,' Lauren says, patting her pocket to check she's got her house keys. 'I don't think she's been home today at all. Her milk's still on the doorstep. I was beginning to get quite worried.'

They hurry down the road, Lauren thinking it's strange that her elderly neighbour hasn't been far away from her all this time. 'I'm surprised I didn't see her when I drove back from work at lunchtime.'

It is gloomy now, dusk has fallen and the air is chilly. Maybe tonight will see the first frost of the winter. 'She was shivering, Mum. We've got to hurry.' Freddie is rushing ahead, turning to encourage her pace.

And then they see her. A hunched, lonely figure, one gloved hand clutching her black handbag on her knees, the other gripping a small case at her side on the seat.

Lauren rushes towards her. 'Margie, have you been waiting here long? If you need to go somewhere I can drive you. It's too cold to stay out here any longer. Let me help you.'

Anna's silence, and the tension in her limbs, tells Lauren she isn't going to get an immediate answer. 'Freddie's here too, Margie. He's worried about you as well. He rushed straight home to tell me you were here.'

Freddie sits the other side of Anna so she is sandwiched between them, their warm firm bodies picking up the trembling of her being. Lauren rubs the bony clasped hands, cold despite the gloves. 'We're taking you home right away, Margie. When you've warmed up, you can tell us what's troubling you. And if you still need a lift, I'll sort it out. Come back with us and you'll feel much better once you've had a nice hot cup of tea.'

Together they help her to her feet and turn towards home. Anna's feet seem frozen to the ground, moving inches at a time. And then she speaks in a frail uncertain voice. 'Meine Handkoffer. Ich muss meine Handkoffer nehmen.'

'What are you saying?' Lauren asks, not quite catching the words.

'It's German, Mum. I think she means her case. I'll carry it for her.' Freddie picks it up in his right hand and slips his left through Anna's arm. 'It's all right, Mrs Wilson. I've got your case right here. It's quite safe.'

They shuffle at such a slow pace back along the street. Every few yards Lauren thinks Anna might crumple onto the pavement, and she wonders if it would be better to call an ambulance after all. But then she tells herself it would take ages to arrive and surely it's better for such an old woman to wait indoors, in the warm, rather than out here in the empty dark. If she needs medical assistance they can sort it out once they're safely back home.

As they near the house, Anna tries to fumble in her pocket for her door key, but Lauren is firm. 'No, Margie, not just yet. I want you to come into our house with us for a bit so we can get you warmed up and check you're going to be all right.'

Indoors at last, Lauren and Freddie lower Anna into an armchair, with cushions to support her back. She is still shivering, despite the heating, so Lauren wraps a tartan picnic rug round her legs and feet and switches on the gas fire. 'There now, Margie, you'll soon feel warmer. I'm just going to make the tea. Freddie will sit with you for now.' She nods at her son and he pulls a cushioned stool close to the chair and props his chin on his fists, his elbows resting on his knees, looking at Anna with a concentrated frown.

She'll be fine in a moment, Lauren tells herself. Just needs to warm up, and she probably hasn't eaten since breakfast time either. She toasts another teacake. It's not a match for Margie's cheesecake or her strudel, but that's all there is. If this doesn't perk her up maybe I'll give her soup or scrambled egg on toast.

As Lauren returns to the sitting room, holding a cup and a

plate, she hears voices. Not loud, just a soft murmuring. That must be a good sign, she thinks, entering the room. Freddie is listening intently, adding a brief comment now and then. Lauren can't understand what either of them is saying.

'That's good, you've got her talking again. Here we are, Margie, tea and a toasted bun. Not up to your standard, I know, but it will do you good.'

'Danke,' Anna says, taking the cup as Lauren puts the plate on the little side table, within reach.

'What's that?' She turns to Freddie. 'What did she say?'

'It's German, Mum. I can't understand everything she's saying, but it's definitely German.'

Freddie is learning two languages at school and the other one is French, which Lauren thinks will be far more use to him. Who learns German these days?

'Has she said much? Anything useful?'

'I'm not sure, but I think she said it wasn't me. I don't know why she'd say that.'

Lauren sits down in the opposite armchair, watching the elderly figure sip the tea then nibble the teacake. Has something happened to suddenly change her normally quick-witted neighbour into a doddery old lady? She knows Margie is very old, but she is now so different to the alert woman she spoke to only a few days ago, and she has never heard her speak anything other than English before. She wonders if German is the language of her homeland and her mind is reverting to its earliest memories.

Is this how it begins? Is this how dementia starts? She'd always thought it crept into the brain quietly, secretly, gradually eroding cells and lobes over time until the subject could barely function. A bit like Colin's cancer, which sneaked in through his prostate and eventually invaded all his vital organs. Though in his case the cancer didn't creep, it marched at a pace, eight months from start to finish, ending his life just after his fifty-third birthday. But in Margie's case maybe she has had a stroke or seizure and dementia has claimed her overnight.

And then she hears that quiet, accented voice speaking. 'Danke schön. Ich muss jetzt nach hause.'

Lauren stares blankly, but her son turns to her and says, 'I think Margie wants to go home now.'

NINE

HAMBURG, APRIL 1945

'Keep the noise down, everyone,' Ursula said. 'We don't want anyone noticing us and barging in before we're finished.' They packed the pram with jars of gherkins, pickled onions, *rotkohl* and sauerkraut. Into their pockets they slipped tins of sardines and canned meat. Ursula arranged the blanket round another sack of rice and a can of cooking oil to give the impression of a sleeping baby. She also tucked more coverings round the jars of preserved vegetables, so there wouldn't be a tell-tale clink or rattle as they wheeled their way back over the ruts in the broken roads.

They had taken it in turns to feel around the dark cellar for the goods. Despite the lantern they'd brought with them, it was hard to see into the furthest corners of the underground store. Anna jumped and squealed under her breath when she thought she felt a rat run over her foot. The basement store carried an odour of damp decay, with a hint of spice, maybe paprika, though they hadn't yet found any. And she was sure she'd trodden on something long dead underneath the cobwebs and dried leaves on the beaten earth floor. But she also thought how cheerful they'd all become, faced with the prospect of another good meal in the evening. 'You won't have to hunt for more rats tonight,' she said to Hermann as they left the ruined shop after rearranging the debris on the floor to hide the trapdoor to the cellar.

He laughed. 'Ha, I might pop a bit of one in just to add more flavour. It's just meat, Etta, and we need to make this haul last as long as possible.'

'There's still plenty down there,' Ursula said, her coat bulging with the packages she had secreted about her person. 'I think we should come back again tomorrow and collect more while we can.'

'I thought you didn't want to draw attention to this place,' Anna said.

'I don't, but if we leave it too long, Etta, there's a risk that others will find the store before we can finish clearing it all out. We aren't the only ones hungry and desperate in this godforsaken city.'

And as they trundled back to the cellar they called home, taking turns to push the heavily laden pram, Anna noticed figures furtively creeping in and out of the ruins, as if the rats of the city had been transfigured into human form, sniffing and poking their way into every crevice in search of anything that could sustain them or make life a little more bearable.

They had nearly reached what she was now beginning to think of as her new home when she became aware of a hunched man limping alongside them. He hastened his steps till he was level with the pram. 'What you got in there?' he asked, peering in and reaching out with a filthy, long-nailed hand. The sleeve of his threadbare coat slid back down his arm, revealing a smudge of ink that could have been either badly etched numbers or a crude tattoo.

'Get off. It's our sick baby brother,' Ursula said, grabbing the pram handle from Ingrid and increasing her pace.

As Ursula marched ahead with her brother and sister, each

gripping either side of the pram with a protective hand, Anna noticed the man was now staring at her. 'Clear off,' she said. 'There's nothing for you here.'

He continued to stare, peering beneath the brim of the stained peaked cap that was too big for his shaven head. He kept walking alongside her while she followed the group and said, 'I know you from somewhere, don't I?'

A chill swept through her stomach and hit her heart with a thud. Could he know her from before? Would anyone recognise her wearing the assortment of ragged clothes she had found? Her hair was covered with a tightly wrapped scarf. She turned her head for a brief glance at him. He was very thin beneath his loose coat, but then so too were most of the city's remaining residents, surviving on their sparse, restricted diet. She hadn't seen anyone who looked well fed for days and days. Perhaps he was an injured soldier, returned from the front. His limp could be a sign that he had seen action. Or maybe he was more than just an ordinary serviceman. Perhaps he had been a guard or a member of the SS and was hoping to slip back into normal life with no questions asked. His face wasn't familiar, but then how many people would resemble their previous selves after the months, and in some cases years, of hardened service to the regime?

'I've never seen you before,' she said. 'You must be mistaken.' She wanted to get away from him as quickly as she could. He couldn't be one of The Others, could he? Surely they had all perished on that long march from the east.

Her words seemed to have an effect and he slowed down and slipped back; but before she had gone much further, he shouted out, 'I bet you're one of them. Your sort all have that haughty tone, think you're in charge and better than us.'

She hoped her new friends hadn't heard him; they were singing as they marched at a pace, eager to share the success of their haul with Gertrud and the children. She ran to catch them up, and kept in step with the group as they rattled along the damaged road. They hadn't noticed her accuser, and when she looked back over her shoulder she could no longer see him. He must have slunk away, like the others who crept through the ruins. But it still unsettled her. She didn't recognise him, but there had been hundreds of them, most of them far more malnourished than he was, so perhaps he was nothing to do with the camp. She just had to hope she wouldn't see him again.

As the group arrived at the steps to their own basement, Anna heard loud groans. She looked around and realised they were coming from below. Ursula heard them too and rushed ahead, leaving her brother and sister to guard and then unload the pram. Anna filled her arms with rice and jars and followed her into the dim cellar. Gertrud was rocking backwards and forwards on her mattress. 'The baby,' she panted, 'it's started.' She moaned again and then gave a deep, wrenching cry of agony, tipping forward onto her hands and knees.

Anna caught sight of little Therese and Stefan coming down the steps, fear creasing their faces at the awful sound. 'Shoo, go outside,' she said. 'We'll bring you a treat in a moment.' She set the groceries down on the makeshift table and bench, checked that there was water in the kettle and put it on the stove to heat.

'Etta, what do we have to do?' Ursula turned from rubbing Gertrud's back. 'I've never helped at a birth before.'

'I've seen it a few times,' Anna said, hoping neither of the girls would ever ask for more details of her experience. 'Let's hope it won't take long. We'll need to keep some water boiling, and clean rags would help.' She knelt down next to Gertrud and encouraged her back onto the mattress. The girl looked exhausted already. 'How long have you been like this, do you think?'

'Since you left this morning—' Her words were interrupted by another pain, through which she gasped and groaned until she could speak again. 'You'd only been gone a minute when my waters broke...' She managed to wave her hand towards a corner of the cellar, where the floor was damp.

'You've been at it for a while then,' Anna said, pouring some of the boiled water into a tin cup and checking it wasn't too hot. 'Here, sip this, then we should take off your dress.'

Gertrud drank a little, her sips interrupted by more pains and loud groans. Then, while she was kneeling, Anna helped her out of her top layer of clothes. Clothing was hard to come by and there was no point in ruining good garments.

In between contractions, Anna folded a thick blanket to make a pillow. Ursula came back with water to refill the kettle and handed over a torn sheet, ripped into large squares. 'Here, Etta. Use it how you wish,' she said, 'and if the baby lives, we'll use this to wrap it until we can find some clothes.' Anna followed her instructions, hoping that this birth would be straightforward and that she would soon be helping a healthy baby into the world.

As Gertrud's labour progressed, Anna was aware of Ingrid or Ursula slipping up and down the steps to stash their successful haul from that morning. In a far corner of the cellar, Hermann dug a pit in the dirt floor and fetched bricks to line the hole, then began stacking some of the tins there.

All the rest of the afternoon, Gertrud laboured until finally she heaved herself to her hands and knees and declared she had to push. 'Good girl,' Anna said. 'You're nearly there now.' She positioned herself behind Gertrud's haunches, knowing that soon a slippery bundle would slither out into her waiting hands. And in seconds there it was, the crowning of a head.

'One more push, come on, you can do it.' Then the little body twisted and with a gush of fluid a tiny baby came out with a rush and as he was lifted, he cried.

'You have a baby boy,' Anna said, wrapping the newborn in some of the sheeting. He gave a lusty cry, his cries echoed by Gertrud's sobs and the cheers of joy from the rest of the gang waiting by the steps.

Gertrud put her lips to her baby's damp head when he was laid in her arms, and kissed him. 'Welcome, little Peter,' she said, putting him to her breast.

Anna heard her words and felt the stabbing pain of hearing that name again. She turned away, unable to bear the sight of Gertrud cradling him. Anna knew she would have to get used to it, hearing the name that meant so much to her and seeing a healthy baby grow.

DER RÄUBERBRÄUTIGAM

THE ROBBER BRIDEGROOM

You won't be getting married, you'll
meet your death. They will chop you into
little pieces, then cook you and eat you all up.

TEN

HAMBURG, JULY 1942

Anna had always liked him. Although she was a little nervous of his strident confidence, she had always admired his very blond hair and blue eyes from when she was young. Even though her brown hair and eyes didn't conform to the Aryan ideal, she thought they still made a good match. She had known Günther almost as long as she'd known her childhood friend Etta, who'd disappeared with her family almost five years previously. He'd played with his companions in her neighbourhood as far back as she could remember. His father was a thickset man who worked in the docks, a hardworking family man, heavy with his hands at work – and at home, so she'd heard.

But much as she had been in awe of Günther from afar when they were children, it wasn't until they were older that he in turn began to notice her. Anna had finally been promoted to the Jungmädelbund, the organisation she and her friends could join until they were old enough to join the League of German Girls. Being a little older, Günther was already a member of the Hitler Youth, enjoying his spare time hiking with other boys, camping and singing patriotic German songs to promote a healthy, strong body and national loyalty.

And by the time Anna was nearly eighteen, wearing her prim straight grey skirt, with her neat buttoned white blouse, trying hard to learn to type and do shorthand, Günther was impressing the girls when he returned home on leave in his shining jackboots and his pressed and belted uniform of erd-grau. How that greyish green suited him with his close-cropped silver-blond hair. She could not help smiling at him, noticing how broad his shoulders were now, how straight his back, how firm his jaw.

'I remember you,' he said. 'Your father's the cobbler, isn't he? I might have to pay him a visit if I need these boots heeled.' He stretched his legs to show off his gleaming black boots.

'They're very shiny. I like the way you've tucked your trousers into your boots. The girls are all saying it's a very dashing style.'

'Are they now?' He flashed his perfect white teeth, turned to look at the group of girls across the street, then smiled again at Anna.

'And I like the badges on your uniform.' She dared to touch the black collar badge with a silvery flash of lightning sitting just below his chin, her knuckles grazing his smooth jawline.

He grabbed her finger before she could pull away. 'That's how you can tell my rank. I'm a Sturmmann now, but soon I'll be promoted to Rottenführer.' Still holding her hand, he moved her finger to point to the straps on his shoulders and also the patch on his sleeve. 'See? All these are symbols of my rank. You like them, don't you?'

She blushed and pulled away from his grasp. Her cheeks were tingling and her hand longed for him to hold it again, which after a few seconds he did. He held her hand, leant forward to kiss it with the lightest touch, then bowed and took his leave of her.

Anna watched him saunter across the street and stop to chat to the group of other local girls, who were soon shrieking with laughter at his witticisms. He lit a cigarette and looked back towards her. She was still standing there, unable to take her eyes off this manly, Aryan figure, so adored by the girls around him. She knew he would not be home for long. He'd been involved in the successful German advance on Stalingrad, but she hoped he wouldn't have to return to Russia once summer was over.

The thought that he might be sent back to the cold Soviet vastness made her bold. She didn't want to cross the road and endure the taunts of the girls, so she continued to stand and stare at him, smiling and making sure her slim legs were presented at an enticing angle. It didn't take long for her alluring pose to work its magic. He returned to her, his cigarette nearly finished; he ground it out on the pavement with the toe of his boot. 'Would you like to take a walk with me?' He offered her his arm and she took it willingly.

It was early evening, and when they reached Jenisch Park it was nearly empty. They wandered arm in arm until they found a secluded corner under the trees where they couldn't be seen, and sank down onto the grass. Günther lay back and propped himself up on one elbow. 'You know I've always really liked you, don't you?'

Anna, kneeling beside him, could feel herself blushing at this handsome boy's words. She still thought of him as a boy, although he must have been nearly twenty-one, almost four years older than her. 'No, I never realised you'd even noticed me before.' She fiddled with the sash of her skirt, winding it round her fingers.

'I really, really like you. Will you be my sweetheart and write to me when I go back to fight for our country?'

Her heart leapt. This was significant. Boys didn't ask for such a commitment unless they meant it, everyone knew that. 'I'd like to do that very much.'

'Good,' he said, reaching for her hand and pulling her down beside him. 'Promise me you won't forget.'

He kissed her and she felt herself melting with happiness. She had a boyfriend, a serious handsome boyfriend. How jealous all the other girls would be when they knew. She kissed him back with such urgency, it felt as if they were melding together. His fingers were tracing the buttons on her blouse and she was too weak with desire to stop him finding his way inside. This was what the other girls on her secretarial course talked about doing with their boyfriends. They giggled about it behind their hands and she, she who had never had a boyfriend before, or even kissed any man other than her father and uncles, had often wondered what it would be like to be kissed passionately. If Etta hadn't gone away, the two of them would have whispered and giggled about when they might have their first real kiss.

Lost in his kisses and the stroking of his fingers on her breasts, she almost didn't hear the bell of the Nikolaikirche tolling the hour. She pulled away, jumped up and straightened her skirt and buttoned her blouse. 'I've got to go. My mother doesn't like me staying out in the evening.'

The sky was beginning to glow, but the evenings were long at this time of year and Günther reached for her hand, trying to persuade her back to him. 'Please stay. We may not have another chance.'

She hesitated, biting her lip. How she longed to lie down beside him, feeling more of the touch of his lips and his hands. 'I really can't. She'll be furious if I'm late. I'll try to stay out tomorrow evening. I'll tell her I'm with friends.'

He rolled onto his back, hands folded behind his head. 'Let's meet right here, then. Our special place.'

Anna hugged herself all that night and all through the following day, trying to concentrate on her studies but feeling her fingers slow on her typewriter every time she thought about Günther.

By the time evening came, she was dizzy with excitement at the thought of being with him again. 'Don't be too late,' her mother said as she was leaving. 'And who are you going to the cinema with again?'

'Berthe and Klara,' she called back, anxious to avoid questions, as she rushed out of the apartment and down the stairs and almost ran all the way to the park. Please let him be there, she repeated to herself as she hurried, knowing she would be devastated if he hadn't kept his promise.

Her heart leapt for joy to see him standing by the trees, smoking. He offered her his cigarette and she took it. Even though she had never smoked before, she didn't want to appear unsophisticated or ignorant. Besides, the paper was wet from his lips.

'I've been thinking about how lovely you are, all day long,' he said, slipping his arm round her waist and pulling her closer to him.

'I couldn't think of anything else,' she said, taking a last inexperienced puff of the cigarette and handing it back to him. He stubbed it out against the bark of the tree, then bent to kiss her.

Anna could feel herself melting into his arms as he drew her down onto the grass behind the trees. They kissed and kissed, while his hands began to caress her breasts, then her thighs. 'You know how much I love you, don't you?' His voice was hot and hoarse, whispering in her ear, his fingers urgently slipping under the elastic of her knickers.

She said she loved him back. This was love, she thought. Real grown-up love, now she had a real lover.

'Give me something to remember when I return to the front, Anna. Let me make love to you right now.'

Almost before she knew it, first his fingers probed her, then something bigger, and he was whispering, 'My darling, you're so wonderful.'

It hurt, she knew it would, but this was what people who

loved each other did, to show their love for each other. She tried to stifle her cry, but she couldn't help a moan escaping her lips and he pressed his lips onto hers to quiet her as he pushed and pushed inside her.

When he rolled off her, he gasped, 'Thank you, my darling. I'll treasure this moment for ever.'

She lay close to him, throwing her arm round him while he smoked again. She felt wet down below and wondered if there was much blood, as the other girls had often said happened the very first time.

When they parted, he kissed her again and stroked her hair. 'You've given me something very special to remember you by.'

'You're not off just yet, are you?' She brushed the damp grass from her creased skirt.

'First thing tomorrow morning so this was the best leaving present you could have given me.' He stroked, then kissed, her cheek.

She gazed at him with tears welling. How could she have denied him when he was prepared to face danger and she was facing nothing more taxing than her final secretarial exam? She tried to blink the tears away so she wouldn't spoil their final moment, and made sure the last impression he had of her, his last glimpse, was of her radiant smile. And then, as she walked slowly home, she checked her skirt wasn't stained and crumpled, so her mother could never suspect that she had experienced a moment of true passion in real life and not one in celluloid on the illuminated screen of the cinema.

ELEVEN

HAMBURG, MAY 1945

Anna stayed by Gertrud's side for the next two days, while the others continued to ferry supplies back from the derelict grocery store. Ursula had assigned her the role of maternity nurse, saying, 'Thank goodness you were here, Etta. The rest of us hadn't the faintest idea what to do.'

I didn't know much, Anna thought, Gertrud did it all by herself. And when the afterbirth slithered out very soon after the baby slid into her hands, only the youngest children turned their noses up at the glistening, meaty mass. 'It looks just like calves' liver,' Hermann said. 'Do you think we could eat it? We haven't had real meat in ever such a long time.'

Ursula peered at the dark red placenta and poked it with her finger. 'Is it safe to eat?'

Gertrud laughed and said, 'If you can eat your fingernails, I'm sure this would be no worse, and probably a darn sight more tasty. I don't mind if you want to eat it. My mother used to give the afterbirth to the dogs, but I know others would bury or burn it.'

'We haven't had good meat in ages,' Hermann said. 'We should cook it. If we don't like it, we'll throw it out and I'll have to find more rats for us. Etta would like that.' He laughed as he glanced at Anna.

The delicious smell of the placenta fried with onions filled the cellar and everyone ate a portion with some of the rice and preserved vegetables retrieved from the shop's cellar. Gertrud usually did the cooking, but now she lay back on improvised pillows with her new son in her arms, resting and supervising the task. 'You've overcooked it just a little too much,' she said tasting her share. 'Like liver, it should be undercooked and still a bit soft.'

Anna thought it quite palatable, as long as she didn't think too much about its origin. But she only took a tiny portion and let the rest of them have the largest share.

Ursula laughed, as she had assumed the role of cook that night. 'And I suppose it should have been served with speck as well, if we had been able to find some?'

'Definitely,' Hermann said, popping a piece of flesh into his mouth and chewing it reflectively. 'Next time, a touch of sage perhaps?' He laughed as he dodged Ursula's playful stab with her fork.

Anna was glad to be given the role of nurse. She remembered her fright with the vagrant in the street; this meant she could stay in hiding, venturing out only to fetch water from the street pump and rinse the cloths used for the baby. The younger children, Therese and Stefan, played outside, stacking fragments of brick in a game of rebuilding make-believe houses peopled with friends and family members they vaguely remembered from the time before the bombing.

Anna kept glancing around the ruined streets whenever she went out. She was afraid of encountering that inquisitive man again. So far, the rest of the group had not questioned her too closely. She just said she had been working away from home for a long time and was trying to find her family, letting them think she might have been prevented from returning. She knew that not everyone would be so lacking in curiosity with the war nearly at an end, but for now it suited her to rest here and help her new friends.

One morning she was just hanging up the makeshift nappies outside on a line strung between two door frames when Ingrid came running up the road, her face red with effort, shouting, 'Gertrud, Etta, have you heard? It's all over, he's dead!'

'What's the matter and where are the others?' Anna peered down the street. In the distance she could see Ursula and Hermann running towards them with the burdensome pram full of supplies, bumping it over the damaged road.

'They're all right,' Ingrid puffed, catching her breath and bending over to hold her stomach. 'But Hitler's dead. He's shot himself.'

'What? How do you know that?'

'People out there are talking about it. They heard it on the radio.' Ingrid pushed past Anna, saying, 'I want to hold the baby.'

Dead? Shot? The man who had been held up as Germany's saviour? Anna was deeply shocked. All of her life she had heard his name spoken with reverence. Why had he taken his own life? Could he not accept the humiliation of defeat? She stepped out into the road to meet Ursula and Hermann. 'Is it true? Does this mean the war is really over at last?'

'He shot himself yesterday,' Ursula said.

'Coward,' Hermann said, spitting with fury. 'He should have waited to face the victors.'

'So that means Germany has lost the war and the Allies will be coming here soon,' Ursula said, looking around as if she expected the arrival of foreign troops any moment.

'Did anyone say which ones are coming here?' Anna felt herself trembling, waiting for the answer.

'Does it really matter? As long as life gets better, do we

care?' Ursula began unloading the pram and pressed the cans into Anna's hands.

'I hope it's the Americans,' Hermann said. 'They'll have more food and chocolate and cigarettes.'

And Anna wished for that too, though she didn't want to voice her deepest fear, that it would be the Russians. Hamburg was far enough east to be near the territory already claimed by the Red Army and with their reputation for harsh reprisals, including rape, she prayed inside that it would not be them who came. But would assault by the Americans, French or British be worse?

Being a few years older and wiser than most of her new friends, she hid her trepidation, saying, 'Let's stow this food away as quickly as possible. We don't want to lose a single bit of it.' As she turned to go down the steps, she heard the baby crying and Gertrud soothing him as she put him to her breast again. New life, new hope; Anna clung to the thought that life could only get better from now on, but the baby's cries and Gertrud's crooning stabbed her wounded heart.

Only a few days later, she heard Hermann shouting. 'We're in luck. It's not the Russians, it's the British!' he yelled, as he jumped down the steps into the cellar. 'Come on, Etta, come and see them march past.'

'Thank God it's not the Russians,' Anna murmured as she joined the gang outside to watch the British troops marching through the streets, thinking how quiet their arrival in the city had been. No bombing, no shooting, just the tramping of battle-hardened feet. Elsewhere on the street, she could see their few neighbours watching too. Children looked curious, some older ones running alongside the men while their mothers held back the youngest. Many of the women glared with faces of hate or fear and the few men who were still living in the city looked ashamed and beaten.

As they watched, they heard the soldiers remarking on the destruction of the city, which had been caused by bombs from their own air force. 'Blimey, it's a bloody sight worse than we thought,' and 'Poor sods. How are they still alive?' But as they tramped past the nervous onlookers, Anna saw how many of the men wrinkled their noses and sometimes put hands over their faces. And slowly she understood that these were expressions of disgust and horror at the stench of decomposition that still pervaded Hamburg, a smell that they, the Ausgebombten Gang, lived with and were surrounded by and to which they had all become completely accustomed.

When Anna also saw them pointing out the optimistic messages chalked on the walls of ruined homes that she had noticed when she first arrived in the city, she was reminded how many had been lost in the inferno. The pitiful scrawls still pleaded for news of missing family members, lost either in the inferno or in the chaos of evacuation and war. Pleas for loved ones to return, to find their families, words of hope that they would be reunited. Was Inge ever found and did Tante Hilde ever return? She couldn't help wondering just how many people had been lost in the war years, how many families had been torn apart, never to be reunited.

As the troops marched past the onlookers, she heard someone say, 'They're taking over the city. The British are now in control of Hamburg. Things are bound to get better soon.' Anna watched the parade pass by, resisting the temptation to scratch the itchy scab that was a sure sign her burnt arm had healed, but thinking that the wounds inside her heart would take far longer.

TWELVE

HAMBURG, OCTOBER 1942

As time went by and Anna didn't hear from Günther, despite her frequent letters to him, she began to worry that all was not well. She knew he had been sent back to Russia and, now that summer was long over and the weather was growing colder, she feared that he would be facing not only artillery, but the fearsome might of the Russian winter as well.

After waiting two months for a letter, even a brief note, she plucked up courage to call on his parents. His mother opened the door, red-eyed with a tear-streaked face. She held a handkerchief to her face as she said, 'Oh, not another one. Go away. You damn girls, all after him and now he's dead. My handsome Günther.' Then she slammed the door shut.

Anna stood outside, frozen. Dead? After only two months? What girls? And she realised with a sickened heart that she might not have been the only one to give him a leaving present. Those girls had all admired his uniform, his shining boots, his broad shoulders and clipped blond hair. They all wanted to be on his arm and enjoy his manly kisses. But did any of the others give him the parting gift he really wanted or was it just her?

A month later, she knew for sure that he had given her a

special leaving present too. And not a welcome one either, however much she might have longed to cherish the memory of their brief time together. He might have left her to fight for his country, but now her own battle had begun; she realised he'd not only left her with sweet memories, but a sweet souvenir in the form of an unwanted pregnancy.

It wasn't his fault, she told herself. *I wanted to do it as much as he did. He didn't mean for me to get into trouble. We both knew what we were doing.* But she fretted and cried and her mother thought she was just pining for her tall, blond boyfriend to return. 'If you think this is bad,' Mama said, 'it's not half as bad as the last time. Mown down in the mud, they were then. At least this time they've got control of the air.' Anna couldn't bear to tell her that the father of the child she was expecting was now dead.

Her college friend Mathilde was the one who came to her rescue, when she learnt of her plight. 'You've heard, haven't you, that there are special homes where young unmarried women can go to have their babies? There's no shame in it these days. They say it's a way of serving our country and giving the nation new life. You'd be well looked after there and they'd take care of you and arrange to have the baby adopted by a good Aryan family.'

'But how could I explain to Mama and Papa where I was going? They're expecting me to get a good job with my qualifications.'

Mathilde tossed her blonde hair and laughed. 'You could say the nursing home needs a secretary. At least that way you'll be able to leave home without them ever knowing about your condition. The BDM will help you find a place.'

All the girls knew about the BDM, the Bund Deutscher Mädel, which she and her friends had all had to join when they were fourteen, just as the boys were recruited into the Hitler Youth. Anna had always been a little timid in the presence of the organisation's most confident girls and leaders, but she followed Mathilde's advice and went to speak to Hildegard, the woman who had lectured and drilled them on how a good German woman was expected to behave.

'You say he was a Sturmmann? Full name?' Hildegard consulted her list and ticked a line on the file, nodding in approval. 'Hmm, we already had him on our list of approved candidates. If you hadn't got hold of him first and he hadn't lost his life in the course of duty, he would have had the privilege of attending one of our special centres.' She looked up at Anna. 'It's a pity you're not blonde, which we would have preferred, but still, you've already done the most important part for us and I can now authorise a placement for you on the Lebensborn programme at Steinhöring. You'll have the child there and everything will be arranged for you afterwards. I'll give you a letter for your parents to say you are doing important work for us. That should satisfy them.'

On the long train journey three weeks later, south to Bavaria, Anna was nervous. How would she be treated there? Unmarried mothers were normally regarded with disdain. She clutched her case and the package of bread and cheese that her mother had insisted on pressing into her hands when she left. She was too worried to eat and spent the entire time staring mournfully out of the window at the landscape as it changed from the northern plains to dark pine forests. She couldn't help wondering if the home would enforce a strict routine, poor food and harsh treatment as punishment for her shameful mistake.

But when she finally arrived, the reality was so different and her fears were dispelled. The unmarried mothers' home looked like an enormous tiered Alpine chalet, surrounded by dark trees and snow-topped mountains, such a contrast to the familiar flat countryside of marshland and pasture around Hamburg. 'Welcome, my dear child,' the matron said, showing her to her warm, comfortable room. 'We are going to make sure you have plenty of rest here and are in the best of health for the arrival of your baby, a glorious addition to our noble race.'

Anna could never have imagined it would be such a luxurious place, scented with lavish arrangements of flowers, nourishing food and a hint of antiseptic in the corridors near the medical wing. As well as rooms for leisure and games, there was a library and a cinema. The food was plentiful and delicious, so she felt cosseted, comforted and cared for, knowing that she only had to count the days till she was free. An efficient but gentle SS doctor in a white coat examined her soon after she arrived and asked her some questions about her family's medical history. Was she aware of any hereditary diseases or imbecility among her relatives? And then she had to sign a document renouncing any claim to her child, which would become the property of the state from the moment it was born.

Her life after that initial examination became a time of leisure, with servants undertaking every task to care for her and the other expectant residents. She could walk the paths that meandered through the well-kept grounds, read books, have baths, watch films and eat wonderful meals. She felt relaxed, lazy and indulged, but a little fattened up like a prize pig for the slaughter too.

Some days the other girls there were tearful, bitterly regretting their mistake, some days they were self-righteous, saying they were doing it for their country, having a baby for Hitler. Although Anna couldn't bring herself to think that way, she thought that her baby was probably going to be genetically purer than any other baby born there at that time. Her parentage, combined with Günther's blond hair and blue eyes, surely meant that her baby would be the cream of the crop that season and would go to a suitably vetted Aryan couple with a good home.

'I'm going to do it again after this,' one of the girls said one day, when they were all sat at lunch in the dining room with its view over the rolling lawns, blanketed overnight with a fresh fall of snow. 'If I'd known it was going to be this cushy, I'd have got myself in the family way a whole lot sooner.'

'You know there are other places even better than this, don't you?' One of the other girls reached for another portion of sauerkraut to spice her roasted pork.

'Oh, that's for girls who aren't already expecting,' said the first.

Anna didn't understand what they meant and when the girls could see that she wasn't following their conversation, the very pregnant young mother, her belly touching the edge of the dining table, said, 'It's a really luxurious place with all the best facilities, like a top hotel. There's a crowd of the most handsome young SS officers and you can decide which one you want to take to your bed. All the men and the girls are carefully chosen so they will make perfect babies. Can you imagine it? Isn't that wonderful?'

'Ooh, how exciting,' her friend said. 'I'd choose the tallest and strongest.'

'But then he might be stupid. I'd choose someone I could talk to, with a lovely kissable mouth.'

'I bet they'd all be virgins,' another girl said. 'They'd have to be untouched and pure, so they wouldn't have any idea what they were doing, so it wouldn't be that much fun.'

'But then it would be fun teaching them how to do it,' the first girl said as they all burst out laughing.

As the girls giggled and speculated on how long after the birth of their babies they might be allowed to take part in this officially approved scheme, Anna thought it sounded like a state whorehouse, albeit full of genetically suitable examples of the master race. Was this, she would think in later years, when she had her first glimpse of the motivation behind her glorious country's governing forces? She should have been more alert, she would tell herself, more willing to question their objectives.

As the other girls imagined their ideal mates if they were selected for this programme, she wondered if she would ever have chosen anyone other than Günther. He was strong, tall and blond; what more could she have wanted? She gazed out at the white landscape dotted with groups of iced fir trees, thinking how wonderful it would have been to walk with him across the pristine snow in the ice-cold January air under the clear blue sky and start afresh.

She dreamt of him sometimes, him and their brief time together. At least she'd done that for Günther before he was sent to the slaughter, she thought. More and more young men were going to the front, many of them dying, although the staff at the maternity home maintained morale by continually telling all the girls that Germany would win in the end.

Anna's time of peace and leisure suddenly came to an end one day in early spring when she felt a sharp pain in her belly. She stood up and it felt as if something inside her had popped, like a big fat balloon. 'What is happening?' she gasped, as she stood there looking down at the very wet patch that spread on the floor, which was followed by an enormous cramping pain. She rang the alarm bell that was installed in all the rooms to summon help.

'We'd better get you into the labour room to see what's going on,' the nurse said, steering her out of the library, where she had been about to choose another book to read lying on her bed. In her advanced state of pregnancy, she slept badly at night and spent most of the day resting, supported by mounds of pillows.

'And let's stay calm and quiet while we get you there. You don't want to alarm the other young girls who aren't quite ready to do this yet.' A wheelchair was brought and swiftly wheeled to a sterile room, where Anna was helped onto a white bed, her legs forced apart so she could be examined.

'It hurts so much,' she groaned as another pain gripped her insides.

'That's perfectly normal,' the nurse said. 'It will get worse before it's all over.'

It seemed to take hours, although it could only have taken a part of one day because Anna was back in her own bed by dinner-time, with a tray on her lap and a thick pad between her legs mopping up the blood. When the pains became really fierce and she asked if she could have some relief, the midwife had admonished her, saying, 'Oh no, you don't need that. You're a healthy young girl. A good German woman doesn't expect to have help like they have in degenerate Western democracies. Be brave, dear. It's a sign that your baby is strong, pushing out into the world.'

But when he was delivered, she heard what the midwife said under her breath to the nurse as she wrapped him in a clean towel after telling her she'd had a son. 'This is one of the special ones. You know what to do.' And she turned to Anna, brightly saying, 'Well done. He's a little jaundiced, so we'll look after him in the special unit.'

She didn't know then what 'special' really meant, when to her it signified her love for Günther. Anna only saw her son for a second, his pink scrunched face peeping from the white towelling bundle as the nurse hurried out of the delivery room. In her head she called her baby Peter, but she never got to call him by his name in person, only in her thoughts and in her dreams. She never saw him again, never even fed him once to ease her swollen breasts.

She begged to see him, to know that he was well, but after a couple of days she was told he had already been taken to a good family. The nurse gave her cabbage leaves to slip inside her brassiere, a crêpe bandage to bind them flat and sage tea to dry up her milk. She cried with the pain of her sore breasts, and cried even more when she learnt that the other girls were allowed to feed their babies themselves for two weeks before the children went to their new homes.

Soon after that Anna forced herself to think about the future. A job, she had to find a job, a good one with accommodation, so she could be independent. Despite her secretarial qualifications, prospects in Hamburg were limited, and she wouldn't be able to afford her own room; she'd have to share with other girls. But there it was, the perfect job, on the maternity home's noticeboard. 'Wanted... Secretary... Own room'. These key words told her it was just what she needed. It was far away from Hamburg and with the war continuing, she probably wouldn't be able to go home regularly. But once she had recovered she could return there one last time to pack her belongings and spend Easter with her parents before her departure to a new job, a new life and a chance to forget her sadness.

THIRTEEN

LONDON, NOVEMBER 2016

'Well, I must say, her day of truancy doesn't seem to have done her any harm,' Dr Morgan says. 'Considering her age, she's in very good shape. I do wonder though if she may have had a very minor stroke yesterday, as that might explain her peculiar behaviour. But I can't see the point of dragging her into hospital and subjecting her to exhaustive tests unless we notice any other cause for concern.'

'Margie does seem more settled back here in her own home,' Lauren says, wondering if her neighbour may suddenly abandon her kitchen and come to join their conversation in the hallway of Margie's house.

'Will you be able to keep an eye on her?' the doctor says, completing his notes and shutting his case. 'Maybe make sure she's eating properly and taking care of herself?'

'I'll do my best, of course. I'm going to ring her children later, but they're thousands of miles away. I've never met them as they've been in Australia for years. I've already rung social services, but they've got a long waiting list, they said. And I have to work in the mornings, so I can only check on Margie first thing and then again when I get back around lunchtime.'

'Well, that should be enough for now. Better if it's someone she knows and she can continue to stay in familiar surroundings.' He paused. 'You said that she wasn't speaking English yesterday evening when you found her. But she seems fine today. Her English is very good, so I assume she's been living in this country for many years.'

Lauren shrugs. 'We don't really know. Since the end of the war, I believe. But it's so odd. Margie's never spoken German to us before, just the odd word for one of her special cakes and so on. And all of a sudden she couldn't seem to speak English. Do you think that means she's developing some kind of dementia?'

'It's possibly an early sign, but as you say, odd it should happen so suddenly.'

'And do you think it could happen again?'

He shakes his head. 'Hard to say. If it wasn't a stroke, maybe something stressed her, or gave her a shock perhaps. She's obviously had a fall quite recently, judging by the graze on her knee, but I can't find any other injuries or symptoms that require immediate treatment. I did notice a scar on her arm though, when I took her blood pressure. Looks like an old burn. Has she ever mentioned that to you?'

'No, but I know she often rubs it, as if it bothers her. Do you think she could have got it during the war?'

'It's possible. I asked her how she did it, but she just pulled her sleeve down again.'

Lauren shakes her head. 'She's a mystery. It was really awkward yesterday too. I couldn't understand a blooming word she was saying. I had to keep asking my son to interpret. He's doing German at school. But I really hope it doesn't happen again when he's not around.'

'Well, that's good he can help, at least. Sometimes the young can relate to the elderly on a different level and have a special relationship with them.'

'That's one way of putting it, I suppose. But he can't be here all the time.'

Lauren sees the doctor to the door and as he is about to leave, she says, 'Do you think she might take off again? I can't bear to think what might have happened to her if she'd stayed outside all night in the cold.'

'I really wouldn't know,' he says as he waves goodbye and heads to his car. 'Let's hope she stays home from now on.'

With a weary sigh, Lauren closes the door and wonders what she should do next. She'd already decided she had to contact Margie's children and had found phone numbers in an old address book next to the telephone on the hall table. And she thinks again about last night and how she and Freddie had encouraged Margie to eat scrambled eggs and nibble toast, then brought her back to her own house. Once she was in the home she had known for so many years, she seemed to relax. 'Ich bin zuhause,' she'd said, taking off her raincoat and hanging it on the hook on the hallstand, next to her winter coat. Then she had turned to them, saying, 'Gute Nacht,' and had begun walking up the stairs, clutching the handrail and carrying her little blue case.

Lauren and Freddie had stood there, wondering if they should follow her. But soon they heard her footsteps in the bedroom above them and the sound of the curtains being pulled across the bay window. 'She must be going to bed,' Freddie said. 'Do you think we can leave her now?'

'Let's wait a minute, just to be sure.' And they both listened until they heard the click of the wardrobe door, the creak of bedsprings and the snap of the bedside light switching off. 'I think it's safe for us to go home. I'll check on her first thing tomorrow.'

. . .

But Lauren didn't sleep well at all that night. Twice she had looked out of her window, thinking she might see Margie leaving the house in her nightdress and slippers. But the house was in complete darkness and all was quiet.

She woke earlier than usual, at five thirty, and the house next door was still silent. As soon as the doctor's surgery opened she had placed a request for the doctor to make a home visit; a rarity, the receptionist said, but in the circumstances they could make an exception. Lauren phoned the nursery to make her excuses and after Freddie had left for school she went to knock on Margie's door, key in hand, nervously wondering what surprises she would find today.

But a rinsed empty milk bottle had been put out on the doorstep and when Lauren rattled the doorknocker, Margie answered promptly. She was dressed, her hair was combed and twisted into her usual bun and she looked as if yesterday had never happened.

'Good morning, Margie, how are you feeling today?' Lauren said, bracing herself for a reply in a language she wouldn't be able to understand.

'I am very well, thank you,' Margie replied. 'Did you need something?'

Lauren was quite taken aback. Where was the confused elderly lady she and Freddie had rescued from the bus stop the night before? Margie looked quite herself again. 'Oh, I just wanted to check you were in. I'll be back in a minute with your groceries from the delivery yesterday.'

She turned away, thinking it was her turn to be confused. What had happened yesterday? Had she imagined her speaking in German? She fetched the few purchases Margie had added to her order and knocked on her door again. This time it took a little longer for the door to be answered, but Margie still seemed bright and cheerful. She had tied her apron round her waist and Lauren thought she could smell coffee and baking. 'Come and join me,' Margie said, leading the way through to the kitchen. 'I'm making *apfelkuchen* this morning. Vill you stay and have some with me?'

Lauren stammered in her surprise at this change in her neighbour. 'That... that would be lovely, Margie. Will it be ready soon?'

Anna looked at the clock on the wall. 'In about ten minutes. I have made the coffee.'

She seems so well, Lauren thought. How am I going to explain that I've called the doctor out? He's going to think there's nothing wrong with her. But she knew she had to tackle the question in case he arrived soon, although the receptionist said it wouldn't be until after his morning appointments.

'I wanted to ask you about yesterday, Margie,' she said. 'Do you remember Freddie and me bringing you back from the bus stop?'

'Did you? What was I doing there?' Anna didn't look at Lauren, but opened a drawer to find an embroidered tray cloth.

'We thought you'd been waiting for a bus, but we think you'd been there for quite some time. You were getting very cold.'

'It will soon be vinter. The nights are getting much colder now.'

'Were you planning on going somewhere?'

'I was probably just resting. I can't quite remember.' Anna busied herself setting a tray with plates, cups and doilies.

'You had a little suitcase with you?'

'Had I?' Anna frowned, as if she was trying hard to think about this. 'A small one?'

'Yes, very small. Like a vanity case.'

'Oh, I sometimes use that for shopping.' Anna poured the coffee into two flower-patterned china cups with matching saucers and they both sat down at the little red Formica kitchen table.

'And the funny thing is... I don't know if you remember... but yesterday, you were speaking in German. I couldn't understand it, but Freddie was with me and he said he was sure it was German, because he's doing it at school.'

'Such a clever boy. He will follow Amy, your eldest, to university I am sure, one day.'

'Yes, perhaps. But you see, we were very worried. We thought something was wrong. So, I called the doctor this morning and he's coming round later to check you over. Just to make sure you are quite well.'

'Is he learning German at school?'

'The doctor? No... I mean, you weren't speaking English yesterday. But yes, Freddie is learning German.'

'Then he must visit me more often. I may have lived in your country for over seventy years, but I have not forgotten the language I was born into.'

'That's very kind, but yesterday we wondered why...' Lauren doesn't finish her sentence.

Anna is checking the oven in a fragrant, steamy cloud of cinnamon and apple. 'Nearly done. You must take some home for dear Freddie and tell him ve must have regular *konversationsunterricht*. We can make a start tomorrow.'

'What did you just say?'

'Conversation classes. If Freddie is to go to university, I would like to help him do vell, the dear boy. And now, I think the cake is ready. Do you think the doctor would like a piece when he comes?'

FOURTEEN

HAMBURG, MAY 1945

'Ingrid shouldn't come with us this morning,' Ursula said. 'She's too young. She's not even ten yet. The authorities might decide to send her off to an orphanage.'

Little Ingrid stamped her foot petulantly at this order. But Anna thought her big sister was right. It was safer for the older members of the little gang to check out the new refugee centres first. The rumour had gone around quickly and there was some admiration for the speed with which the British were assuming control and establishing administration.

'We're sure to get more food now,' Hermann said. 'No more rats for us!' He gave Anna a cheeky grin. 'But maybe I'll catch one now and then as a special treat for Etta.'

But would they get more food? Anna wasn't so sure. The centres were being established to help the thousands of displaced people flooding into the city now the war was over. Forced labourers and former prisoners, far from their original homes, were all seeking help. The thought of who those refugees might be made Anna nervous. Was it possible that some of The Others might be among them, if they had survived that long march in the coldest months of the year?

Anna didn't think the members of the Ausgebombten Gang would qualify for assistance. They were still in the vicinity of their original home and they were German citizens. They hadn't been imprisoned, enslaved or starved, however much they might complain about their poor diet. They were more desperate than some people in Hamburg, but only because they had been careful to avoid the authorities, who had managed, with typical German efficiency, to keep the majority of the city's remaining residents reasonably well fed. So, she was sure the British wouldn't be handing out precious rations to them.

Hermann had heard talk of several centres being set up, but the main one was located in the Zoological Gardens, not too far away. 'We'll go along and try that one first, with Etta,' Ursula said. 'And if they don't like the look of us and we can't qualify, maybe they'll take pity on Gertrud and the baby another time.'

When the three of them arrived at the centre, they weren't surprised to find an enormous but orderly queue snaking around the grounds of the zoo. The condition of the hopeful refugees varied tremendously. Some were barely clothed, some were emaciated, some were still strong. 'Don't get too close to them,' Anna whispered. 'You can't see disease, but it's sure to be lurking close by.' She stood well back from those in the queue, hoping germ-laden lice weren't jumping from one body to another. A tell-tale sign of lice looked like dandruff sprinkled over the shoulders; you could see it on those with dark clothing.

As they drew nearer, Anna realised the line of desperate people was being divided into groups of fifty, bringing back terrible memories of previous occasions when hungry unfortunates had to stand in groups of ten while they were counted and counted again, some to the left and some to the right, some sent to work, others to their fate. Ahead of them she could see desks where two or three uniformed men were seated. They appeared to be efficiently taking notes, stamping cards and waving those they'd registered straight through. But a pair of armed soldiers stood behind each checkpoint in case of trouble, making her feel even more nervous.

What information did the clerical officers need to know before people could benefit from their charity? Anna wanted her young friends to take advantage of this opportunity; they had already suffered so much. But she was feeling wary, anxious that too many questions might be asked. Where have you come from? What have you been doing for the last five years? And what powers might be exercised if the British scented trouble or suspected the truth?

'I'm not sure this is going to work,' she said. 'They'll soon see we're not real refugees. I'm sure they won't help us.' She pulled her headscarf low over her forehead and around her cheeks, hoping her face wasn't easily seen.

'No, don't give up yet, Etta, let's wait a bit longer,' Ursula said. 'We'll be able to see and hear more as we get closer. I think they're giving everyone a special card.'

'It must be a ration card,' Hermann said, straining his neck to see to the front of the line. 'We'll definitely get more food if we play this one right.'

By the time they were only a dozen or so people away from the desk, Anna's fears were confirmed. She could hear that the army clerks were asking for names, home addresses and information on the individual's unfortunate circumstances. She could lie to them, of course, but it was too close for comfort. She could feel her heart racing, her palms sweating. It would be like lying to one's trusting parents, a teacher or, worse still, the police. And the consequences of being found out might be severe.

'I don't think I should go through with it,' she said. 'I honestly can't claim to be a refugee, so I might harm your chances. But you two should carry on. You might be lucky.'

And before they could protest or stop her, she turned and quickly walked away. She was desperate to run as fast as she could, far, far away from the questions and those who might not believe her story. But running might have drawn unwanted attention, so she forced herself to walk off at a steady pace. She looked back for a second and saw that Ursula and her brother had reached the desk together. The worst that could happen to them was that they would be told to clear off. The worst that could happen to her was far, far worse.

Back in the cellar, Anna fetched water and stoked the stove to heat it. 'I'm surprised you didn't want to stay and find out for certain, Etta,' Gertrud said when she told her that she could tell from the questions being asked by the army clerks that she wasn't going to be in luck.

'I think I would have spoiled the chances for the other two. None of us are really refugees, so we aren't entitled to help. But they are both much younger and might bluff their way through. Better that they did it without me, I thought.' She kept her head turned away, not wanting Gertrud to look into her eyes and see the truth hidden there.

'If they come back with good news, I might feel strong enough to take little Peter along with me and try for myself. Surely they will take pity on a new mother and her tiny baby?' Gertrud picked up her son and bared her breast. He was feeding well and she seemed to have plenty of milk for him.

'It's worth a try. I'm sure they will help.' Anna poured boiled water into a tin bowl, trying to ignore the deep pain she felt at the mention of her own baby's name. Her Peter had never fed from her breasts, never even been held in her arms. 'You can use this for his wash when you've finished feeding him. And here's a clean cloth to wrap him.'

'He's a dirty little beggar, he is. But I think this time he'll live all right.'

Anna took a sharp breath. Had she heard correctly? She knew that these last few years of straitened circumstances in wartime had been extremely dangerous times for little ones. Even more so in places like the ghettos and camps, where they weren't welcome; but had Gertrud been anywhere like that? She'd given no indication that she was anything other than a regular citizen of Hamburg. 'Do you mean to say he's not your first baby?'

'He's my third. I started young.' Gertrud stroked her baby's downy head as he suckled.

Anna tried to digest this information. It sounded as if Gertrud's first two babies must have died somehow. She felt sorry for her and thought maybe they had both been stillborn. And the only thing she could think of saying was, 'Your husband will be pleased to hear you've had a healthy baby this time then.'

'Husband? You must be joking! If I had one, I wouldn't be in this line of business.'

'But they have the same father?'

Gertrud shrugged. 'Not a clue. One of the drawbacks of the job.' She covered her breast, put her baby to her shoulder and patted his back. Milk bubbled from his mouth and he gave a tiny belch.

And in that moment it dawned on Anna, with a sickening feeling of dread, that this was why Ursula had talked so eagerly about Gertrud going back to work soon. She wasn't working in any of the factories that had resumed operation since the bombing; she'd had to resort to working on the streets, selling her body for money. And now that the city was filled with foreign soldiers, far from their loved ones at home, there was likely to be plenty of work for an attractive young woman, even one such as Gertrud with milk-filled breasts.

. . .

Much later that day, when Anna had folded a small pile of fairly clean nappies for Peter and Gertrud had begun to make their evening meal, Ursula and her brother ran joyfully down the steps into the cellar, waving their registration cards.

'We did it! The Zoo Camp was wonderful!' Hermann yelled.

'Did they give you any food to bring back here for us?' Gertrud looked at the pair, sizing up their transformation. 'And you've got a change of clothes!'

Ursula twirled to show off her new dress and jacket. The garments were too big for her skinny frame, but they were clean and in good condition. 'The British are forcing the well-off Hamburgers to donate their spare clothes. Ours were filthy, so we've got new ones. Ta da!' She curtseyed at the end of her performance.

'And we've been cleaned up,' Hermann said with a grin. 'We were dusted with lice powder and showered.'

'But the best thing was the food! Thick soup with sausage and a piece of bread as well.'

'That's it, then. I'm going off to the Zoo Camp tomorrow as well,' Gertrud said. 'I could do with a good wash. And I bet they'll have proper nappies for babies too. He's getting a little sore. I'll lay it on thick and they're sure to be generous.' She turned to Anna. 'What about you, Etta? Do you want to come with me and give it another go? Maybe we'll take Therese and Stefan. They could do with some new things to wear.' Gertrud peered at the two younger children, whose garments seemed filthier and more threadbare by the day.

But Anna thought about the desks, the pens, the forms, the armed soldiers and the inevitable questions, then shook her head. 'I heard talk that the British have set up camp in the old Luftwaffe barracks at Bahrenfeld. The troops get generous allowances there, so it might be worth seeing what I can get for free to bring back here.'

'Good idea,' Ursula said. 'We've still got to feed the rest of us. We ate well today, but we have to think about the whole Ausgebombten Gang, not just us two. It would be wonderful if you could help.'

Gertrud looked over her shoulder and winked at Anna. 'Soldiers get lonely and go looking for company, Etta. You might do very well up there.'

And with a feeling of dread, Anna understood the meaning of Ursula's remark and realised that whole gang was expecting her to earn her keep by turning her hand to the oldest profession, if she was to stay with them. With no other prospect of work, did she really have to be like Gertrud and sell herself to survive?

FIFTEEN

LONDON, NOVEMBER 2016

'Do you think you'd like to practise your German with Margie?'
Lauren hands Freddie a plate with a large piece of the apple
cake she had been given by her neighbour earlier that day.

'If she keeps giving me cakes like this, I will.' He falls on the
cake, holding it with both hands and eating it in a few quick
mouthfuls, then dabs his finger in the sugary crumbs.

'I think she really meant it, about helping you learn the
language. And I feel it might be good for her to have some
regular company. Maybe that's her real problem – she's on her
own far too much. The doctor couldn't find anything definitely
wrong with her. She is quite extraordinary.'

'Can I have another bit?' Freddie reaches out for another
slice, but Lauren taps his hand.

'What's that for?'

'I'm doing lasagne for your tea. You'll spoil your appetite if
you eat too much cake now. Save it for tomorrow.'

Freddie scrapes the kitchen chair back on the tiled floor and
gulps his mug of tea. 'Did Margie say anything else in German
today?'

'No, it was very strange, after yesterday. Well, she spoke the odd word, like the German word for apple cake and so on, but otherwise it was all English, just like she always used to be. She didn't even seem to remember what had happened and whether she'd really been expecting to take a bus somewhere.' Lauren sips her tea. 'I don't know what was going on in her mind yesterday.'

'Maybe she forgot which country she was living in.' Freddie rinses his mug and places it upside down on the draining board. It might earn him another piece of cake sooner than tomorrow.

'The doctor couldn't really say why it had happened. Though he did think perhaps she'd had a shock and was very stressed. But I've simply no idea what was going on. I mean, why was she out all day? Where did she think she was going? She had that little case with her too.'

'Maybe she wanted to go back to a happy time. Early in her life.'

'Huh, I doubt whether much of it was happy, love. The very early years, when she was a child perhaps, but she lived through the war, you know. It was bad enough here, but over there it was terrible.'

'We did a bit about the Blitz and evacuating children in Year 6.'

'That was very hard for people over here, but not the same as having your country invaded.'

'I think we do more next term. I'm sure they said we do the Second World War.' Freddie is thoughtful for a thirteen-year-old – well, pushing fourteen.

Lauren notices his serious expression. It reminds her of when Amy used to ask questions at about the same age. Lauren had hoped the children would not be shown the most distressing images of the Holocaust. She knows it has to be done, that only by teaching the mistakes of the past can they be avoided in the future. But it is hard to think how upsetting the lessons might be when it comes to explaining the causes and consequences of the war.

However, her sensible son, still so much a child and not yet a sullen morose youth, says, 'Maybe Margie can tell me about what happened where she was in the war, as well as helping with my German. Talk about what it was really all like back then. That would be cool.'

And Lauren smiles. He's right. 'Good idea, love. She might not want to talk about it much though. I've never known her say anything about her past. But you never know, it might help her.'

'Cool. I'll ask her about it when I go round hers tomorrow for my German lessons.' He slopes off and she hears him pick up his rucksack in the hall. 'Going to do my homework now,' he shouts, 'then can I have another piece of cake?'

'Course you can,' Lauren shouts back. 'I'll call you when tea's ready.' She smiles to herself. He'll be all right, she thinks. The kids have had it hard with Colin going so young, but they're both coping. Amy is doing well in her first year of university at Exeter, with her English and French. And Freddie will do GCSEs in a couple of years and then maybe he too will do his A-levels and be off.

But they have to live their own lives. They can't hang around here with me forever. And I left home at eighteen, she thinks. Teacher training college, not that I've done much with it in recent years. Nursery school isn't the same as real school, so perhaps once Freddie's on his way I'll rethink my life too. If Colin was still here I probably would have already got a proper teaching job, but for now part-time nearby is enough.

Lauren begins preparing the lasagne by dicing onions for the sauce. Always home-made, though she's very happy to use the easy fresh pasta sheets she can buy from the supermarket these days. When she first learnt to make it years ago, the dried pasta had to be boiled and then drained and it was a slippery job layering the wet sheets of pasta with Bolognese and cheese sauce. She quickly realises that she has made far too much of the meat sauce and, rather than freezing it as she usually does, she decides to make a dish for Margie. She's always so generous to us, she thinks, giving us her lovely cakes. I'll make a separate one for her. She might be tired after yesterday and not think of cooking a proper meal for herself.

She hums as she assembles the filling dish, beating the roux for the béchamel sauce, stirring the mince, then grating some fresh Parmesan over the top of the layers. She pops both dishes into the oven and once they are cooked, bubbling with a topping of golden cheese, she calls to Freddie from the bottom of the stairs. 'I'm just popping next door for a minute. The lasagne is out the oven, so help yourself when you're ready, but leave some for me!'

She hears thumping steps on the stairs as she slips out of the back door holding the small dish with thick oven gloves. She could have taken it there uncooked, but if Margie is feeling tired and frail, how much nicer for her to know she has an instant hot meal tonight. The front of the house is in darkness, so Lauren goes round the back to the kitchen. The light is on and she can see Margie sitting at the kitchen table where they had coffee and apple cake earlier in the day. She isn't eating or drinking a cup of tea, she is sitting with her head in her hands.

Lauren hesitates, wondering if she should intrude. But the lasagne is hot, ready to eat, and if Margie is distressed, she wants to help her. She taps on the window, but Margie doesn't stir. So Lauren taps again and this time Margie's head jerks round and she looks alarmed. Lauren tries the door handle, which is usually still unlocked even past lighting-up time. But today the door won't open and Lauren calls out, 'Margie, it's only me. I've brought you a freshly cooked lasagne for your tea, it's just come out the oven.'

Anna puts a hand to her heart and shakes her head, then

comes over to the door and unlocks it. 'My dear, you gave me quite a fright.'

'I'm so sorry I made you jump. Can I come in? I made far too much and I thought you might like it for your supper tonight. Save you cooking again. It goes well with a green vegetable or maybe a bit of salad.'

'You are really very kind.'

'Oh, it's nothing much. It's a bit of a thank you for all the lovely cakes you're always giving us. Freddie was very happy to find your apple cake when he came in from school today.' Lauren sets the dish down on the table. 'It's still hot so it's ready to eat right away if you want to.'

Anna turns to the cupboard and fetches two plates, then opens a drawer for cutlery. In that moment, Lauren realises she is expecting them to eat together. 'Oh, I can't stay though, Margie. Freddie is waiting for his tea back home. Another time perhaps.' She feels awkward, wondering if she really should keep her neighbour company.

'Of course. I didn't mean...' Anna shakes her head. 'Sometimes I forget there is no one else here.' She pauses as if she can't remember what else she should say. 'Once there were so many of us and so little to eat. I was thinking about them, trying to remember how it all was...'

'I can stay for a moment, though, if you want to talk for a while.' Lauren hovers by the back door, clutching the oven gloves to her chest, knowing she looks anxious to leave.

'No, my dear. You must go home. Feed your child and make sure he eats well and grows strong.' Anna waves her away.

Lauren steps outside and just before she closes the door she says, 'Freddie is really looking forward to practising his German with you tomorrow, Margie.' And the old woman nods and smiles.

DER WACHOLDERBAUM

THE JUNIPER TREE

So the stepmother chopped the little boy into
pieces and stewed him for his father's supper.

SIXTEEN

HAMBURG, EASTER 1943

Anna had resolved not to see any of her old friends when she returned home from Bavaria at Easter for a last visit before starting her new job as a secretary, far away to the east. Now Günther was dead, the only other person she would have enjoyed seeing again was her childhood friend Etta, the dark-haired girl with whom she had shared so many games, dancing with their dolls across that threadbare patterned carpet. But she had not seen Etta for more than five years and had no idea how she and her family were faring in France under German occupation.

Mama grumbled about the expense of Easter traditions, but clung to them all the same. 'When I was growing up in the countryside we thought more about our spring cleaning at this time of year than all this extravagant nonsense. And we all ran out into the fields to have our great big *Osterfeuer* to burn all the rubbish that had gathered over the winter and welcome the coming of spring. Every year, we did that, so we'd all have a clean, fresh start.'

Anna had heard her tell the same story every Easter for as long as she could remember. As a child she had pictured a huge bonfire with all her aunts, uncles and their children linking arms and dancing around it. When they used to pay their annual visit to her mother's village in the height of the summer, before the war, her cousins gleefully pointed out where the fire had burned with flames as high as the farmhouse. But Anna could see no sign of it; there was nothing, not even a patch of scorched ground, to mark where it had all been, just new green grass. Mama also liked to remind her and Papa that rural folk were far more frugal than those in the city, where people revelled in chocolate eggs and lavish decorations. 'We always wrapped our eggs in onion skins to colour them. That was good enough for us.'

If I'd had brothers and sisters, Anna thought, these holiday times would have always felt more special. And if I'd returned to my parents with a grandchild in my arms, would they have celebrated a new life or would they have been appalled and said I'd brought shame upon them? As it is, we are going through the motions of the Easter traditions without any sense of joy and celebration.

The Thursday before Good Friday, known as Gründonnerstsag, Mama prepared one of her family's old country recipes, a soup made with various green herbs and vegetables. 'Your grandmother and great-grandmother always made green soup at this time,' she said. 'I expect your aunts are still making it on the farm even now. But it's far easier to prepare out in the open countryside, where you can just go out into the kitchen garden at any moment and pick all the herbs you need. Seven-herb soup we always called it. We used dandelions, chives, sorrel, everything.' She ladled portions out into bowls set before Anna and her father. 'But you try and find seven herbs these days, in the market here in the city. You'll be lucky.' She shook her head in dismay at how little Hamburg had to offer. 'I've had to make do with just spinach and parsley. Two-herb soup we'll have to call it.'

Anna sipped the thin green broth from her spoon. It tasted much the same as every year, whether Mama found two herbs or the fabled seven. She thought she could detect something like onion, whether leeks or shallots she wasn't too sure, plus a hint of grated nutmeg, which her mother always used with spinach. The soup was watery and not at all full of flavour, but at least it was more palatable, she thought, than her mother's other traditional Easter speciality for this particular day of the year – eggs in green sauce. The very sight of the white, hard-boiled eggs sitting like shiny bald heads in a thick puddle of green gloop had always made her feel sick and she felt queasy just thinking of it now.

'Well done, Hilde,' Anna's father said. 'You are an excellent housekeeper. I think your family would be proud of you for keeping their country ways alive.'

'Huh,' Mama snorted, 'my mother would turn in her grave if she could see how little we can buy in this wretched city. I can't even grow my own herbs here in this dark apartment. No balcony, barely a windowsill even. It makes me wonder what on earth they think they will gain with this war after losing the last one.'

'Keep your voice down, Hilde. You mustn't talk like that. We don't want the neighbours hearing you. I don't know who to trust these days. And please be very careful what you say in public when you go to the market. Any criticism of the Reich will not be tolerated. You know that could be dangerous.'

'I'm only speaking the truth. It's going to get a whole lot worse before it gets better. And you know it is.'

Papa shook his head. 'There is no point in complaining. At least my skills are in demand. The army marches on its feet and they need strong boots. I can barely keep up with the work.' Everyone knew that the war wasn't going well. One of the latest disasters had been labelled the Palm Sunday Massacre as it happened just before Easter, when aircraft on their way to rescue troops stranded in Tunisia were shot down by the British.

Anna listened to the bickering while she spooned her soup. It was the accompaniment to every meal she had ever taken with them. Despite their hard work, her parents never seemed to improve their life, never had anything to spare for luxuries. It was always about managing to keep going.

'Well, I'm glad I still have plenty of work too,' Mama said. 'My ladies can't spare money for new fabrics, if we could even get hold of the material. But there's demand for alterations and remodelling often enough.'

Throughout Anna's childhood her mother had made and refashioned ladies' garments on the dining table, which was always spread with fabrics and threads, alongside her hand-cranked sewing machine. Only on feast days, like now, was the table cleared of lint and pins and set with the family's best plates; Mama would bring out the white porcelain with gilded edges, which had been a wedding present. She wouldn't let Anna wash it, and insisted on replacing it in her china cabinet as soon as she'd carefully dried each piece herself.

If I'd brought them a grandchild for Easter, Anna thought, Mama would have made a dress embroidered with bunnies for a girl, a romper suit for a boy. She might have knitted a bonnet and a shawl too. And Papa could have cut a sliver of soft red leather to make little buttoned shoes or fleece-lined slippers, just like the ones he stitched for me one Christmas when I was very young. And maybe Peter is wrapped in a hand-knitted shawl with his new parents right now, as they enjoy the start of their Easter feast too. And next year, when he has passed his first birthday, they will give him his first little taste of chocolate as a sign that good things are sure to come.

Lost in thought, she was startled when her mother nudged her, saying, 'Eat up your soup! It's nearly cold. Here, mop it up with some bread.'

She quickly wiped her bowl with a slice of dark-brown Graubrot, then helped her mother clear the table. 'Thank you, Mama, for such a good meal. I shall certainly miss your cooking when I've gone.'

'Where is it you're going again?'

'It's over in the east, beyond Danzig.'

'Huh, Polish then. Well, you won't get this kind of food there. And why couldn't you have found a nice job in Hamburg with your qualifications? Do you really have to take a position in a prison? There must be plenty of good jobs here for a skilled girl like you.'

Anna shook her head. 'There's very few, Mama. There are plenty of jobs in the factories, but not office jobs like this one. And I'll be tucked away in an office typing all day, I won't be working with the prisoners. Besides, it will pay very well. And they include all meals, laundry and accommodation, so I might even be able to save some money to send home. That would be quite a help, wouldn't it?'

'A little more would be very welcome. I can't see prices dropping while this wretched war continues.'

Every meal that Easter concluded with a mild interrogation of her plans. After the Good Friday dinner of salmon with sauerkraut and green cabbage, Mama said, 'And what about coming back here when the war is over and all the young men can come home. You'd like to marry a nice boy from round here, wouldn't you?'

Anna swallowed hard at that point and changed the subject. Surely even Mama knew how many eligible men were losing their lives at the front. And she'd never dare tell her parents that the man she loved was lost, fearing she might burst into tears. Then, when they had lamb with juniper berry sauce on Easter Sunday, Mama said, 'If you don't hurry up and get married, there'll be no point in me trying to teach you all my old family recipes.'

Papa had interrupted then, saying, 'Hilde, for goodness' sake, the girl's only just passed her secretarial exams, she's young, she's only eighteen. There's plenty of time for all that. We've got a war to win first.'

Mama had shaken her head and said, 'Girls used to want to marry and have children while they were young and healthy, not leave home to work in offices.' Anna held her breath and hoped she wouldn't ask any more searching questions about the man she had hoped to marry. But Mama turned instead to the topic of recipes and food. 'And I've made my *lammkuchen* again this year, baked in the special tin my grandmother always used for her Easter cake.'

And despite her grief, Anna softened at this gesture. 'I love your lamb cake. It always looks so lifelike. Thank you for making it. And of course you must pass the special lamb tin on to me one day, so I can keep on baking it, just like you do.' Her mother smiled at this, proud that her family traditions would survive. 'And when I leave after Easter, can you give me some of your home cooking for the journey?'

'I'll make a food parcel for you and I'll bake some lebkuchen as well and put them in a tin so they'll keep well. That'll remind you of home.'

SEVENTEEN

HAMBURG, MAY 1945

Anna had done her best to improve her appearance; boiled water to wash her face, her hair, her armpits and down below. But there was no soap and it seemed as if the greasy, smoky grime was just shifted from one place to the other. Still, she combed her hair, tied it back from her forehead with a strip of cloth and fashioned a bow in some semblance of style. In the cracked scrap of mirror that was all they had to check their appearance, she thought she looked most unlike the girl who had begun her journey back to Hamburg over a month ago and certainly nothing like the girl any of The Others might remember.

Gertrud had looked her up and down before she left to visit the British barracks and said, 'Lordy, Etta, you won't have any luck wearing that filthy, shapeless coat. Here, take my jacket. At least it will show you've still got some curves. They'll like that.'

Anna shook her head. 'I don't know what you're talking about. The British aren't the Russians. They're not like that.'

'Etta, all men are like that,' Gertrud said with a knowing cackle.

But Anna accepted the offer and as she buttoned the loose

jacket across her breasts, she thought that the weight loss of recent weeks had only accentuated her waist. 'I'll take the little ones with me this time. I just want to go along there to see what it's like and nothing else. Come on, you two.' She held out her hands to Stefan and Therese, who were eager for an adventure and scampered up the steps to the street.

Was this wise, Anna asked herself, as they walked to the encampment to the west of the city centre. The children skipped alongside her, chattering with excitement about what treats might be in store for them. 'Will there be chocolate, Etta?' they kept asking her.

'Who knows what they may have hidden in their big rucksacks?' she said, catching their eagerness. 'You saw the soldiers marching through the city the other day with those bulging bags on their backs. And trucks of supplies have arrived now to feed all those men, so they may well have something to spare for cheeky little monkeys like you.'

But as soon as they reached the barracks, with its high wire fences and guarded main entrance, Anna realised she wasn't the only one to think that this was a good place to come for handouts. Quite a crowd of children was gathering at the gates, calling out for chocolate, and as soldiers marched to and from the camp, shifty older men hobbled alongside them begging for cigarettes. 'Come with me,' she said to Therese and Stefan, 'let's take a look around. There might be another way in.'

They skirted the perimeter fence, peering at the substantial, well-designed barracks that had originally been built for the Luftwaffe, looking at the soldiers parading, sergeants shouting, tanks and jeeps driving back and forth. A tempting smell of roasting meat wafted from a nearby building, which Anna guessed must be the cookhouse. The fence was just a fence, the lines of wire were barbed but not electrified, there were no lookouts with machine guns ready to fire from watchtowers, so she could let her fingers grasp the metal strands, avoiding the spikes, longing to be closer to the wonderful aroma of whole-some food.

As she peered, her nose absorbing the delicious smells, the children clutching the fence alongside her, an army cook came out of the building, wiping his hands on his white apron. He lit a cigarette, then leant back against the wall, his face to the sun. And then he noticed her and her young charges. He took another puff, wandered across to her, looked over his shoulder, then offered her the lit cigarette.

'There's more where that came from,' he said, 'if you know what I mean.'

She couldn't understand his words, but she understood the meaning of his gesture when he pouted a kiss and winked. She took his offering, the first she'd had for many months, and put her lips to the still-damp paper.

'That's it, gel, you put your lovely lips right where mine were. Good, eh?' He winked once more and then looked around again. 'No fraternising, Sarge says, but what's a fag between friends, eh? Wait right there and I'll be back in a jiffy.' He walked back to the cookhouse and minutes later emerged with his hands hidden under his apron. Then, like a magician producing a string of coloured flags out of a hat, he thrust a small loaf through the fence. 'Come back tonight and there'll be more of the same, if you're feeling friendly like.' He tapped the side of his nose, making it clear they shared something secret together.

Although she had no English, she understood exactly what his words implied and thanked him, quickly breaking off pieces of the crust for the children, who grabbed it from her hand and silently began munching the fresh bread. Anna watched him walking back to his workplace. As he reached the entrance, he turned and blew her a kiss.

Anna turned to go herself, thinking about his crude suggestion. Was this what she was reduced to? There was free food to be had if she took the risk and registered at the refugee centre in the Zoo Camp. Or she could go to any of the city's communal kitchens and take a chance on being questioned. But would the pickings here at the barracks be more plentiful for the group and safer for her? Could she bear to give herself to such a crude man for whatever he was prepared to offer?

She was preoccupied all the way back to the cellar. Rumour had it that food supplies would soon peter out, despite the best intentions of the British, because they had dismissed all the city officials who had managed to keep a steady flow of rations coming into Hamburg ever since that terrible bombing. If that were true, they would all need to be more resourceful than ever, and if the only currency a woman had was her body, should she refuse to use it to benefit the group of young people she was growing to care about? She hadn't been able to do much more than smuggle crusts of bread to help The Others, but these youngsters might come to rely on her and maybe this way she could do some good.

When they returned to the cellar, Gertrud was boiling water to wash Peter and change him. 'Is that all you managed to get?' she scoffed when Anna showed her the loaf. 'You'll have to do better than that. Go back tonight and hope you have more luck. This place will be running out of food soon, now those British idiots have sacked all our officials. You've heard, haven't you? And the ration cards they're handing out won't be much use if there's nothing to get in the shops!' She waved a card under Anna's nose.

'You went to the Zoo Camp and registered?'

'I certainly did, much good it's going to do me.' She laid Peter down on her bed and removed his soiled napkin and wiped his skin. 'Still, we had a good wash and a nice dusting of powder and I got some clean clothes and nappies for us. Could be worse, I s'pose.'

Anna winced at the roughness with which Gertrud scrubbed her baby's flesh as he cried. She knew she'd have been far gentler with her own child. She poured some of the hot water into a bowl, added a little cold, then handed it to Gertrud. 'I'll go back later tonight and see what it's like there. The man I met today was a cook. He must have access to all the food supplies at the barracks. And he had cigarettes.'

'Then if you get nothing else, try and get cigarettes. That's as good as cash these days. I heard one of the Brits at the Zoo Camp say he could get a suit made for two hundred cigarettes. If we can get plenty of cigarettes, we'll use them to go hamstering in the countryside.'

Anna hadn't heard that phrase in a long time. It was what her mother used to say when they were taking a trip out into the country, coming back laden with fresh eggs, ham, butter and cheese. 'If things get as bad as you think they will, the farmers will soon be able to charge whatever they like.'

Gertrud looked up at her from her freshly washed baby son. 'From now on, we must concentrate on searching not just for food, but for goods we can barter. By the time winter comes, the greedy farmers will be asking for fur coats for their wives and Turkish rugs for their pigsties.' She laughed but Anna knew her words bore the truth. The city folk were now the deprived poor and the farmers were getting rich on their hardship.

EIGHTEEN

LONDON, NOVEMBER 2016

Lauren isn't used to making international calls and is flummoxed by the different time zones for Australia. She decides she should ring before she goes to bed. How much simpler it would be if she could find an email address. But, not surprisingly, Margie's address book only has street addresses and phone numbers for her two children, Peter and Susan. Margie once told her their names were chosen because they were English, yet similar to names she had grown up with. She looks sad when she talks about them and the grandchildren and great-grandchildren she has never seen in person, and Lauren can't help wondering why they are not only distant in terms of where they've chosen to live, but emotionally distant from their elderly mother.

A woman's voice answers and Lauren says, 'Is Peter there? I'm calling from London on behalf of his mother.'

'She hasn't gone and died, has she?'

'No, it's not bad news. She's okay, but I need to talk to him. Is he there?'

'No, he's not. I'm Rosemary, his wife. He left early this

morning. Dental appointment before his round of golf. I can get him to call later.'

'I'm Margie's neighbour, Lauren. I had to call the doctor out for her today and thought Peter should know.'

'Is she seriously ill?'

'No, but she's been behaving a little strangely.'

'Oh, thank goodness for that. I need to keep him calm. It's his heart, you know.'

'Oh, I'm sorry to hear that. Tell him not to worry too much. The doctor said she's in good shape for her age. But maybe you could tell his sister, Susan?'

There was a big sigh of resignation. 'Susan? Yeah, I suppose I can do that. Not that she'll be interested and do anything.'

'Thank you. That would save the cost of another call.' Lauren is shocked by the woman's indifference. 'You can tell Peter I'm keeping an eye on his mother for now.'

She finishes by asking Rosemary to take down her contact details, including email, 'Just for the sake of convenience,' she says, doubting they will ever be in touch. Do they really not care? And is it just coincidence that both of Margie's children moved so far away?

She puts down the phone, then feels Freddie come up behind her and rest his head on her shoulder. She pats his hair with her other hand. 'You off to bed?'

'In a minute. Can we have a dog?'

She laughs. 'I've told you before. I haven't time to look after or train a dog.'

'But I'd look after it. Really, I would.'

'Oh yeah. At first maybe, while it's a novelty. But then it would be down to me to do all the walks and clear up the mess. And what about your schoolwork?'

'I could walk it before school. Charlie's just got a dog. It's a cockapoo.'

'Expensive dog then. Why couldn't they give a rescue dog a good home?'

'Dunno. They wanted a cute puppy, I suppose.'

'Well, cute puppy or mangy mutt, they're all hard work. Besides, a dog's not just for while you're still at school, you know. I'd be left picking up the poo once you've gone off to uni or college. So the answer's definitely no.'

'I knew you'd say that.' He steps back and slouches off towards the stairs.

'Night, love,' she calls, but there is no reply from him.

Lauren smiles to herself. He will get grouchy as he grows, she knows that, but for now he is still her little boy. Maybe she should allow him to have a dog. How hard would it be? Could she manage to walk it in the mornings if Freddie was running late? It wasn't like she worked every single day. Might do me good, she thinks, remembering how she'd loved walks with Barney the golden retriever when she was about Freddie's age and still lived with her parents. An eager, panting dog makes the experience of walking an enjoyable task, whatever the weather. Colin had always said they'd get a dog one day, when they weren't both so busy and had more time. He'd have liked a big dog, to make him go for long walks and help him lose weight. A Labrador or a boxer perhaps.

As she tidies the kitchen before going to bed, covering the remains of the lasagne, washing up the dishes, putting out food for the wandering cat, she notices that all the lights in the house next door are blazing. Margie is normally careful with her electricity. Lauren shakes her head and thinks it is none of her business. But then, as she switches off her own lights after making a calming cup of camomile tea to take upstairs, her neighbour's lights suddenly go off too. She checks her back door is locked and is about to leave the room when she glances out of the window; and there, over the low fence dividing their gardens, lit only by the light of the risen moon, she sees Margie. The old lady is standing still, just outside her house, her head tilted up at the sky. She holds her hands clasped under her chin and seems to be looking upwards, unmoving.

Lauren watches her, wondering why she is out in the cold at this time of the evening. It isn't terribly late, not even ten o'clock yet, but it is odd to see her standing there. And then she realises that Margie is gazing heavenward. And maybe her clasped hands mean she is praying. But for what? Is she praying for herself, for others, for her children to return so she can meet her grandchildren?

It pains Lauren to see her doing this. Goodness knows, she has prayed herself, both before and after Colin's death. Prayed that she wouldn't soon follow him, but would live long enough to see her children educated and set off on life's journey. Her prayers have been answered in that she is still, at the age of forty-seven, reasonably fit and healthy, still able to enjoy her friends, though she's far from feeling ready, even though they've urged her, to try the risky path of online dating. She isn't yet ready to move on from Colin's memory, despite his final hope that she would find another partner one day. But she doesn't step outside in the dark to pray, she does it in her local church and in her bedroom before going to sleep.

And Lauren comes to the conclusion that Margie needs more in her life, what little she has left. Apart from her short excursions to the corner shop and the church, her exchanges with the milkman and visits from her neighbour, she has no one. Freddie's visits will be welcome of course, but she needs more, and Lauren is now resolved to help her as much as she can.

NINETEEN

LONDON, NOVEMBER 2016

Anna reaches under her bed for her little blue suitcase. She hasn't looked at it since the day Lauren and Freddie found her and brought her home. She slid it back under her bed last week and hasn't looked at it again till now. She knows she felt an intense need to escape, coupled with a fear of being found out, but she can't remember exactly what prompted her to leave the house that particular day.

She slides the case out from its hiding place and lifts it onto the bed. With slow, steady movements, she stands up from kneeling and sits on the soft candlewick bedspread. Such bedding seemed so luxurious when she first came to England and she has always liked the soft, carved pattern; even now her hand strokes the tufted ridges. She opens the case on her lap and removes the contents one by one, as if she is checking that they are all still there.

But she isn't really checking, is she? No, she's looking for something, trying hard to remember – and there it is, right at the bottom, below her underwear and toiletries, a manila envelope filled with newspaper clippings. For years she has kept watch, knowing that The Others might point Them out, might one day stand in court to point accusing fingers and make their memories known. On the whole she has not recognised the faces in the reports, although there was a long-ago year when one was all too familiar. A jowled female, with a sulky expression, her hair no longer blonde as it was in the younger image alongside her older self.

Looking again at the picture of the thickset woman, Anna wonders if she softened in her later years, or did her incendiary temper mark her out all her life? In the newspaper cutting she is named as Birgit Schuetz, now Birgit Maurer, a former prison camp guard, accused of ill-treating prisoners on work details at a camp where thousands died. You can tell just from looking at her photograph, Anna thinks, tell that she enjoyed her work. And she was one of the guards who left early to accompany the long march taking most of The Others to their deaths.

Some, Anna now knows, were sent onwards to other places of hell, but some were crowded into the ships that were bombed by the British just before the war ended. How could the pilots have known that the craft were filled not with enemy troops, but with starving prisoners in need of salvation and not drowning?

Which is worse, Anna wonders, swimming for your life, if you even had the strength, in the icy waters of the sea, or dying of starvation and typhus in huts putrid with waste and disease? She thinks she'd have preferred the cold, clean waters of the Baltic, the Ostsee, washing away the filth and giving the swimmers a small chance of saving themselves. In the huts The Others could never have stood a chance.

She puts everything but the stuffed envelope back in her case, then bends with great difficulty to slide it back under her bed. She probably won't be needing it now. She's proved to herself that she can't manage to get much further than the bus stop. That, the corner shop and the church are the full extent of her world now. Once she had been able to walk great distances for days, over four hundred miles back to Hamburg, but now her life has shrunk and is limited to these three destinations. There is no escape for her now but death.

Anna reads again the latest news cutting she added to her collection. She recognised his younger self. He was a little older than her then, a gentle man, but compromised as they all were. The man had worked in a bank until his retirement and latterly lived in a care home. He was ninety-seven years old and he recently pressed the button on his electric wheelchair and ran it along a jetty and right into the River Elbe. Luckily for him – or not so lucky, she thinks – he was rescued by passers-by, who thought his chair had malfunctioned. But she knows it was a deliberate act. He was afraid of what was going to happen. The prosecutor said he could still be charged, as his act clearly showed that he was of sound mind. Sound enough, Anna thinks, to want to escape the accusations. He was young back then, only in his mid-twenties, he was following orders and he was merely an accountant. He was good with figures, not with firearms. He never harmed anyone himself with his own hands, but was he complicit in the fate of many?

She slips that report too back into the envelope. The man died a week later after his dip in the icy river. Delayed shock or hypothermia, who knows? But he escaped. And was that justice, or would it have been better if he'd stayed alive to testify about his experiences?

But there can't be many more like him, she knows. They are all dead or are dying. Both the accused and the accusers are dwindling in numbers, so soon there will be no one left to tell how it was back then. She wonders if any of The Others are still alive. They weren't meant to live, they were meant to die, if not deliberately with gas or a bullet, then through wilful neglect. But a handful did survive, she knows, and testified to their ill-treatment at the hands of Birgit and others like her, to ensure that her kind were justly punished. Birgit was hanged, but some served penal sentences from which they were released for good behaviour.

And what was good about their behaviour, Anna asks herself. That they kept quiet, followed the rules, didn't foul their cells? Did they deserve to live at all, if they'd had a hand in the punishment or death of many? But an accountant, a man who'd counted the numbers and tallied the figures, what did he deserve? He'd lived an ordinary life after the war until his death, keeping quiet and harming no one. And he died at ninety-seven, rather than in the prime of his life.

Anna tries to turn her mind away from The Others, but there were so many of them it is very hard to forget. She tries to think about the rest she helped, like the Ausgebombten Gang and how eventually debasing herself brought them bread and a little more time to grow stronger after the trials of the inferno. They weren't many, compared to The Others, but she is glad she contributed to their survival. She has never forgotten the feeling of shame she experienced lowering herself to the same level as Gertrud, but she reminds herself that she wasn't the only young woman in Hamburg who had no choice but to use the only currency available to her. And at least she received help, she remembers with a smile, thinking of her first night abroad on the city's streets and the night she made some new friends.

DAS MÄDCHEN OHNE HÄNDE
THE GIRL WITH NO HANDS

She held out her hands and her father chopped
them both off. But when the devil returned,
she had cried so much that her tears had
washed the stumps clean and
the devil could not claim her.

TWENTY

HAMBURG, MAY 1945

Blazing lights illuminated the grounds of the British barracks that night, but the areas surrounding the perimeter fences were largely in darkness. Anna slipped past the main entrance, its gates guarded by sentries, as a barrier lifted to allow vehicles to enter. She passed unnoticed to the section where she had been given the bread earlier in the day.

It was quiet and still and she shivered in her tight jacket and dress. She stood close to the fence, her face almost touching the wire. There were sounds of laughter further away, within the camp, but no eager men came towards the boundary, arms outstretched, ready to drop their trousers at the first sight of a pretty girl.

Anna heard rustling in the bushes behind her and a woman came and stood beside her, while a shadowy male figure slipped away in the background. In the reflected light, Anna could see a heavily made-up face, though where she had managed to buy cosmetics she couldn't think. Maybe it was soot defining her eyes and juice her pouting lips.

'You'd think they'd be keen to have a bit of fun now they've won the war,' the woman said, turning to Anna and looking her up and down. She sniggered, then began laughing aloud. 'You're not going to get much business looking like that, love!'

Anna took a couple of steps away from her, but didn't speak.

'You haven't done this before, have you? Well, as you're no competition for me, dearie, I'll give you some good advice. Payment first, then get down to it. And use your hand if you can. It's quickest and safest, but that's also the cheapest.' The woman held out a friendly hand. 'Lili – pleased to meet you.'

As Anna stepped forwards to shake her hand, half wondering where it had been recently, Lili moved into a beam of light and Anna could see that she was really much younger than she had at first thought. Was it the harshness of life for everyone in this ruined city or her life on the streets that was eroding her youth, etching hard lines around her mouth and eyes?

'My name's Etta and I'm not really sure I want to do this,' Anna said. 'But I know food supplies in the city will run out before long. The British may have won the war, but they won't win us over if we end up starving.'

'Too right. But at least they won't take advantage for free. Not like the bloody Russians. Damn Soviets don't care how old or how young. If it's got a fanny, they'll fuck it.'

Anna was shocked by Lili's language. 'Can you be sure the British aren't like that too?'

'Nah. They're mostly decent. And if they pay us in cigarettes, we'll do all right. That's practically currency these days.'

'That's what my friend Gertrud says. I think she'd be down here too if she could be, but she's just had a baby.'

'Gertie? She got dark hair?' When Anna nodded, Lili shook her head and said, 'She's a one, old Gertie. Fearless, she is. I remember one time she took on three men, all at the same time if you know what I mean. The two of us started out in Tante Kitty's when we were both young and fresh. Down by the docks. Plenty of clients down there in the old days. It's all gone now, of course.'

'You both worked in a *bordell*?' Anna had heard of such establishments, but couldn't imagine what it would be like to work in such a business.

'Yeah, it was hard graft all right, but old Tante looked after us, she did. Food, doctor, bedding, baths, all of it included. And Auntie didn't stand for no nonsense from the punters, so we all felt safe there. You didn't get much hard cash for yourself, but you were well fed and had a roof over your head, so it wasn't that bad. Better than the streets like now.'

Lili sighed, 'I wish I was back there, but it was bombed out. Tante was burned to death and we all just about escaped in our flimsies. I was just about to do a Luftwaffe pilot when the siren went. Shame that. He'd have been my fiftieth that month, which would have made me the highest scorer in the house.' She shrieked with laughter, a laugh that was accompanied by a rattle in her throat and a wheeze in her chest, a sure sign of festering tuberculosis.

Behind them, they then heard another female voice calling out, 'I'd know that cackle anywhere, Lili,' and a second woman emerged from the bushes, followed by a soldier buckling his belt.

'Rita!' Lili shouted, opening her arms to greet her friend. 'You must have started early tonight.'

'Yeah, I thought I'd come and check it out.' She jerked her head at the soldier, who was wandering off. 'I told lover boy there that I'd be here every night from now on with a couple of friends. He'll put the word round and by tomorrow we'll be in business.' She studied Anna's face. 'You look like a new girl. Just starting out, are you? They'll like you.'

'I'm not sure yet. I've never done anything like this before.'

'But you've been with a man, yeah?' Rita scrabbled around in her handbag and brought out a cigarette. 'Here, got a light?'

'I've got one,' Lili said, striking a match. 'You got more than one fag for that fumble, I hope?'

'Course I did. They get them as part of their rations, along with Lumelle. Don't want them getting the clap, do they? And that one didn't even smoke!' Rita's raucous laugh floated in the night air, then she poked Anna in the ribs. 'Here, you didn't answer my question. Have you done it before or haven't you?'

'Just the once,' Anna whispered. 'He was killed.' She thought of Günther, his plea for them to be bonded in love before he left for the front. She could never have said no to him, knowing he was sure to face the Russians while she only had to face a speed test for her typing.

Rita took a drag on the cigarette, then passed it to Lili, who inhaled deeply and offered it to Anna. She declined. 'You sure, Etta?' Lili said. 'Warms you up and it's gonna get chilly tonight with no knickers on.'

'No thanks, I'm not that keen.' She didn't want to offend either of them, but the thought of TB germs being passed from mouth to mouth was really what she wasn't keen on. The chances were that Rita was also beginning to suffer in the same way.

'Suit yourself then,' Lili said, taking another drag before passing it back to her friend. 'Ooh, hear that?' She turned her head in the direction of male voices. 'Looks like your bloke's put the word out, Rita.' Both the girls giggled and undid another button on their dress fronts, thrusting their breasts forward.

Anna looked behind her and saw several soldiers coming towards them. She felt cold, shivery and very scared. Was she going to go through with it? And for what? Shame, pain and maybe disease? 'I'm going to go,' she told the two girls. 'They're all yours.' She ran past the men, running as if she was being hunted, faster and faster.

'Over here, lads,' Rita yelled.

'Form a queue, boys,' Lili shouted.

TWENTY-ONE

LONDON, JANUARY 2017

It's not easy being a single parent, Lauren thinks. She'd never expected to finish raising her children alone. Colin had been there for the early sleepless nights, some of the time, present for the terrible twos and the saucy sixes, but gone by the time they entered the teenage torments. And his passing only added to her children's troubles.

So, is that why, she asks herself, why I feel I have to try extra hard to be a good parent? Do all single parents, well, the conscientious ones that is, alone through choice, abandonment or bereavement, feel they have to perform the role of both parents? It's not as if, truth be told, Colin could even have been here all the time, with such a huge workload and his overtime. Police work doesn't really make allowances for being a dutiful dad, though he did manage the nativity and school sports day most years. But with him gone, I always feel like I have to try extra hard to make up for his absence.

She was always a dutiful mother, even before Colin's death. Amy was an easy baby, but Freddie with his hip problems, the joint encased in plaster, was fractious. She tried so hard to do her bit, always made costumes for World Book Day on time, although one year she stayed up most of the night gluing layers of green and blue tissue scales onto the Little Mermaid's tail; she also stitched name tags onto uniform and made crispy chocolate cornflake cakes for charity sales. And with her husband no longer around, she devoted herself to running the children everywhere for swimming classes, ballet lessons and drum sessions. Oh, the drumming, how could she forget that time of having drums in the house? They were finally expelled to the garage, where they now lie under a dustsheet, never to feel the out-of-time rhythm of Amy's drumsticks ever again, thank goodness.

And now Christmas has been and gone, Amy has returned to halls and Freddie is reluctantly hauling himself out of bed to start the new term. Margie seems to have settled back into her normal routine of a weekly order of flour, sugar and butter, plus potatoes occasionally. She joined the family for the holiday, with gifts of stollen and lebkuchen. She does not appear to have suffered any further lapses of memory or delusion and has returned to her regular baking, walks to the corner shop and attending church, where she also cleans and helps with the flowers.

Freddie returns from his first day back at school after the Christmas holidays, slamming the front door and letting his coat and bag drop with a crash at the bottom of the stairs. 'Mum,' he shouts, 'Where's Amy's drum kit?'

Oh no, Lauren thinks. Please not that again. Though she's heard that the violin can be worse for parental ears. 'Why'd you want to know?'

He slouches in the doorway. His shirt is untucked and hangs down below his school jumper and blazer. So untidy, Lauren thinks, longing to shake him up and tuck his shirt in. His cheeks blaze pink from the cold wind outside, so she also longs to warm him up with a hug.

'Me and Charlie are starting a band.'

'Just the two of you? Won't you need more people?'

He shrugs. 'Maybe. Once we get started, we'll see.'

'And what does Charlie play?'

'He doesn't yet. He's having guitar lessons.'

His poor parents, Lauren thinks, but she says, 'You'd better start practising then. It's in the garage.'

'Can't I bring it inside? It's freezing out there.' He heads for the internal door that leads through to the garage.

'Certainly not. It stays outside. But I'll let you put a heater on, just while you're out there. Don't leave it on all the time though. We're not made of money.'

'Oh Mum, I'll still freeze.'

'Wear gloves then,' she shouts as he disappears. She may be a doting mother, but she knows when to put her foot down. Besides, he'll forgive her when he comes in for his tea and finds she's made his favourite, shepherd's pie. Which, she tells herself, she had better hurry up and finish making. The meat is cooked, with chopped carrot and plenty of onion, so she strains off the gravy to thicken later and starts peeling potatoes. As the slivers of peel fall from her knife she can hear the uneven thud of the drums and the clash of the cymbal. He'll soon tire of it, she hopes, as she prepares herself for an evening of discordant rather than syncopated rhythm.

Later, when the shepherd's pie is baked, with crisp brown ridges on the potato layer, juice oozing underneath the topping, thick gravy steaming in a jug on the table, she calls Freddie inside. He appears, huddled with cold.

'Didn't you put the heater on, like I told you to?'

'Yeah, but it didn't make any difference.' He blows on his hands to warm them, then wraps them round the hot gravy jug.

'And you didn't put your gloves on like I said.'

'Drummers don't wear gloves, Mum. That's so lame.'

'Maybe not for performances, but I bet they sometimes do for warm-up sessions.'

Freddie grunts and takes the plate of food she passes across the table.

'Anyway, how was your first day back? Anything new to tell me?'

'It was all right.' He shovels a large forkful of food into his mouth, finding it too hot, which slows him down. 'German was good though. That's because of Margie.' He blows on the next forkful.

'That's lovely. You must tell her. She'd like to hear that your sessions with her are helping.' Lauren pops a large spoonful of the neglected cabbage onto Freddie's plate. He has never been one for filling up on green vegetables.

He mashes the cabbage into the shepherd's pie so it can hardly be seen. 'And in history, we've got to read this lame book this term.'

'What's that?' Lauren knows Freddie is a reluctant reader, much as she tried to tempt him with Harry Potter, which Amy loved from the first.

'It's this girl's diary. I don't want to read some girl's book. And nor does Charlie.'

'But what's it called?' Lauren sneaks another spoonful of cabbage across to his plate. It's like feeding a toddler sometimes, she thinks, but she's only doing her single-mother best to keep him healthy and help him grow.

'Anne somebody, I think. Her diary about the war.'

'Do you mean *The Diary of Anne Frank*? Is that it?' Lauren finally manages to eat some of her own food, including plenty of cabbage. She knows what's good for her.

'Yeah, think so.' He pours more gravy.

'Mmm, I read it years ago.' Lauren thinks a boy Freddie's age is not going to find it easy. She remembers struggling a little with it herself at first, until she went to Amsterdam. 'And I went to her house, when I was a bit older than you. Did your teacher tell you why she wrote the diary?'

'Something about hiding from the Germans in the war.'

'I went to the house where she and her family hid in an attic. I can't remember how long they were there.'

He looks interested; there's a faint spark in his eyes. 'For the whole of the war?'

'No, unfortunately not. A couple of years maybe. I think someone told the Germans they were there, so they were taken away from their hiding place. Her father survived, but Anne and her sister and mother didn't.'

'Why did you go there?' Freddie has finished his plate of food, but is picking crusty edges of crisp potato from the edge of the baking dish.

Lauren taps his hand to stop him peeling off all the crispy bits. 'Our teacher organised a school trip. I was older than you and I was doing history A-level.'

'Cool. Wish our teacher would do that. Better than giving us a lame book.'

'Don't say that, Freddie. It's a very famous book. It's been sold all over the world.' And then Lauren has the idea. 'We could go there, Freddie. Would you like to do that?'

'Go where?'

'Amsterdam. We could go to the very house and see the actual rooms where Anne and her family hid. We could go at half-term. What do you think?' And Lauren thinks that her single-parent credentials have risen considerably with this suggestion.

'You mean we'd go in the attic where they were all hiding?'

'The very same. And we'd see some other things as well, if there's time.'

'Wait till I tell Charlie. He's going to be so jealous.' He dashes away to call his friend.

Lauren smiles to herself. She's just seen her late husband Colin in Freddie's triumphant grin. She doesn't see him so much in Amy, but now and then when Freddie frowns or smiles, it hits her. He's becoming more and more like Colin. The good parts, she hopes, as he finishes his call and returns to the pounding drums.

TWENTY-TWO

HAMBURG, MAY 1945

Anna ran and kept running away from the barracks with the ogling soldiers and the parading girls, until she could run no more and had to stop for breath. She bent down, hands on her knees, a pain constricting her side. When she stood up again, she realised she was in a park, Jenisch Park, where Günther had made love to her the one time with unforgettable consequences.

It was also one of the havens to which people had fled that terrible night of the inferno nearly two years previously, when British incendiary bombs rained down on the city. How many had found sanctuary in this cool, green space and how many had gasped their last breath here? Some had managed to race from the burning streets, clothes and hair on fire, but even the cool green grass could not save them, as they sank to the ground in their dying moments in agony.

She herself sank onto the damp grass, trying to understand whether she had made the right decision in escaping from the lustful men. She knew that desperate times called for desperate measures; hadn't she seen that time after time, women throwing themselves at guards for a crust, to save a family member or to buy themselves another day of life? My honour doesn't matter, she told herself, I must do what I can to help the young friends I have made so recently, who gave me shelter when I needed it.

But the more she thought about it, the more she felt that the coarse embrace of other men would be a betrayal of Günther. Their union here in the park that summer had been so brief, but so sweet. 'This memory will give me strength to face what is coming,' he'd said, kissing her again on the lips. But that had been at the beginning, the year after Paris was taken in the summer of 1940, when she was only seventeen and it had seemed that the Reich would triumph. And soon after he had left, her own battle had begun, when she'd realised he'd not only left her with sweet memories but a sweet gift too, in the form of an unwanted pregnancy and the birth of her baby.

How long ago was it now? Four years or more? But she suspected her child had never reached his fourth birthday. The imperfect ones didn't last long. She'd heard what the midwife said under her breath to the nurse as she'd wrapped him in a clean towel. But even if she'd fully understood then what was meant by the word 'special', what could she have done? Demanded to see him, feed him and keep him? Take him home to her parents, who would have thought she had brought enough disgrace upon the family without the additional burden of a child who must have been disabled in some capacity? She'd already signed the documents before he was born, confirming that he was a child of the state and not hers from the moment of his birth. She knew now that his imperfection might have been as minor as a cleft palate, perhaps. But no, better that she continued to imagine he was perfect, that he was adopted into a loving family and that he was having a happy life.

She cried a little for her lost son and then she cried some more for all who had died here in Jenisch Park in the middle of this struggling city. She was lucky not to have been in Hamburg at the time of the bombing, being instead far away to the east, but she had heard the terrible stories. Ursula and Hermann had been old enough to understand and to remember, the younger ones less so.

Only the other day, she had found Ursula sitting outside the cellar on the crumbling wall, quietly crying. She had slipped her arm round the tearful girl, saying, 'Whatever is it? Can you tell me?'

Ursula had sniffed and wiped away her tears with the back of her hand. 'I was remembering,' she said, 'how dreadful it all was the night of the bombing, Etta. I sometimes think it was better that our mother died so quickly. We saw such awful things as we ran to safety in the park.'

'Where did you all run to?'

'Jenisch Park. We had to get as far away from the flames as we could. They were everywhere. It was a *flammensee*.' She cried a little more. 'Some of the people escaping their homes were naked,' she said. 'I don't know why. Do you think their clothes caught fire and they had to pull them off?'

'I suppose if you couldn't douse the flames, you'd be desperate to stop yourself burning. Or maybe the force of the explosions had torn their clothes from their bodies.'

'We saw some of them jumping in the water to put out the fire.' Ursula put her face in her hands.

'I've heard people say balls of fire raced through buildings and along the streets. It must have been so terrifying.' Anna looked across the damaged street to the ruins on either side, imagining the flames, the heat, the whole conflagration.

'I keep dreaming about it. Being chased by a ball of fire. Etta, it was so hot and people everywhere were screaming and shouting. We just had to run as fast as we could.' Anna hugged her. 'You did the right thing, you brave girl. The three of you survived. And were Therese and Stefan with you then as well?'

'No, they were already in the park. We found them here on their own. They were terrified, huddled together, and told us they were waiting for their mother. But she never came. I've looked after them ever since that time. They don't ask for her now, but to begin with, they kept asking where she was and when she was coming back.'

'What about Gertrud? Was she here that night as well?'

'I don't know. Stefan and Therese found her walking down our street one day, a long time after we'd started camping in the cellar. They thought she was their mother at first. Maybe to them she does look a little like her. They wanted her to come and live with us and when she said she'd be able to bring in a little extra money, we let her stay.'

'You've managed really well, you know. Many people wouldn't be as brave and resourceful as you.' Anna peered at Ursula's face, hoping she'd see even the shadow of a smile, but there was nothing but a slightly trembling lip. She was barely sixteen, little more than a child, but she'd had to grow up fast in this devastated city.

'Maybe we should all go to the authorities and let them send us off to live in orphanages. At least then life would be a bit easier and we wouldn't have to hunt for supplies all the time. And we could go to school then.'

'Is that what you'd like to do?'

'Not the orphanage. But I liked school. I liked learning.'

'Me too, when I was your age. I even went to secretarial college—' Anna stopped there, afraid she might say too much and encourage questions.

'I'd like a proper job, Etta. Somewhere clean, where I could wear nice clothes. I don't want to do what Gertrud does, even though what she brings in is very helpful.'

Anna thought how she didn't want to do what Gertrud did, or had done before the later stages of her pregnancy, either, but if it made the difference between eating and starving, she knew she'd have to. 'You mustn't follow her example, Ursula. You're doing all you can with your salvaging and foraging. And now some of you have ration cards, you should never have to think about going on the streets. You're far too good for that.'

'And you're not? I know Gertrud thinks you should follow her example.'

What could she say? That she felt such a burden of guilt that she had to do good in whatever small way she could? That trying to help this little gang of misfits was but small compensation to atone for what she had done? 'It's too late for me,' she said. 'I've already seen and done too much. But you can be saved. Please stay that way.'

Ursula threw her arms round Anna. 'Oh, Etta, I'm so glad you've joined us. I feel better just talking to you.'

'I'm glad I can help. You can always talk to me, about anything. Anything at all.'

'Thank you. It's been so hard, trying to stay strong for all of them. Do you think one day the nightmares will go away?'

Anna thought her own worst nightmares would never disappear completely. The thought that her baby had been carelessly disposed of because in some way he was not of the required standard, the memories of the beaten, filthy prisoners, the ragged women lined up and marched away in the freezing cold – no, she would be conscious of these images forever. 'I'm sure they will,' she said. 'They'll keep fading and be replaced by the good things that will happen when normal life is restored. The end of the war is just the start of recovering.'

'I hope so. I want to forget. I so want to forget the night of the bombs with the screaming, burning people.' Ursula shuddered. 'And I want to stop seeing the naked woman running towards us. She ran across the bridge over the water, then fell down on the grass in front of us. She didn't have any feet left, Etta. No feet, just charred stumps. They'd been burned off, but she'd kept on running for her life.'

Anna's heart felt as if it had stopped. She had seen some dreadful sights, but nothing like that. 'You will forget in time,' she said. 'Even that will fade.' But all she could do was hope. She knew her own nightmares would never leave her, the sight of The Others stumbling in the snow, the bodies left behind, consigned to a pyre, and the thought of her child, not permitted to live. These images were burned into her memory and would never disappear or be forgotten.

TWENTY-THREE

AMSTERDAM, FEBRUARY 2017

Lauren has the urge to cover Freddie's eyes as they find their way through the narrow backstreets of Amsterdam, looking for the Anne Frank House. She hadn't realised that the directions she'd been given would lead them through the red-light district with its vulgar, blatant displays of lurid sex aids, as well as the infamous girls posing in curtained windows.

Some of the cramped rooms really do have red lights, giving the bored girls a healthy glow, while other larger premises feature girls dancing in showroom windows, clad only in PVC, thigh-high boots and strategically buckled black leather straps. The large plate-glass windows are like high-street shopfronts, displaying the goods to advantage with a live show.

Really, Lauren thinks, we've only just had our breakfast and they're all cavorting about, showing off their bits and pieces at this time of the morning, pretending not to be bored. Surely a city like this has other job opportunities to offer? What makes girls come here to live like this? Are they so very desperate?

It's all so sordid and sad, but tourists are already gawping at the windows and laughing at the displays and there is a steady stream of visitors to the nearby Sex Museum, which Lauren also finds disturbing. 'I'm sure I've gone wrong somewhere,' she says, checking the directions on her phone again. 'I'm beginning to wish I hadn't brought you here.'

'It's all right, Mum. We've all seen this kind of stuff online. Everyone in school has. Think of it as another part of my education.'

Lauren laughs. 'Cheeky! Still, I suppose your friends are all expecting you to visit this area. They probably think it's one of the main sights of Amsterdam. And when you get back after half-term, they're bound to ask you if you did a tour of the red-light district as well as the Rijksmuseum. Just tell them how sleazy and tacky it all is, please. I don't want anyone from your school thinking I approve of this.'

'Too right. But they'd think it was a bit lame if we didn't do it.' He peers ahead to the next bridge. 'Is the house much further, do you think?'

'It's just round the corner, I think,' Lauren says as they take a right turn. 'Wow, look at that huge queue. Aren't you glad I booked tickets?' A long line of tourists is waiting to enter the Anne Frank House, which Lauren had definitely wanted to include as part of this morning's experience. Since Freddie told her that his class was covering twentieth-century history this year and would be including the Holocaust, she has been determined to bring him here. She can remember how much of an impact the cramped attic rooms made on her as a teenager, when she came here on a school trip as part of her history A-level.

But it looks so different now. Back then, she and her chattering friends had entered the house through an ordinary front door that opened straight off the street. Climbing the steep stairs and ducking through the narrow secret entrance hidden behind the hinged bookcase, they had become subdued, almost hearing the hushed voices of the terrified family hoping that their presence would never be revealed.

They had moved freely through the upper rooms, sensing how the occupants had maintained their reduced existence. Her group was small enough for it to seem that they too were experiencing this small, restricted life of daily boredom, trying to maintain a semblance of normality with lessons for the girls and the preparation of food. And Lauren remembered thinking, as she peered at the magazine cuttings of film stars Anne had pinned to her bedroom wall, how like her she was, just an ordinary girl full of hope, bursting with life, excited at experiencing her first relationship with a boy.

But now, visitors are jammed in tight queues on the steep, narrow stairs and into the attic rooms, in a hubbub of loud chatter and crowded bodies. The air is stuffy and it is so warm that Lauren has to wriggle out of the padded coat she'd needed outside on the city streets on such a chilly, early spring day.

Years ago, when she and her schoolmates had emerged from that shrunken, disciplined life, they had immediately entered a place of horror, where the worst of the Frank family's fate, and that of so many others, was graphically displayed with images of skeletal bodies, starved faces and heaps of corpses. It was shocking and awful, but impossible to avoid or forget.

But now, Lauren feels the house and its sad story have been sanitised to make it more palatable to the parties of students. There are photographs and written information available to those who choose to look, but she thinks none of it can convey the overpowering impact she experienced years before.

Is this the rewriting of history, she thinks. Do the facts have to be watered down before schoolchildren can learn about the real horror? She had prepared herself for Freddie to find their visit upsetting, but now she thinks he may not gain a full understanding of the inhumanity inflicted in that dreadful time.

She grabs Freddie's hand and they decide to stop for refreshment before carrying on to the Our Lord in the Attic Museum, another must-see sight that she realises, with a sinking feeling, may necessitate trailing through the red-light district again. Perhaps they can march past the lurid windows quickly this time; and she hopes the church won't be filled with noisy, insensitive students as well.

In the museum café – yes, even the Anne Frank House has to have a café – Lauren pays for their expensive drinks. 'What did you think of it?' she asks Freddie, as he stirs his thick, strawberry milkshake with a paper straw.

'Yeah, it was cool.' He shrugs. 'But think – no TV, no internet, no phones, no Xbox. It must have been so boring!'

'You don't think you could have stood being cooped up like that then? Anne Frank's friend Peter was in there too, and he was about your age, maybe a little older.'

'Yeah, I know. But they had to stay there, didn't they? I suppose if you know that the only way to survive is to hide and keep quiet, you just have to do it.'

'I think so too, love. They had to make a difficult choice. It was that or risk being sent away. At least they bought themselves some time, and her father actually survived. It's thanks to him that her diary was published.'

'Yeah, we've started doing that in school.' Freddie stares into the depths of his thick, cold shake.

'How are you getting on with it?'

'I didn't think I liked it, but now we've been here, I think it will make more sense. More like seeing the book through her eyes.'

'Well done.' Lauren pats her son's hand, cold round the chilly drink he has chosen for a wintry day. She sips her strong, hot coffee. 'I'd have found it tough up there without my regular coffees, I can tell you, let alone all the stuff you said you'd miss.'

'You'd be all right, Mum. You always look on the bright side.'

Do I, she thinks. Or have I just made the best of it because I've had to? Since Colin died, I've always tried to be bright and positive for the children, when at times I've felt like falling apart. Is that what the Frank parents tried to be, faced with the prospect of annihilation for themselves as well as their daughters? What would I have done in those circumstances?

And then she realises Freddie is still talking. 'What, love? Sorry, I wasn't listening.'

'I said I want to talk to Margie about all this. I'm going to get a card or something to take back for her. I want to know if she knew what was happening to Jewish families at that time.'

'That's a great idea. I'm sure it's good for her to talk.' Lauren pictures that neat figure, her tidy hair, her pressed clothes, and wonders whether she will ever find out what Margie might have experienced when she was younger. They still don't know why she left the house that cold morning in November and they also don't know anything about her early life. She may be able to speak German but they don't even know for certain if that is her native language and Germany is the country of her birth. And she hasn't had any further incidents that would suggest a confused mind. In fact, on the contrary her life has resumed its orderly pattern. Lauren made sure she was well supplied with groceries before she and Freddie left on this four-day trip.

But as Lauren thinks about her neighbour, she begins to wonder. Was the past so very dreadful for Margie that she can never bear to talk about it? Will a conversation with Freddie encourage her to open up or will she clam up even more, or revert to speaking a language Lauren can't understand? She can see Margie now, sitting at her red kitchen table, passing Lauren a slice of freshly baked apple cake, sprinkled with icing sugar. And then she remembers how Margie often rubs that scar on her arm, as if she is trying to erase something. She can see her doing it now, rub, rub, rub— and then Lauren suddenly feels as if the breath has been sucked out of her. How could she not have realised before? It's blindingly obvious to her now. That scar has obliterated something she wants very much to hide and forget. Margie's past must be a nightmare she has tried to escape.

Lauren glances at Freddie, slurping the final dregs of his shake, licking his lips. He may now be a teenager with worldly knowledge in some ways, but he is still an innocent boy too. How will he cope if, in talking to the elderly woman he more or less sees as a third grandmother, he uncovers some horrific facts? Should she tell him her suspicions or just watch, close by? He is sensible and still tells her his worries. So she tells herself she must let him go ahead, let him talk to Margie and see if he can find out the truth for himself. She trusts him to tell her what he discovers, however terrible.

TWENTY-FOUR

HAMBURG, MAY 1945

'That's it then,' Hermann said a couple of days later. 'The war's all finally over. Everyone's saying Grand Admiral Dönitz has announced the end on the radio.' Hermann had just returned from the Zoo Camp after taking Ingrid and the younger children there to be deloused.

'Are you sure?' Anna said. 'Is it official?'

'The announcement was made by Grand Admiral Dönitz himself. He's the only one left in charge now, isn't he, since Hitler shot himself.'

'About time too,' Gertrud said. 'Bastards like him need hanging. It's all their fault, damn Nazis.' She banged the saucepans angrily, demonstrating how she'd like to punish those who had brought Germany to its knees. 'When I get back to work, if any Nazis come my way, I'll knee them in the balls and rip their peckers off. Arrogant pigs.'

'And I don't think we can blame the Allies for the bombing here, either,' Ursula said. 'They wouldn't have had to do it if the Nazis hadn't started the war in the first place.'

Anna kept quiet. She knew that Dönitz had been appointed President after Hitler's death. And he had been applauded for his command of the seas, with U-boats hunting for convoys in groups known as wolfpacks. But for Anna it was enough just to hear that the war was really over at last. Although that was likely to mean equally dangerous hordes of former prisoners and soldiers roaming the countryside, not to mention desperate Nazis trying to hide to avoid retribution from those who blamed them for Germany's collapse. It should have been a time of celebration, but who knew what was going to happen next and whether the victory of the Allies might fill life with even more uncertainty?

Gertrud banged the pans again. 'We've hardly anything but tins to eat tonight and nothing to help us celebrate. You lot had better get down to the communal kitchen or the Zoo if you want to eat.'

She turned and pointed a finger at Anna. 'And you, Etta, you'd better start earning your keep, miss. If you're not going to bother to queue up for a ration card, you've got to go and smile nicely at some soldiers and do whatever it takes to keep us fed. I'll be doing it myself once I'm properly back on my feet.'

'But I brought us fresh bread the other day.'

'Well, that didn't last long, did it? One loaf between all of us.'

'I'll go back to the camp later tonight and try again. There were a lot of other girls there the other night. It was too busy.'

Gertrud sniffed, 'Then you've got to show them you're the best of the bunch and worth paying for.'

Anna realised the gang members were watching her expectantly. They needed her to do it. The numbers crowding the displaced persons camps were growing and supplies even there were stretched.

'You'd better get some work there while you can, Etta,' Gertrud said. 'I'm betting there'll be more competition everywhere soon, once everyone gets desperate. With no men earning and some not even back from the front yet, in who knows what kind of sorry state, mothers are going to be telling their daughters how it's done and soon they'll all be at it.'

Anna knew she was right. In the aftermath of war, even very young girls would go with soldiers just to survive. 'I'll go back there tonight,' she said. 'I don't want you to go out while Peter needs you so often.' The baby wouldn't settle and Gertrud was constantly trying to soothe him after he'd fed from her leaking breasts. Anna longed to help her and sometimes took him outside to walk up and down, whispering his name, that precious name, in his ear, as if he was her own long-lost Peter. She could hold him, rock him, change him and try to calm him, but she couldn't feed him herself.

The day was nearly over and all around the neighbourhood stoves and fires in basements and makeshift shelters were being lit to cook the evening meal, such as it was. Anna supped a little of the broth from their stew, wiped her face, then left the cellar. She had tied her hair back this time, hoping that with each change of hairstyle her appearance was nothing like it had been and she wouldn't be recognised if someone from the time before managed to reach Hamburg. She could see the tell-tale plumes of smoke wafting in the lowering light, showing her where families were settling down for the night, while she had to head out, wondering if she had the nerve to touch another man's bare flesh for cash, cigarettes or food.

When she reached the barracks, she could tell that word had obviously gone around among the street girls that this was a good spot for business. She could see several new faces hovering around the back of the buildings, close to the fence, softly calling to the soldiers: 'Come over here, lovely boys. We'll make you happy. We've got lots of tricks up our sleeves.'

Anna hung back, wondering whether it was even worth joining the crowd of strutting girls, their hands on their hips, their blouses enticingly unbuttoned. Pairs of soldiers were shuffling towards them and as they came up behind her she felt some pat her hips, squeeze her waist and pinch her bottom. But then they headed towards the main parade of willing girls.

She was beginning to think it was pointless to try competing with those who had experience of living and working on the street when she became aware of a figure much shorter than herself coming right up alongside her and putting a hand on her elbow. She turned round to see little Ingrid, mesmerised by the scene ahead of her.

'What do you think you're doing here?' she hissed. 'Go back this minute.'

'I wanted to see why Gertrud was making such a fuss. Why are all those girls here, Etta? Who are they?'

'They're old friends of Gertrud's, I think. Listen, you shouldn't be here. This isn't the sort of place for girls as young as you.' Anna put her arm round Ingrid to protect her. She guessed that, if Ursula was maybe sixteen, Ingrid couldn't be much more than nine. And then she sensed another presence behind them both. A taller, male presence that spoke in low, soft, enticing tones. 'Let me help you. If you like, I can take her somewhere safe for a bit, keep her company, if you want to stay here for a while and get on with your business.'

Anna turned round to see a smiling soldier slipping a hand through the crook of Ingrid's arm. 'Why not let her come with me for a while?' he said with beguiling softness. 'She'll be all right with me.' He lowered his head to Ingrid's ear and whispered something, then looked at Anna and said, 'I've told her we've got to find out where the chocolate is hidden in the barracks, but I can pay you as well if that makes you feel any better about it.'

'No, you don't.' Anna pulled Ingrid back towards her. 'She's far too young. She has no idea what's going on here.'

'Suit yourself.' He gave a careless shrug. 'Soon learn though, won't she?' He started to walk away, but threw one last piece of advice over his shoulder before he left. 'As she's fresh to the market, you could make a packet. More fool you.'

Anna felt sick. What had she nearly wandered into? Hamburg had always had its red-light district, particularly around the harbour and shipyards, but was it now so debauched that it was acceptable to sell girls who were only children?

'Etta, I want to go with that nice man. Why can't I go with him to get some chocolate for us?' Ingrid was craning her neck to look for him as he disappeared into the gloom around the swarming girls and soldiers.

'Because he wasn't really very nice and I don't think he really had any chocolate either. It's more likely he wanted to show you his *schwanz*. And that's not a good idea.' Ingrid may have been able to help with their foraging on the street, but she had little idea about the other business of the streets in the dark corners of Hamburg. Anna hugged this innocent child, glad she had been present to fend off such a dangerous predator and he hadn't pounced on Ingrid earlier.

'Come on, let's go back home. And promise me you'll never come here again, or follow me anywhere else either.' Anna was anticipating more withering looks from Gertrud on her return empty-handed, and was already thinking that she might have to find another place to pitch for business, if the barracks was becoming too well frequented by the regular street girls.

But seconds later, a booming voice disturbed the negotia-tions and shook those already in the middle of transactions out of the bushes. 'No fraternising! And that's an order! You girls clear off and you lads behave yourselves!' The ladies of the night sauntered past the sergeant, fluttering their fingers and blowing kisses, while the men of the battalion retreated, shame-faced, buckling their belts, into the shadows.

Anna and Ingrid had gone some distance beyond the barracks towards home when they heard Lili calling to them, accompanied by the clatter of her heels on the road. 'Hang on a tick, Etta, I've got something for you.' She caught up with them, saying, 'Good thing that sergeant didn't turn up earlier. I was doing all right till then. Here, have some.' She held out three packs of cigarettes. 'I know it's not cash, but it's good as.'

'Are you sure? I couldn't have stayed there anyway. Not with this one turning up.' Anna held up Ingrid's hand; she was holding her tight so she could make sure the young girl got back safely and wasn't tempted by any further thoughts of hidden chocolate.

'Yeah, go on, take it. I've done enough for one night.' Lili peered at Ingrid. 'I saw that creepy bloke eyeing her up. He's an odd one, not to be trusted. Though I dare say in these tricky times he'll soon find someone ready to sell their daughters, however young.'

Anna shuddered at the thought. Older girls and women she could understand, but not ones whose breasts had yet to bud. 'I hate to think what might have happened if she hadn't found me straight away.' She hugged Ingrid close to her, shuddering at the thought of that perverted worm touching her young friend.

'Here, me and Rita were talking after you left the other night. We both think you're too good to work the streets. It's all right for us, we're used to it. But you don't have a clue. You'll be in deep shit in no time, you will.'

'I'm not completely innocent. I do know what I'd be letting myself in for.' Anna didn't want to be too explicit with Ingrid by her side.

'No, you don't. You don't know the half of it. Weirdos, some of them. So, we reckon you need to do your business somewhere safe indoors. And we know just the place. They won't rip you off and it'll be safer than throwing yourself to the wolves like you almost did back there. You go and see Rolf and tell him Lili and Rita sent you.'

TWENTY-FIVE

HAMBURG, JUNE 1945

Anna hung her day clothes on the hook on the back of the bedroom door. She never let the younger Ausgebombten children see her in her work clothes and always left the cellar wearing a plain summer dress. Here in the rooming house Lili and Rita had recommended only a few weeks before, near Hamburg's main station, she changed into a flimsy negligee that she could never have worn to attract customers out on the street. She always covered her head on her way there, but once she'd entered the house she knew she was unlikely to encounter anyone from her previous life. She didn't ask questions of her clients and they never asked questions of her, other than what was she prepared to do for them and at what price. And no one ever queried her scarred arm, as many carried their own scars, both of the body and the mind, from the years of war.

The room only cost a small proportion of her takings; it was sparsely furnished, but it was clean and the bedding was free of bugs. Rolf always left her a jug of warm water on the washstand, and emptied the chamber pot hidden beneath the bed when she'd finished work. Once she'd turned on the bedside table lamp and the light filtering through its red shade filled the bedroom with a rosy glow, she felt safe and warm, ready to greet whoever Rolf sent upstairs to her.

Gertrud had also gone back to work, but complained that her milk-heavy leaking breasts were discouraging her punters. 'They can smell it on me, that and the baby sick. Puts most of them right off, dealing with a milk-cow. Though there's the odd freak who likes it and wants to suck my tits.' So she only worked the odd evening for a couple of hours, because they badly needed the extra money to buy food on the black market.

That month there were no potatoes to be found or bought in the whole of the city. Transport links were still so badly in need of repair that supplies could not be brought in by rail or road. The whole population of Hamburg was growing more and more desperate and many a day was spent wearily trekking out into the surrounding countryside to barter for increasingly expensive produce. A man might be able to buy a tailored suit for two hundred cigarettes, she thought, but what use was that if he couldn't buy eggs, cheese and bacon to feed his family?

Anna's first customer in her new surroundings had been a shy young man, even more inexperienced than her. He had been sweet and gentle and very quick. It was not an awful or painful encounter; she had felt sorry for him, fumbling with his condom and then reaching a climax almost as soon as he had entered her. They weren't all like him, of course, but Rolf, downstairs at the door, was good at sniffing out the drunks and troublemakers and so far, she hadn't had any awkward customers. But she knew that a quick scream or a blast on the rubber-bulbed hooter hidden beneath her bed would bring Rolf running to her aid.

Being further away from the British barracks, she rarely saw many soldiers; she supposed they were being well cared for in the tender embrace of the likes of Lili and Rita. Here, near the city's train station, she tended to attract the attention of local businessmen, not vengeful former prisoners or enslaved workers. They came seeking a little comforting recreation after the stress of trying to re-establish their bombed enterprises. All around the city, companies were struggling to rebuild; some had the support of the British, others who'd had connections to the war effort found their efforts hampered.

And one such businessman was Herr Reiser, or so he said. He didn't tell her his full name, but said he was in the wine trade and was looking to reacquaint himself with his old contacts. He was refined, elegant, clearly cultured, and said he had travelled widely before the war. His well-cut suit and silk tie suggested a lucrative enterprise, though she couldn't help noticing that his shirt cuffs were starting to fray at the edges.

She assumed he probably had a wife and family, as he must have been in his mid-fifties, but he was a regular customer and paid well, so she didn't ask questions. Their union was unexciting, perfunctory even, and afterwards he would often lie back smoking, telling her with the glimmer of tears in his eyes how he could not believe his life had disintegrated to this degree. Once he had been widely respected and admired, he said, but now his colleagues were scattered across Europe or no longer in a position of influence.

He came to see her every Tuesday and Thursday at six o'clock, wearing dark glasses and a black homburg hat. His appointment suited her very well because it meant she could usually be back with the gang in the cellar before dark. Once or twice he had asked to stay the night, which also suited her because the bed here, despite its creaking springs and rattling iron frame, was more comfortable than the thin, stained mattress she had to sleep on in the crowded Ausgebombten Gang basement. And in the morning when Herr Reiser swiftly departed, dear Rolf would bring her some ersatz coffee, then run her a hot bath in the shared bathroom, where she also had the luxury of a flushing toilet rather than the hole in the ground in the crumbling ruins of their wrecked neighbourhood.

'I'd like to stay again tonight, if I may, Etta,' Herr Reiser said, lying back on the pillows after he'd finished heaving himself off her passive body. He was perspiring and panting from his exertions, but still lit a cigarette.

'Of course you can stay. I'm completely at your disposal on the evenings you visit. Shall I send out for beer and wurst? Rolf usually knows where to find some, though it certainly isn't cheap these days.'

'If you like. I don't suppose you've had much to eat today.' He patted her slim thighs and peeled off some money from a roll of notes.

Anna took the cash and wrapped herself in a silky green dressing gown. She opened the bedroom door and slipped down the stairs in bare feet to find Rolf. He was not in his usual chair near the open door at the entrance and she peered into the ground-floor room that was his main abode. It was empty apart from a sliver of hard cheese and a corner of black bread on a plate on the table. She broke off a piece to eat, hoping he would turn up soon. Maybe he was taking the air or smoking outside. And then she heard his footsteps in the hall as he came back into the room.

Anna quickly wiped the crumbs from her lips. She guessed he'd seen, but she knew he wouldn't be annoyed. They were friends and she could trust him. 'Can we send out for beer and sausage?' she asked, holding out the money.

Rolf nodded towards the ceiling. 'Your regular still upstairs, is he?'

'Yes, he's staying with me tonight. I don't think he's very hungry, but I certainly am. Would you mind seeing what you can get for us? Anything will do.'

He tucked the cash into his trouser pocket. 'Of course, Etta. I'll go right this minute. But I'm going to lock the front door.

There's some odd types out there tonight and I don't want anyone barging in while I'm gone.'

'Thank you, darling.' She leant forward to peck his cheek, smelling the musky scent of cologne that she knew had earned him a harsh sentence in a labour camp, where he was lucky to have survived.

Anna ran back upstairs to her room. Maybe Rolf was right about tonight feeling odd. It was all very quiet. None of the other rooms were yet occupied. She was used to hearing the creak of the stairs, the opening and shutting of doors and the banging of headboards on bedroom walls all night long, coupled with the occasional animal groan or squeal.

Herr Reiser was no longer on the bed. He was looking out of the window, down at the street. 'Your queer bloke doing your bidding, is he?'

'Please don't talk about him like that. Rolf is very sweet and I feel very safe knowing he's keeping an eye on me here.'

'He's harmless enough, I suppose. Certainly won't be helping himself to the goods, will he?' Herr Reiser yawned and sat down again on the protesting bed to light another cigarette.

He passed it to her, but she declined, saying, 'Not right now. But can I take one for later?' She always did that and she didn't think he realised that she was collecting them to add to her takings from his visits.

He settled himself with the pillows behind his back, then tilted his head towards the door. 'It's a bit quieter than usual tonight, isn't it?'

'Yes, I was thinking that too. There's normally at least a couple of other girls in by this time of the evening. But maybe they're finding plenty of business elsewhere. It's lovely weather, so perhaps they've decided to stay outside. I think the troops like being in the parks on these summer evenings.'

He frowned and seemed to be listening, his cigarette ash growing and threatening to fall on the sheet. Restless, he suddenly got to his feet and went to stand by the window again, looking down on the street with its lengthening shadows as the day faded. 'There's no one out on the street at all. It's strangely empty.' He stubbed his cigarette out in the ashtray on the bedside table, going on, 'I've changed my mind, Etta. I don't think I'll stay after all.' He pulled up his trousers and reached for his suit jacket and, at that point, they heard the front door opening.

'Oh don't go,' Anna said. 'That'll be Rolf, returning with our supper.'

But the next minute there was a thunder of boots on the stairs and the door was flung open by an officer in British army uniform, followed by two armed soldiers. Anna squealed and shrank back against the wall in horror, thinking they had come for her at last. But the officer focused on Herr Reiser and said, speaking with a slight French accent, 'Joachim von Ribbentrop, I believe. I am arresting you for crimes against humanity. You will face an international military tribunal.'

The man she knew as Herr Reiser simply nodded acceptance, as if he had been expecting this all along. He finished dressing, taking his time knotting his tie and straightening the cuffs of his shirt. He smiled at Anna, who was frozen with shock, and tossed his roll of banknotes onto the bed. 'I doubt I'll see you again, Etta. Thank you for your company.'

'You, madam,' the officer said, 'are not in trouble. I believe your evening meal is on its way to you.' He led his captive out of the room and Anna sank back on the sagging bed, trembling. She now knew exactly who had been in her arms only moments before. He was not Herr Reiser, formerly an international wine merchant, he was one of the most senior Nazis and one of those most trusted by Hitler. His name was well known to everyone during his time as Minister for Foreign Affairs. And all this time, there he'd been, lying on her bed, feeling sorry for himself and smoking cigarettes. And all she could think was how she'd felt sympathy for this once-successful businessman with his fraying shirt cuffs. How Gertrud would scoff if she told her later that she'd let him pay for her services many times, without ever exercising any kind of brutal punishment. She couldn't help but smile at the thought.

TWENTY-SIX

HAMBURG, 14 JUNE 1945

'Did you know who Herr Reiser really was?' Anna joined Rolf in his room downstairs to share the simple supper he had bought with her client's money.

He nodded. 'Sorry if it shocked you, Etta. But I couldn't warn you. The Brits had been keeping an eye on him for a while, apparently. Knew he was a regular here. They said he'd already tried to get out of the country into Denmark a couple of times, over the border at Flensburg. Approached an old contact in the wine trade who didn't want anything to do with him. Coward, on the run. I don't mind admitting I helped them.'

'I had no idea who he was. He gave the impression he was trying to re-establish his business connections. I almost felt sorry for him.'

'Well, don't. He'll get what's coming to him. He and the other madmen who got us into all this damn awful mess. Those that haven't already scarpered to South America, that is. They'll give him a fair trial, but he won't get off. He'll hang, for sure.'

Anna chewed a mouthful of the hard, black bread and dry wurst. 'But he was so polite, so well behaved. He seemed to be such a gentleman.'

Rolf laughed, spluttering beer and crumbs over the table. 'Good manners don't stop you from being a monster. You could say that about all of them, the sick bastards. They created a system that gave mankind's worst traits free rein. Anyone with a taste for brutality was free to exercise their vilest fantasies.'

She considered him, this man who was kind to her, who had been imprisoned because he liked to lie with men more than women, who had lost the sight in his milky eye when he was savagely beaten. 'They treated you very badly, I know that. But do you think everyone who joined the Nazi Party and everyone who fought is to blame?' She asked the question fearing the answer.

'I think they all had a part to play, some more than others. But ordinary people let all this happen, Etta. They didn't realise it was a creeping infection that would destroy all sense of moral code and decency. Most of the population of Germany were hypnotised into thinking those at the top knew best. It was like one of those terrible folk tales where a spell is cast and no one can wake up. The British are going to make sure the whole world hears what Germany did in its thirst for land and power. How we, a civilised nation, beat, starved and murdered millions in cold blood.'

Anna felt a chill in her stomach. If this was Rolf, her trusted friend, talking like this, what about The Others – if any of them had survived that long death march? And what were the British saying? What were they going to do with the thousands who had worked in the camps, flocking back to the cities, their homes and their old lives? Would they all be called to account?

'You know, Etta, before I was arrested, like everyone else I thought the camps were more or less legitimate prisons for political opponents and anyone else they thought was antisocial. How wrong I was! I saw some of it for myself, but nothing like they're saying really happened. Since the British liberated that hellhole Bergen-Belsen, everyone's been able to see the truth for themselves. I saw people worked till they dropped and beaten to death, but not trainloads shoved into gas chambers, not piles of skeletal bodies.'

Anna picked at the crumbs on her plate. The dry food was hard to swallow and she tried to take a sip of beer, but began to choke.

Rolf thumped her on the back until the choking and sputtering stopped. 'Don't go upsetting yourself, Etta. It's not your fault Ribbentrop did what he did, or mine. Besides, if you hadn't kept him happily occupied upstairs, he wouldn't have been arrested so easily. The Brits have got you to thank for that. You're in the clear.'

She took another gulp of the warm beer, not wanting this conversation to go any further. 'I think I might finish for the night. Do you mind if I take this food back with me? It's not the best, but my friends are always in need of a little extra.'

'Of course. Take the lot. It's dreadful stuff and it cost the earth too. If it carries on like this, we'll be in for a terrible winter.' He turned his head at the sound of a girl and a man entering the front door and heading upstairs. The house would soon be filled with heaving bodies and creaking beds again.

As she left the building, Anna noticed the streets had returned to their normal night-time rowdiness, with slender girls in thin dresses competing for business and men lurking around corners, smoking and arguing. There must have been a military cordon around the house for a time, deterring the usual melee. Shouting and the occasional burst of song followed her as she walked back to the basement, clutching Herr Reiser's money and the poor-quality food it had bought. Now that he'd been arrested, she'd lose that source of income and have to rely on other men finding their way to the rooming house. She'd done well out of him, but now, knowing who he really was, knowing she had been intimate with one of the architects of that vile regime, she felt sick, and if she'd had more in her stomach she'd have retched and thrown up in the gutter.

Was Rolf right? Was she to be thanked for Ribbentrop's arrest? Did the capture and ensuing punishment of one of the ringleaders of the country's downfall and shame mean she was exonerated, even though she'd had no knowledge of his true identity? But was it her fault and that of the ordinary German people that such a punishing war had been forced upon them and that the regime had taken its fierce desire for control to such dreadful lengths? Hadn't they all, from an early age, been schooled in the language of supremacy, with compulsory membership of the League of German Girls from the age of ten?

She thought again of Rolf's words – *legitimate prison.* That was what she had also thought when she'd read the advertisement. It had seemed too good to be true. Excellent pay, all accommodation and food provided at a nominal rate, social facilities; it had seemed perfect. And what was the alternative? Returning to her parents' home and taking a job in a factory with no prospects?

And then she thought of Etta, her dear friend of years before. They had known each other since childhood, played with their baby dolls when they were very young, before progressing to talk of the real babies they would one day have. Etta who came to her house in tears when they were both thirteen, distressed by the rioting on the streets that had smashed the windows of her uncle's shop in another city.

'We don't condone that kind of behaviour in Hamburg,' Mama had said, to comfort her. 'There are people among the working class who do not defend the Jews, but the majority of decent people disapprove of such callous acts.' But despite her kind words, when Etta left, Mama had discouraged Anna from seeing her as she used to. 'Keep out of it,' she'd said. 'They're all trouble.'

And that kind of talk didn't help Etta complete her education or find a good job, and now Anna wondered what had happened to her. She had believed the family had left for France long ago, but perhaps they'd been hiding in Hamburg when the aircraft came over and dropped their incendiary bombs. Maybe they'd been trapped in a secret room or attic, unable to escape and roasted like a chicken in the oven. Or was she sent away like so many others, to work until she fell? Or were she and her family incinerated deliberately, even though they had escaped a flaming city? So perhaps I am partially responsible for her fate too, Anna thought, wearily trudging the streets back to the only group she could now think of as family.

TWENTY-SEVEN

LONDON, FEBRUARY 2017

'You're very quiet today, Lauren.' Yvonne gives her colleague a curious look. 'I thought your half-term trip would have perked you up.'

'Sorry. I was miles away. The holiday was great, but it's given me a lot to think about.' The two of them are treating themselves in McDonald's, after a morning of wiping little noses and ferrying little people to the little toilets at Tumbly Tots Nursery.

'Like what?' says Yvonne, delicately removing the gherkin slices from her Big Mac. 'Not Freddie, is it?'

'No, it's not him. He's doing well at school and we had a great time in Amsterdam. He's a lovely travelling companion. We agreed the whole trip had to run on "Amsterdam rules", meaning no lying in bed late, to make the most of every minute there.'

'Good idea. And he didn't object to getting going every morning?'

'No, he was totally up for it! He was keen to get down to the great breakfasts they did.'

'So, what's the problem? Do you want to tell me about it?'

'Mmm.' Lauren struggles to finish the big bite she has taken of her burger. 'It's not Freddie who's worrying me at the moment, it's my elderly neighbour. Seeing the Anne Frank House in Amsterdam has made me wonder about her past. I think I've always known she was a war bride and came to live here after the war, but I've never known any more than that. And then she had an odd episode a few months ago and it's got me thinking it would be good for her to talk about her life.'

'Is she all on her own now?'

'Yes, her husband died around fifteen years ago, I'm sure she gets very lonely. And her children are both in Australia, so there's no one close to her. Just us, really. We're both widows, me a bit sooner than I should have been, sadly.' Lauren pauses, gazing across the busy restaurant, where Colin probably had more burgers than he should have done, grabbing a quick meal when he had a moment, often finishing it in the car on his way to another incident.

'It never leaves you, does it?' Yvonne notices Lauren's distant gaze. She's a single parent too, a mother of five boys, though in her case she's never married and the boys have different fathers.

'And I keep thinking, we should learn from the older generation, shouldn't we? Freddie's grandparents are no longer around on either side and Margie is like another grandmother to him, she's known him that long. She babysat for me years ago, when my two were both small.' Lauren dips a skinny fry into the little pot of tomato ketchup, wishing it was bigger.

'But is it always good to go back into the past?' Yvonne says. 'Is it good for her, or for you and Freddie?'

'I think it would be helpful for Freddie to learn about times that were really hard, not just like nowadays, when he moans about not having enough money for a McDonald's or a new pair of trainers! And I've always felt like I've got to do the work of two parents, ever since Colin went – I've got to try extra hard to bring up my kids well and give them moral guidance.'

'Don't I know it!' Yvonne slams her banana milkshake on the table. 'You try doing it with five boys! Though I'm not sorry their fathers were never around to be role models. I didn't want my boys turning out like any of them.'

'You're a wonderful role model for them all, Yvonne. Look at what you've achieved with Tumbly Tots. They must be very proud of you.' The nursery has a waiting list, with babies being registered as soon as they're born. And all of Yvonne's sons have made their mother proud, qualifying as an electrician, plumber, decorator, carpenter and accountant, so she can rightly boast that she can always make swift repairs and maintain the nursery premises to a high standard, as well as ensuring that the business is financially solvent.

Yvonne smiles shyly, saying, 'And your kids are proud of you too, though your Colin was also a great example to them, loyal, kind and hardworking.'

'Too hardworking, I think now. He should have slowed down before it all caught up with him. But he would never have listened to me.' Lauren fishes down the bottom of the red pack for the last of the thin crispy chips. This lunch is a rare treat.

'But this neighbour of yours, maybe she doesn't want to remember her life before she came over here. Maybe there are things she simply wants to forget. Or it would be too painful for her.'

'I know. I wouldn't want it to be distressing for her, but I have this niggling feeling that she has to, how do I put it, cleanse her soul or something like that. And it would be good for Freddie too and she's very fond of him. She's even helping him with his German. I know I regret now never asking my grandparents about their early years and the war. I never even knew much about my dad either, just that he was evacuated to Devon.'

Yvonne puts down her half-eaten burger. 'I remember my grandma telling me stories about the overseers, that her grand-mammy told her. So, it goes way, way back. It's history, real history. And you don't want them stories lost forever, do you?'

'Exactly. You can read books and learn stuff in school, but it's not the same as hearing it from someone who was actually there and saw it for themselves.'

'Well, maybe if you flatter her, tell her how much Freddie likes her and really wants to hear what she has to say, she'll do it. Can you ask her?'

Lauren thinks again about the strange state Margie was in back in November, her reticence about her past and her rubbing of that old scar. 'Maybe I could. I'll approach her carefully. I don't want to upset her. I have an awful feeling that she may have had some terrible experiences.'

'Be gentle then. Get her to talk to you first, before you go encouraging Freddie to rush in full of eager questions. That might be the best way forward.' Yvonne takes one last noisy, spluttering slurp of her milkshake. 'It often pays to be subtle.'

Anna had already heard the rumours that were now unsettling the Ausgebombten Gang. Rolf and some of the girls on the streets were all talking about it. 'The British are demanding that all the residents of Hamburg donate their good winter clothes to the refugees,' Ursula said, her face red with indignation. 'And, Etta, we've also heard they've already requisitioned some of the better houses.'

'But they won't be taking anything from us,' Anna said. 'We've got hardly anything for ourselves for a start, so we can't go donating to charity. The British are only talking about the families who are better off. The ones we see now in good clothes visiting the theatre. There are some here around the city who were hardly touched at all by the bombing.'

'We're definitely not moving out of here,' Gertrud said. 'We're better off staying in this old cellar than in some smart house. They'd push us out after a while, I know it. At least here, no one can tell us what to do.'

Anna tried to calm her, saying, 'They don't mean people like us have to give up their decent clothes. They mean the ones who weren't bombed out and have continued to live in comfort. You mustn't worry so much.'

'Well, I'm hiding my winter coat right now and you'd better do the same.' Gertrud's defiant expression made it clear that she would not stand for such measures. 'And think about it, Etta, you won't be able to work if you can't keep yourself warm this winter. Why'd you give up that cosy room anyway?'

Anna had told the gang about Herr Reiser's arrest but she couldn't explain why she had left the comfort of Rolf's house soon after that. Was it because she felt safer on the street, being free to run away, rather than trapped and locked in a room if she was under suspicion? There was constant news of trials, of war crimes, of sentences being passed for those considered responsible for the piles of corpses. Some were sent to serve relatively light sentences of only a few years for their sins, others were condemned to hang. The Allies were demanding retribution as well as homes and good winter coats, it would seem. The news made her nervous and every day she wondered if, once the guards and the highest-ranking offi-cers had been punished, they would move on to the lower orders.

'I reckon I can make more money if I'm free to move around,' she said. 'It was cushy there, but Rolf took quite a cut. I think I'm better off on my own. I can always go back if it doesn't suit me in the winter.'

'Maybe you're right,' Gertrud said. 'You don't want someone like that having a hold over you. Next thing, before you know it, they're pimping you out and grabbing all your takings, leaving you with nothing to show for all your hard work.'

Anna knew that would never have been the case with Rolf, but she could also imagine how his circumstances could change. If he was persuaded to go into partnership with some of the less savoury types hanging around in the city, she might well be treated differently. It was right for her to leave, now she was more confident in selling her body. Besides, she didn't have to do it that often now Gertrud was working again. She had got into the habit of handing Peter to Ursula in the evenings after she'd fed and changed him, leaving a flask of breast milk in case he grew hungry.

'I'm sure Rolf would never have taken advantage like that, he was always very good to me. But I prefer the freedom of being outside. I thought perhaps I'd go back and check out the British camp again. At least there's always the chance of extra food there too.' She tucked her hair back under the little grey hat Ursula had found for her earlier that day in an abandoned house. She was acquiring quite a variety of hats and scarves to vary her appearance and was beginning to feel more confident that she was unlikely to be recognised now. She was thinner in figure and face than at the beginning of the year and her street clothes were quite unlike the uniform The Others would have remembered.

'You do that, Etta dear,' Gertrud said. 'I'm off to the port. Plenty of pickings down there and the chance of a few more cigarettes too.'

Anna left the group in the cellar to walk to the camp, taking her regular route along a busy throughfare, where girls of the street were beginning to gather for an evening's work. She took little notice of them but, suddenly, there among the thinnest waifs she recognised a sturdy blonde-haired figure who appeared to be in charge of a group of girls.

Anna slowed down and held back. She felt sick and was afraid she'd been seen. It was a face from her past, a face she'd hoped never to see again. She could well remember the weight of that heavy hand on her shoulder, the thick fingers digging into her flesh. She'd thought and hoped that hefty Birgit Schuetz was gone from her life for good when she'd left early in the year. But here she was, still bossing, still in charge, just as she used to as a guard in the camp. What was she now? A pimp or a madam?

And after a terrifying few seconds, in which all around her seemed to stand still, that surly face slowly turned towards Anna and their eyes locked. Perhaps Birgit thought she'd spotted a new recruit for her henhouse. Anna was unable to move, praying Birgit wouldn't shout her name. But she didn't smile or beckon Anna across, although it was clear from the narrowing of her eyes that she recognised her.

Anna felt she couldn't breathe, afraid Birgit might welcome her into her strong, meaty arms to become part of her harem. But after a moment, she gave only the slightest nod of recognition, then turned back to her young charges. It was obvious to Anna. Birgit didn't want to be acknowledged either; she too was trying to slip away into a new life.

Anna stirred herself and walked away at speed to the nearest park, where the trees were still full of green leaves although autumn was not far off. Here she could at last breathe freely and recover from the fright of meeting her tormentor again.

As she grew calmer, she felt convinced that Birgit would not pursue her. Her heart quietened and she began to take in the early-evening light and enjoy the last warmth of the day. And at that point, she noticed a man in British army uniform sitting on a nearby bench looking at her. He nodded in a respectful way and, in perfect German, said, 'It is a beautiful evening, is it not?'

She smiled and took a step or two closer to the bench. Maybe she wouldn't have to walk all the way to the barracks tonight after all. He wasn't one of the ordinary soldiers; he was quite a bit older than most of the young men she'd encountered, with a neat moustache and well-combed dark hair.

He waved his hand expansively at the verdant shrubs and trees around them. 'Nature is simply amazing, is it not? I gather that everything here was scorched and blackened only two years ago and now look at it. I'm told that when the trees burst into new leaf just a couple of months after that blasted inferno flattened your city, it was hailed as a miracle.' He turned to look at her again, his brow furrowed, as he asked, 'Were you here at the time to see it recover?'

What should she say? If she said she hadn't been here in Hamburg then, he'd probably want to know where she had been, so she just said, 'Yes, it was a wonderful sign that life goes on.'

'I'm sure that was so, after the dreadful time we gave all of you. Terrible business, bombing such important cities on both sides. Dresden, Coventry, just dreadful.'

He shook his head, looking sad and reflective, then gestured to the space on the bench beside him. 'Would you like to sit here with me for a while? It would be so nice for me to talk to someone who knows the city well.'

She accepted his offer and willingly sat down. He wasn't her usual kind of customer at all. In fact, he looked more like the men who had been handling the registrations at the Zoo Camp; he seemed clerical, studious, thoughtful.

'It's so hard to understand,' he said, 'why all this terrible destruction had to happen. You know, our chaps couldn't see exactly what was going on down below, coming over at night. They couldn't risk daytime flights with your sharp fellows on the lookout, could they? It must have been sheer hell for all of you.' He fumbled in his pocket for cigarettes and offered her one. As usual, Anna took it and allowed him to light it for her, but she let it go out quickly, so she could save it.

'I couldn't believe my eyes when we first arrived in Hamburg. London was bad enough after the Blitz, but nothing compared to what happened here. Total destruction every- where. Almost nothing left standing. And the awful smell! I'm sorry, my dear, but it assaulted the nostrils, that smell of decomposition wherever we went.' He took a quick glance at her. 'How on earth did you manage to get through it all?'

She shook her head as if she was distressed. She felt uncomfortable lying to him, when so many had suffered so terribly in the city, but she was also aware that he was curious and she ought to be careful. 'The park, many of us ran straight to the park. The fire was everywhere, in the buildings, on the roads. Only the parks and the canals were safe.'

'And your family?'

She looked down at her hands, holding the cigarette. 'I am the only one left. Our house is gone. My parents didn't manage to get out in time. I live with friends now. We have made ourselves comfortable in a cellar.'

She couldn't help noticing his expression of distaste and added, 'It's really not that bad. We manage quite well, apart from the shortage of food supplies. That is always a huge worry.'

'My dear, I'm so very sorry. War is one thing man to man, but civilians are another matter entirely. Dreadful business.' He looked into the distance, smoking but silent.

She watched the pigeons cooing as they jostled for space in the trees for the night. Although it wasn't a cold evening, the park was already quiet and empty. Most residents were trying to make a meal of some sort from whatever they had managed to find that day. Ursula and the children would be sharing out another kind of *eintopf* made in one saucepan from scraps, Peter might be waking and wanting milk, Hermann would boast of his rat-catching skills. Suddenly she thought how she missed them all, her little ragbag family of misfits, and she stood up, ready to leave. 'Thank you,' she said, 'It was very nice to meet you.'

'And you, my dear. Perhaps our paths will cross again.' He held out his hand. 'Reginald Wilson. Known as Reg. I come here most days at the end of my shift. Just to sit and think, you know. I'd appreciate talking to someone who could tell me what the city was like before its destruction.'

Anna shook his hand and hesitated over how to introduce herself. It would be impolite not to tell him her name. And he really did seem pleasant and she had meant it when she said it was nice to meet him. A good, decent man was a rare find these days. 'Margarete,' she said, 'Etta for short.' But should she give him her whole name, as he had done? The Ausgebombten Gang accepted her for who she was, so she hadn't needed a surname until now. She glanced at the cigarette pack lying on his lap. Wherever had he managed to find them? They were Ecksteins, the Jewish brand that had struggled to survive both ostracism and the Nazi creed of healthy living that so disapproved of smoking and any sinful habit. 'Margarete Eckstein,' she said, thinking she'd just added another layer to her disguise.

TWENTY-NINE

LONDON, FEBRUARY 2017

'Well, what did Margie say about the postcard you gave her?' Lauren turns from stirring the pasta sauce she is making as Freddie comes through the back door.

He looks puzzled and slumps against the door as he clicks it shut. 'She didn't say anything that made any sense.'

'Oh dear. She's not having another one of her funny turns, is she?'

'No, she's behaving normally – well, fairly normal. She's speaking English most of the time, except when I want her to speak German, to help me practise.'

'Sit down and tell me what happened from start to finish. I'll put the spaghetti on now. And I've done garlic bread for you as well.'

'Oh, good, I'm starving.'

Lauren shakes her head at this frequently uttered remark. Freddie is always 'starving', a normal condition for all teenage boys, she assumes. 'Wasn't there any cake at Margie's today?'

'Oh yeah, she always gives me cake. But I couldn't be greedy and ask for an extra slice, could I?'

'What kind was it today?' Lauren thinks Freddie's regular

visits motivate Margie to bake and that his company and eager consumption of her cakes must be good for her. It's a kind of kitchen therapy for both of them she decides, talking and baking.

'It was different to the usual apple cake. It was like apple crumble on top of sponge cake. With almonds on top as well. Really nice.'

Lauren's mouth waters at the sound of it. Maybe she should pop next door tomorrow and hope there is some of this cake left for her to sample. 'But didn't she say anything about the post-card? You told her that we'd been to the Anne Frank House, I assume?'

'Of course I did, Mum. I'm not stupid. She'd have wondered why I'd gone round with this random postcard if I hadn't explained it to her.'

'Sorry. Of course you did, dear.'

'And she just stared at it, so I explained who Anne Frank was, about her diary and stuff and why it's important to remember her and that.'

'And then?'

'And then she changed the subject. She started talking about how her son and daughter always used to like this apple crumble cake or whatever she called it and how she hadn't made it for a very long time.'

'Didn't you try again to explain why we'd gone there, to see the house?'

'Yeah, I said we're doing the Second World War in history now at school and that I thought as she was old and had lived in that time, she could help me with that as well as my German.'

Lauren smiles to herself. Freddie's candour amuses her, but she's not sure if it's the most tactful way to explore Margie's past. 'Maybe she doesn't want to be your tutor in everything.' She slices tomatoes and onions for a salad and passes the plate to her son. 'Here, drizzle a bit of olive oil over this, will you? And don't forget to add seasoning.'

Lauren is preparing Freddie for his time at university just as she did with his sister. Bit by bit he'll have learnt to prepare a short menu of dishes he can cook for himself and friends, to stay healthy and well fed during his time away from home. When Amy came back at Christmas she said her ability to cook had greatly increased her popularity and widened her social circle and that many of her friends could make little beyond eggs, toast and bacon sandwiches.

Lauren drains the pasta and tips it into a large bowl, then serves the Bolognese sauce in another dish so they can help themselves. This was Colin's favourite too, she thinks. Before they had children she'd made it every Saturday, a quick, easy supper so they could enjoy a video, a bottle of wine and an evening of leisurely lovemaking. And the tradition had continued throughout their short married life, though the love-making was less frequent and more likely to occur in the bedroom than on the living room sofa. And it probably would have carried on if he hadn't been carried off prematurely, poor Colin.

'Do you think anything you said about our visit to Amsterdam registered with Margie?'

'Mmm,' Freddie says, through a mouthful of garlic bread. 'Whenever I said how awful it was that Anne Frank's family was arrested and sent to Auschwitz, or said why didn't anyone stop it, she just said no one knew.'

'Really? That was all she said?'

'That, and "life was hard" was another thing she said several times.'

'I can't decide whether she doesn't want to talk about those times or she simply doesn't remember. What do you think?'

'How would I know? Can I have another bit of this bread?'

He's already reaching for the crisp golden baguette before she can answer.

'Didn't she even tell you where she'd been during the war or where she was born?'

'No, Mum, she didn't tell me anything. If you're so keen to find out, why don't you go round to see her?'

'I might just do that. I'd better go there before you nip back and finish off her cake, you greedy, starving monster!'

The following day is Sunday, and Lauren knows Margie always attends church in the morning. She decides not to intrude on her day of rest and reluctantly thinks she should wait till Monday before visiting. She can use the excuse of finalising her grocery delivery for the next day.

Knocking on her back door on Monday afternoon, she sees Margie in her neat apron, mixing something in a bowl. An unsliced cake is sitting on a plate on the countertop.

'I just wanted to check if you need anything added to this week's order,' Lauren says, opening the door a little.

'How very kind. Do come in. I have been making *karottenkuchen*. I think Freddie vill like this. It was very popular at the last church coffee morning. It's not at all like the carrot cake that is made in your country, as it doesn't have any flour. And I don't put cream cheese icing on top.' She drizzles the sugary syrup she's just made over the top of the fresh cake.

Lauren laughs. 'I doubt there's a cake that boy doesn't like, Margie. He said the apple cake you made at the weekend was delicious. Did he eat it all up?'

'I have a little left here.' She pats a red and white cake tin on the shelf. 'Would you like to try that one first?'

'I'd love to,' Lauren says, thinking this is her chance to sample two cakes in one fell swoop and blow her attempts to eat fewer carbs this week.

Margie opens the tin and takes out the apple crumble cake to cut a generous slice, which she places before Lauren on a plate with a fork. 'It is really better served warm, with *schlagsahne*, but I don't have any cream here today.'

'I could order some for you? Our delivery comes tomorrow.' Lauren tastes the sweet apple, spiced with cinnamon.

'You are very kind. I won't order any cream, but I would like to add sugar and flour. Those bags are quite heavy for me.'

'Of course. And at the rate you are making cakes and Freddie and I are eating them, I think we should be buying the sugar and flour for you.'

'No, no, it is entirely my pleasure. You are so kind and I greatly enjoy Freddie's company. He is such a thoughtful boy.'

'It's very nice of you to say so, Margie. Teenage boys can sometimes be very difficult, but I think he's doing all right so far. I hope he didn't ask you too many questions yesterday, did he? I know he wanted to ask you about the war, because of his schoolwork.'

'Did he? I don't remember.' She cuts a slice of the glazed carrot cake and slides it onto Lauren's plate alongside the few remaining crumbs of apple cake.

'But he gave you the card he bought in Amsterdam? From the Anne Frank House?'

'Anne's house? I know we talked a lot, but I don't remember much.'

Lauren knows she won't get much further with this line of questioning. 'Mmm, this carrot cake is really good. I think you're right to do it with this light drizzle-style glaze rather than the thick frosting it usually has. It's delicious.'

Margie is busying herself filling the kettle to make tea. 'You must take a piece back home for Freddie. He will be hungry when he comes out of school.'

'He always says he's starving. As if they don't have decent school dinners!'

Margie puts two cups of tea on the table and sits down. Reaching for her cup, Lauren knocks the handle and spills hot tea in the saucer. 'Oh, that was stupid of me.'

Margie is about to get up and wipe the spill, which has slopped onto the table, but Lauren stops her. 'No, you stay there.' She pulls a tissue from her sleeve to mop up, then goes to throw the sopping tissue in the kitchen pedal bin. When it pops open she finds herself staring at the face of Anne Frank. The card Freddie bought has been torn in half. There it is, in the bin, stained with tea leaves.

THIRTY

HAMBURG, SEPTEMBER 1945

'We're not supposed to fraternise, you see, Etta,' Reg said. 'But I think if we don't talk to the local people, don't try to get to know them, how can we possibly begin to understand what has happened in this country?'

Their third meeting in the park and already he had told Anna to call him Reg. 'All my friends do.' And already he was talking to her as if she was indeed an old friend. Was he lonely, a little apart from the other soldiers? He was certainly older, though not very old, maybe in his mid- to late thirties, so fifteen or so years older than her.

'I mean, I know that dreadful, truly terrible things have happened during this war, some of them not so very far away from here too. Bergen-Belsen is what, maybe only sixty miles to the south of the city? Did no one really know what was going on there? But I say, if we don't ask the German people how this came to pass, how will we know how to stop it ever happening again one day?'

She knew exactly what he was referring to. Maybe this was how The Others had met their end after marching away. The horrors of the camps were public knowledge now; witnesses to the desperate plight of the starving and the barbaric treatment of the dying were confronting the people of her country. And searching questions were being asked. How could the ordinary Germans not have known, how could they have allowed this systematic extermination to happen in the first place? And with every question she held her breath, wondering when the spotlight would be turned onto her.

'Are you feeling all right, my dear?' He seemed to be trying to examine her face. Did he suspect her as well?

'Yes, I'm all right. I just find this all a bit upsetting. Everyone you see, they say they just didn't know about it.'

'Don't distress yourself, Etta. Perhaps it's better if I don't talk about such things any more. I'm guessing that with a name like yours, you may have encountered some deeply unpleasant behaviour at times.'

She hung her head, thinking of her friend Margarete, her dear childhood friend, who had been pushed and shoved, her hair pulled, just because of who she was, even as a young girl. Then not allowed to continue her education; and where was she now? And Anna knew she was betraying her by pretending to be other than she was. 'It's been hard,' she murmured. 'I don't really like to talk about it.'

'Of course you don't. I don't even like to think about the terrible things you must have seen and experienced, you poor girl.' He reached for her hand and she let him hold her little hand in his for a minute. 'We can talk about other, pleasanter things instead. Perhaps we could go to see a film, or would you prefer a concert?'

'I'm just happy the war's all over, but I do like listening to music.'

'A concert it is then. I'm sure there will be something on soon. I'll see what might be happening and let you know the details next time we meet. You'll be here tomorrow, I hope?'

'Yes, and I would like a concert very much.' Uplifting

music, something to transport her away from a world of blackened buildings, the frantic search for food and the increasingly hungry faces.

'Look,' he said, delving into his coat pocket, 'I hope you won't be offended, but I imagine you are finding it pretty difficult to manage at present, so here's a little something I thought might help.' He brought out a pack of butter, some bread and chocolate. 'You must share that with the friends you're living with.'

'Oh,' she gasped, 'that's so kind. Thank you very much.'

'It's nothing and I can get more for you if you need it. We're not supposed to hand out even so much as a crust of stale bread to ordinary Germans, but I can't see the harm in it, myself.'

'That would be wonderful. We are always hungry.'

'And the barracks is very well supplied with food. The men have everything they need. And I know how much all of you are struggling. And please take this as well.' He pressed some banknotes into her hand. 'That should help too, if you can find anything at all to buy on the black market. I know how tough it must be.'

She stared at the money. She hadn't had to do anything other than talk to him on a park bench. She hasn't had to touch his bare flesh or remove a single item of clothing. The cash wouldn't go very far on the black market – prices were going up by the day – but his generosity was saving her from the streets, saving her from the possibility of disease and even physical abuse. She felt tears spring to her eyes. She hadn't cried in such a very long time that she'd thought she couldn't cry any more. But this very simple act of kindness, without any thought of asking for a favour in return, touched her to the heart and she could feel tears trickling onto her cheeks.

'Don't cry, my dear,' he said. 'I'm not asking for anything from you. I simply want you to know that there is still generosity and kindness in this world. It's the least I can do after all you have suffered.' He reached into his pocket again and took out a clean handkerchief and gently dabbed her tear-stained cheeks.

Anna sniffed, then tried to laugh. 'Thank you. I'm overcome by your kindness, that's all. It's been so hard for such a long time.'

'I completely understand, my dear Etta. You don't have to say any more.' He pressed the handkerchief into her hands. 'Keep it. Now, I'd best be off. Shall we say until tomorrow?'

'Yes, that would be nice.' She pushed the hankie up her sleeve and as the fabric rucked and rolled back, she was conscious that his eyes registered the itchy scar on her arm. She hastily pulled her sleeve straight and then she kissed his cheek, very lightly, very briefly. 'Thank you so very much. You are so kind.'

He looked a little startled but also pleased. 'What a charming girl you are, Etta. If only there were more like you.'

As she returned to the others, Anna wondered if she should tell them that she wasn't really out working the streets any more. But did they ever need to know how she came by these gifts? It was the same as currency and cigarettes, wasn't it? And cash was still cash whatever she'd done to earn it. But all she had to do now was be pleasant, make conversation and look grateful. She laughed to herself. What would Gertrud think if she told her she hadn't had to drop her knickers once these last few days? No, she'd better not tell her or Gertrud might want to share in her good luck, and she could already tell that Reg wasn't that sort of a man.

THIRTY-ONE

HAMBURG, NOVEMBER 1945

Anna felt her very being tremble with the vibrations of the intense orchestral music in the Grand Hall. Hamburg's first concert since the war had ended had been initiated by the British, in an attempt at restoring harmony in the city, and every seat was filled with excited ticketholders.

She scanned the tiers of seats for a sign of Reg, who'd given her a ticket the previous evening. 'I won't be able to sit with you, I'm afraid,' he'd said. 'Fraternisation is still being discouraged, so it's best that we are discreet.' She couldn't tell which of the rows of hatless, dark heads was his, but told herself she could enjoy the concert even if he wasn't allowed to hold her hand beside her.

She had tried to smarten herself up for the occasion, washing thoroughly with a scrap of soap she had saved from Rolf's house, but she suspected that she smelt no better than the majority of those around her. The odours of stale sweat, unwashed clothes and the sour breath of the hungry filled the air, which would once have been scented with perfume, hair oil and the camphor of ladies' furs. She stared at the white specks on the shoulders of the dark suit of the man directly in front of her. Was it dandruff or signs of lice? She couldn't see movement, but thought probably everyone in the hall that night would be carrying tiny passengers.

'I'm so sorry I couldn't sit with you for the concert, Etta,' Reg said as they strolled to the park when the programme was over. He patted her hand, tucked into his arm. 'We're still not allowed to mix with Germans, so I'm afraid I can't risk being seen with you. Not when I'm meant to be setting an example to the men. Though I doubt some of the younger chaps have any qualms, considering the number of women and girls we've seen regularly gathering around the camp perimeter.'

Anna was instantly reminded of her early attempts to obtain work on the streets. Were Lili and Rita still visiting the area? If so, she wouldn't dare venture near the camp in case they spotted her and called out, alerting Reg to her former occupation. 'I quite understand the problem,' she said. 'You don't need to explain. But it was still lovely being there in the Grand Hall, just listening to live music again.'

'Jolly good, weren't they? It's all down to the Brits, you know. It's so important to establish a rapport with the people and music and radio are such a good way to do that.'

'I enjoyed all of it. I had a lovely evening.'

They had reached what she had begun to think of as 'their' bench in the park and they sat side by side in the almost dark of the evening, with the moon rising through the trees. Reg never attempted to do any more than hold her hand or, when they parted, kiss her cheek, and they sat decorously, like an old married couple, hands clasped.

'I couldn't help thinking this evening,' he said, 'about the power of music. Such an expressive, emotional tool.' He paused, pulled his hand away from hers and lit a cigarette. He was still smoking Ecksteins, she noted. 'So powerful. Like with that infamous concert in Berlin, not so very long before the war ended. Maybe you haven't heard about it, my dear?'

She had no idea what he was talking about, but she found it soothing to hear him rambling on, as if, once all the disruption of the last five years had been dissected and understood, life would become uneventful and peaceful. 'A concert?' she said. 'And it was nearly the end of the war?'

'The Berlin Philharmonic, on the twelfth of April, I believe. They were playing Wagner's *Gotterdämmerung*.' He made a slight sound of disbelief, a tiny hint of amusement, at the title of the piece. 'Appropriate, eh, given the fate that the members of that elite audience were all facing? Twilight of the gods and all that?'

Anna just sat and listened to him, even in the silences when he was reflective and drawing on his cigarette.

'And can you imagine what happened at the end of that concert? Hmm?'

She shook her head. She had no idea. Tonight, when the final notes of the programme of Beethoven and Brückner had played out and the conductor had taken his bow, the audience had applauded with great enthusiasm, gathered their coats and left the hall chattering and smiling. Didn't all concerts end in a similar fashion if the music had been appreciated?

'My dear Etta, on that particular occasion, when the music finished members of the Hitler Youth organisation, healthy young lads, prime examples of the Aryan race, walked among the audience offering baskets of free cyanide pills. Can you believe it? Astonishing, isn't it? Not cigarettes, not chocolates or flowers, but deadly poison. Free, on the house. They did a good trade apparently. No one knows how many of the high-ranking political and military figures attending that night went home after their enjoyable evening, perhaps had a last glass of schnapps, lay down in bed and killed themselves, but I hope that the youngsters distributing the pills didn't follow suit. They couldn't have fully understood what their role in this whole sorry mess was. They'd all been indoctrinated since the cradle.'

'Is that all really true?'

'I have it on good authority that it is.' He took another reflective drag on his cigarette. 'Though I suppose it's more likely that those who took advantage of this gesture kept the cyanide in a safe place for future use. After all, this was what, nearly three weeks before their esteemed glorious leader committed suicide.'

Anna absorbed this information, thinking about those young blond lads in the Hitler Youth, strong from gymnastics, tanned from summer hikes, bred to reinforce the country's pure population and for the war effort, boys like Günther when he was younger. 'Do you think that if Britain had been about to lose the war, your leaders would have killed themselves?'

He squeezed her hand tight. 'No, not us Brits. It's not in our nature to give in. We're a stubborn breed. We'd have kept buggering on, as Churchill liked to say. Sorry, my dear, that's indelicate language.'

Anna didn't really understand what he had said or shouldn't have said. She was thinking about why a whole concert hall of important leading figures, instrumental in the shaping of the Reich, would want to take their own lives. Could they really not have faced the humiliation of losing the war, or was it the shame of being forced to face their crimes that would make them want to leave this Earth? And yet again she could not avoid thinking about her own responsibility and guilt. Everyone knew about the trials that had just finished at Lüneberg, passing death and prison sentences. And in that moment, an image of Herr Reiser, her well-dressed gentleman client, flashed into her mind, of him resting back on her pillows, smoking a cigarette and telling her about his dealings in the wine trade. He too had been found guilty at his hearing. He would not be given a paltry custodial sentence; he would surely hang. Everyone was talking about the hunt for Nazi war criminals and, if they weren't arrested and punished by the Allies, then the huge numbers of former prisoners from the camps and the embittered slave labourers freely roaming the countryside were more than ready to exact justice.

'My dear, you're very quiet. I'm sorry to talk of such depressing things. I didn't mean to upset you.' Reg was regarding her with concern, trying to determine her expression. It was already dark and the lights along the park's path were dim.

'I must say, I do find it very upsetting. So many terrible things, the things we are now hearing about. I don't understand how it was allowed to be like that. How can life ever be normal again?'

'The human spirit, my dear. The human spirit has the will to live and to make a good life for us all. Look around you and see how women are clearing the streets, stacking bricks to rebuild your city, making homes of sorts among the ruins. There's hope and determination for you, not despair and the easy option of taking a pill.'

Anna sighed, her voice wavering. 'Some days it just seems so hopeless. It's hard to get enough food and with winter coming on, it's going to get even harder.'

He stroked her hand, warming it in his. 'Etta, my dear, there is little I can do to help you face the winter, but I can help with supplies, as you know. And... well, it seems a little soon to be saying this, perhaps, but I have developed a deep affection for you.' He reached to lift her chin with the tip of his finger so she had to look at him, gaze upon his kindly face. 'It may not be possible for a while, but I am hoping that you would like to come back to England with me in the not-too-distant future.'

'To live there, with you?'

'Not just to live there, but to be my wife. Etta dear, I'm asking you to marry me.' He raced on, while her mind was still spinning round. 'I'm sure, that before too long, the authorities will allow it. I know I'm not the only serviceman here thinking like this. Girls like you are so serious, so dependable. My demob is coming up next autumn, so I'll still be here to help as much as I can through this winter, and once I was back home I'd make sure you had a decent place to live and I'd go back to my old job teaching history too. I might even take on a group for German, now I've had so much practice.'

Anna stared at him intently. He really did mean it, she could see that. This sincere man, who'd already told her that his parents had died in the Blitz, whose sweetheart had changed her mind and married another man, this decent, reliable man would look after her. He had made her a genuine offer. She knew that she didn't love him; she would always hanker for Günther, her first love. But if she didn't accept his proposal, what sort of life could she have here? Once he left Hamburg she would have to return to working on the streets, running the risk of disease, abuse, pregnancy and maybe accusations.

'I'd like that very much,' she said, leaning forward and planting a kiss on the dry lips below his little scratchy moustache. He smelt of soap and tobacco, while she thought she probably smelt of smoke from the cellar's stove, unwashed clothes and the cheap scent Rolf had given her when she said she was leaving the rooming house for good.

'We'll be happy together, Etta, I know it,' he said. 'Some of the other chaps are in the same boat. They say they'd rather have a hardworking German girl for a wife than a hoity-toity English miss any day!'

Reg gave Anna another dry peck on the lips. It wasn't the kind of kiss she'd had from Günther, nor from some of her customers, but it wasn't threatening, it was reassuring. She thought that not only could she escape the ruins, Gertrude's snide remarks and the pressure to manage with so little, but it was also her chance to leave Hamburg, leave Germany and never be discovered.

'I'll help you get the right papers,' he said before she left. 'Come to the Zoo Camp tomorrow, and I'll see you're sorted out.'

THIRTY-TWO

LONDON, FEBRUARY 2017

Why did I do that, Anna thinks, holding the two halves of the postcard. Freddie meant well. He wasn't to know that he pricked my conscience with this picture and his questions.

She knows that Lauren noticed the card in the bin. Hopes that she will not say anything to Freddie. As soon as Lauren had gone, she'd retrieved the stained card, wiped it carefully and tried to stick it back together with Sellotape. The sticky film wrinkled across that sweet, optimistic photo, taken in a carefree moment when Anne couldn't have had the slightest notion of the fate that would befall her and most of her family and friends.

He will think I am ungrateful if he finds out, Anna tells herself, shaking her head. He will tell his mother I am an irritable, unkind old woman. But I replied to his questions, didn't I? Not extensively, it's true, but I answered honestly. We didn't know in the beginning and it wasn't our fault.

She props the card against the canister marked Tea and considers it as she unfolds her ironing board. Maybe the steam iron will soothe her mind, even though she cannot smooth out the creases on the card, nor completely wipe away the stains. She sprays starch onto the embroidered tray cloth she likes to use when serving her cakes. She presses the back of the embroidery first, as Mama once taught her, then turns it over and presses the front, nudging the nose of the iron around the shape of the stitched flowers. She sewed this cloth and others like it when her children were young and she had an hour or so to herself while they were in school. Mama would be proud of her for maintaining her standards of housekeeping.

A double sheet is next, which Lauren helped her to fold when she brought in her washing from the line in the garden. She can still manage to peg out her sheets, but they are too big for her to fold correctly on her own. Reg helped her once he'd retired, but never seemed to quite get the hang of matching the corners. Susan and Peter used to fold too, but were always impatient to rush away to see their friends, do their homework and in the end leave home for good. If she'd been more lenient, would they have stayed? Probably not, she thinks, as the iron steams and presses the slightly damp linen.

She knows only the top edge of the sheet will show, but she can't help herself; she has to iron the whole thing, section by section. Smoothing out the tiny creases left by the wash and the breeze, it feels as if she is ironing out her life, removing its problems and putting all in order.

Anna is surprised that neither Lauren nor Freddie have ever asked her again why she was away from the house so long, when they found her at the bus stop. And they've never asked her what was in her little case. She doesn't want them to ask, but she still finds it surprising. But maybe they assumed her mind had slipped its moorings that day. She is sure that is what the doctor thought when he checked her over the next morning. She could hear them murmuring out in the hallway, talking about her as if she wasn't there.

They must have thought I was showing the first signs of senility, she thinks. Maybe I was, but I think it was the shock that confused me. That and the cold. It does funny things to the mind. I've seen it among the old people in the church, unable to find the hymn numbers and looking blank when the collection plate is offered.

What was it that Reg used to say? 'If I get forgetful in my old age, Margie, just leave me in a corner of the pub. I'll be quite happy there.' He always made me smile when he said that. But I'd never have left him there, I'd have popped in before closing time and walked him home, the dear man. And I said he could let me drop down in the garden. I'd be happy falling asleep in the rose beds after a morning's weeding.

But maybe I should pretend I'm not right in the head if any questions are ever asked. What could they do if I said I couldn't remember? It wouldn't be so surprising after all this time, at my age. I expect quite a few felons have used that excuse in their time. They could never prove I can remember. I suspect they can't even prove who I really am.

But I can't pretend to Lauren and Freddie, can I? They are dear to me and I don't want to lie to them. And the fact is, I do remember. I can recall everything all too clearly, however much I may wish to forget. That is my curse, my punishment, that I will always carry with me.

Anna's iron slows as she thinks and gazes at the postcard staring at her. She frowns and wonders what Freddie would think if he knew that the girl's name was very like her own. That girl was young, of course, younger than Ursula was back then, maybe about the same age as Hermann. Their faces become again so clear to her and she realises she has stopped and the iron has scorched the sheet. Not quite burnt, but a faint smell rises from the fabric, reminding her that purgatory awaits those who have not mended their ways.

She puts the hot iron aside and examines the sheet. Luckily the brown scorch is not along the top edge with its drawn threadwork. Like her, the shameful mark is not visible and will never be seen.

THIRTY-THREE

HAMBURG, MARCH 1946

Winters in Hamburg were always bitterly cold, with freezing winds blowing in from the northern seas, but by March the snows had melted. Reg suggested that instead of a concert or sitting at their favourite park bench, they should take a drive out into the countryside.

'It would make a change to get a breath of fresh air,' he said, making Anna think that he must be still conscious of the stench of decay that continued to haunt the city. Even now, nearly three years since that terrible night of bombing and fire, whole bodies and body parts were still coming to light, whenever builders excavated the ruins to begin the reconstruction of homes, offices and businesses.

'Where are we going?' she asked as they trundled away out of the city in a rattling car he'd obtained by some means unknown to her.

'Aah,' he replied, tapping the side of his nose, 'it's a surprise. A good one, I hope. But it might mean we'll be secure for the rest of our lives, Etta. I don't want you to worry about how you will find the means to live ever again. Life will only get better for you from now on, I can assure you.'

Anna had to be content with that mysterious reply, and tried to relax and enjoy the views across the green fields filled with young crops, calves with their mothers and lambs with ewes. It was all so different to the ravaged streets of Hamburg. It felt like life was starting afresh and, knowing that Reg was still determined she would be joining him in England, she could be optimistic about her future – once restrictions on British soldiers marrying German girls were lifted. She also felt fresh and clean like the spring countryside, as Reg had been able to supply her with a precious bar of soap – and not just harsh carbolic soap either. She held her wrist to her nose, enjoying the treat of breathing in the faint scent of roses.

When the car eventually rumbled into a deserted village, where many of the houses were badly damaged, with shattered windows, she wondered why on earth he had thought they should come here. If he had been one of her former clients, or anyone other than decent, reliable Reg, she might have been filled with trepidation, fearing he was going to assault or perhaps even murder her in this desolate spot. But this was no murderous assailant, this was Reg, the man who had helped her survive the cold of the last winter, given her cigarettes as currency for bartering, brought extra food whenever he could, even managing to give her eggs and milk to nourish baby Peter and the two older children. Of course he wasn't going to harm her.

'Over there,' he said, opening the car door for her and doffing his cap as if he was her chauffeur and she was really a lady of breeding, not a shabby dweller of bombed-out buildings. He pointed to an abandoned inn, a provincial bierkeller, which was in slightly better condition than the nearby ruins. 'No one else knows about this at present, Etta, but I've no doubt they will before very long.'

He took her hand and they entered through a heavy door armoured with a round iron handle and studs. Their feet rustled the dry leaves littering the stone floor inside. A shaft of sunlight filtered through the broken windows, revealing upturned chairs, dusty tables and hastily strewn beer tankards. It looked as if the revellers had left their rousing party, loud with drinking songs, in a terrible hurry.

Anna looked around at the scattered debris, thinking that although the drinkers were long gone, she could still smell their tobacco and spilt beer and almost imagined that she could hear an echoey chorus of that popular song, 'Wunderbar', too.

'Why did you want to bring me here?'

'Because, my dear Etta, this isn't just an old, abandoned inn.'

Reg took her hand again and steered her to a small door round the back of the bar. When he opened it, she could see steps leading down into a dark cellar. 'I'll go first,' he said, switching on a torch he'd pulled out of his coat pocket.

She gripped the rail attached to the wall and gingerly felt her way down the narrow stairs, into a dry basement piled with boxes and crates. As Reg swung the torch beam around, it caught the gleam and sparkle of glass and bright metal in every corner.

'It's hard to believe, isn't it? All of these goods secretly stashed away, waiting for the war to end. There's all sorts here, all of it valuable. Contax cameras and Zeiss Ikon binoculars; there's crates of oil paintings and then all this gold and silver, look.' He whipped away the cloth wrappings covering the contents of one of the boxes to reveal shining gold plates and candlesticks.

Anna had a strange feeling of déjà vu. This was not the first time she had seen such a heap of loot. She peered into several of the crates. Every single one was full. This was a treasure trove of stolen trophies, hidden away either for the benefit of the Reich or as personal insurance for some unscrupulous individual. 'But however did you find all this?'

'Luftwaffe deserter, came into the office recently. I was the only one there on duty at the time. He insisted on bringing me here. Said if I could give him a new identity it was mine to do with as I liked.' Reg brushed the dust off one of the cameras and shone his torch on the gleaming lens, admiring the precision.

'This chap had been let off desertion charges by the SS so long as he stayed here and guarded this hoard till the war was over. But he's heard nothing since and was desperate to get back to his family, so he was prepared to hand it all over to us if he could go free. What do you think, Etta? No one is going to object to us helping ourselves, are they?'

Anna tried to assess the huge amount of stolen goods stored in the cellar. And then she stared at Reg, while he fondled the expensive cameras and binoculars. A creeping feeling of dread filled her heart. Suddenly this formerly decent man seemed less decent, less respectable. Was every man, suddenly offered the chance of unlimited wealth, so easily able to abandon his moral principles?

'But where do you think this has all come from and what makes you think you have a right to take any of it?'

Reg blew out his cheeks. 'Well, if I don't help myself, someone else is sure to. I can't possibly manage to take much, so there's plenty for everyone. All the chaps are collecting trophies and souvenirs, while they're here, you know. No one thinks anything of it. They've picked up German cameras, watches – you name it, they've got the lot. If they don't want them for themselves, they say they'll be able to sell them for a decent sum once they're back home. It's fair game, Etta, after all they've put us through.'

She was silent, thinking about the significance of this hoard. She had seen something like it before, on her long trek back to Hamburg. It made her think there must be stores of stolen treasures, hidden all over Germany during the course of the war, then forgotten in the mad race to victory and the escape from the humiliation of defeat.

But where had it all come from originally? Some of it, like the cameras and binoculars, had to be stock from shops that had been forced to close when the owners were arrested and maybe deported. But the paintings, the gold plate; that had to have been requisitioned from wealthy homes when the occupants were imprisoned or forced to flee the country.

And among the gold and silver, she thought she recognised the kind of branched candelabra that she remembered seeing in Margarete's home, that she had been told was called a menorah. It sat in the centre of the polished sideboard and her friend had told her how the candles were always lit for their special dinner every Friday.

Anna felt a sick shiver of distaste, hoping the excitement of this discovery wasn't revealing Reg's true nature. She could see how thrilled he was by this treasure trove. He didn't appear to realise what its existence actually signified. He probably hadn't thought about the pleading hands that had tried to hold on to it and how many deaths were associated with this vast haul of gold. 'No, this is all wrong,' she said. 'I think this should be returned to the real owners. You should do the right thing and report it.'

Reg shook his head, 'But how on earth can we know who it belonged to? And are they even likely to be alive still? Come on, Etta, it won't do any harm just to take a little of this. Look how much there is! We could never take all of it, but a little could make all the difference to us in the future. Some of it is worth a fortune.'

Anna just stared at him, despising his pathetic pleas. She was tempted to tell him she knew for a fact that there would be a written record of this treasure somewhere. He didn't realise that the thefts undertaken in the name of the Reich weren't surreptitious, but were fully documented, so the owners could be traced if someone did the research. But if she pointed that out to him, might it reveal too much about her knowledge of the workings of that ghastly system?

'We shouldn't take any of it,' she said. 'Not a single thing. You know only too well that it's all stolen property. All of it, stolen from Jewish businesses and families who now have nothing, who probably aren't even still alive. You know they were probably gassed as soon as they reached the camps or died of starvation and typhus. You mustn't touch a single thing. We should leave it all here. Let someone else help themselves and then live with the guilt, or ask the authorities to trace the owners.'

She turned on her heel, marched back to the stairs and rushed up and out into the fresh air. She felt sick and took deep breaths, trying to calm herself, leaning on the bonnet of the car. Up to now, she had thought of Reg as her trustworthy saviour, but she didn't like what she'd just seen.

And she couldn't help remembering what had happened before, when there were new arrivals off the trains and lorries, filthy, shaking with fear, forced to undress, shower and change into prison uniform. Their clothes were carefully searched for the gold sewn into hems, the banknotes lining shoes and hats, the jewels tucked under collars and in the lining of pockets. All the little hidden tokens of currency that might mean the difference between life and death: an extra crust, a lighter work detail, maybe even a pardon or an escape. Everything of value was ferreted out and stripped away, documented and stashed, just like this secret hoard of treasure.

After a few minutes she heard Reg coming up behind her. 'I'm so very sorry, my dear, if you didn't think this was a good idea. I suppose I was just overwhelmed by the enormity of it. I've never seen such wealth in my whole life. But I suppose you're right; there's no honour in trading on the misfortune of others.'

He opened the car door for her and as he did so, she noticed that the inner pocket of his greatcoat was bulging. He realised she had seen and he frowned, then pulled out a pair of binoculars. 'I'm sorry, Etta. I couldn't resist them. They're first-rate quality. I'd never be able to afford a pair like this at home. I'm a twitcher, you see, a birdwatcher. Can you please forgive me?'

Tight-lipped with fury, Anna didn't say a word. At least the binoculars had probably come from a shop's stockroom and not the ripped hem of a terrified prisoner's coat. She just hoped he hadn't slipped any of the stolen gold into his pockets as well.

DIE SECHS SCHWÄNE

THE SIX SWANS

As a punishment the wicked mother-in-law
was tied to the stake and burned to ashes.

THIRTY-FOUR

HAMBURG, OCTOBER 1946

At last, the city was beginning to recover. All around them they could hear the sounds of construction; diggers shovelling, builders shouting and whistling, the drone of drilling, as shattered streets and homes were raised from the rubble.

'We can't stay here much longer,' Ursula said one morning. 'This street is scheduled to be razed next. We're going to have to give in and let them rehouse us.'

Much as she had appreciated being accepted by the Ausgebombten Gang, Anna also thought it was time for them to go. They couldn't face another winter without proper shelter and heating. All of them had suffered from the cold during the long freezing months of winter. Little Peter had endured cough after cough, leaving him pale and sickly, despite the help they'd received from the Zoo Camp centre and the extra supplies of food courtesy of Reg. She hoped for herself that she would be able to leave well before the end of the year, now that restrictions on marriage between British and Germans had been lifted, and Reg was confident that she would be able to join him in England soon after his return. He was due to leave in November and his continued generosity encouraged her to forgive his momentary lapse in the secret treasure hoard. She just hoped that the cash he frequently gave her wasn't the result of transactions with stolen goods from elsewhere.

'I don't want to leave here and be told where I've got to live,' Gertrud said. 'We've managed perfectly well all this time. You lot can go, but I'm staying put.'

Peter was crawling on the dirt floor. He tugged at his mother's skirts and she picked him up and bared her breast. Even though he was well over a year old, she was still feeding him because of the lack of milk and fresh food. Gertrud winced as his little teeth bit her, and admonished him, saying, 'Don't bite Mutti's titty. Any more and that will be the last time.' He gazed at her with eyes that were still the baby blue he'd had when he was born and she stroked his blond hair. Anna watched this image of Madonna and child with a pang of regret that she'd never been able to feed her own son even for a day. If he was alive, she knew he wouldn't still be feeding from a warm breast, but in truth she'd long ago had to face the fact that he'd never had the chance to suckle at all.

'Well, Hermann and I are going to leave soon,' Ursula said. 'We're taking the children with us to the Zoo Camp today and asking them to rehouse us. I don't care where it is. As long as it's warm and there's water, we'll be better off than we are here. And then the children will be able to go to school.'

Anna thought that the once-confident girl who'd greeted her and involved her in their looting missions when she first returned to the city now looked tired and defeated, worn down by the months of harsh survival. She hadn't yet told them that she'd be leaving before long too.

'I think you are right to go,' she said, 'before we have another cold winter. Everyone says that Hamburg is sure to have a big freeze this year, judging by the number of berries on the trees and bushes in the parks.'

'It's a pity we can't eat all of them, Etta,' Ursula said. 'The hips are good and we've had all the blackberries now, but nothing else is edible.'

'If it wasn't for the little extra I'm able to bring you, we'd really be suffering,' Anna said. 'Have you noticed how many people are looking quite ill? Everyone's thin and yellow. There's just not enough food coming in for the huge numbers in the city now.'

'That's it, I'm not waiting any longer,' Ursula said. 'I'm off to the Zoo Camp as soon as I've gathered up our belongings. They won't be able to rehouse us straight away, but they have some rooms and dormitories there. It's got to be easier than struggling on in this dump.'

'But you always said we had to wait here for Father to come back,' said Hermann, who'd been quiet and thoughtful so far.

Ursula spun round. 'Are you that stupid? Don't you realise? He's never coming back. He would have found us by now if he was still alive and wanted to come home.'

Hermann's shoulders sagged and he put his face in his hands.

'Does that mean we're all orphans now?' Ingrid looked at her older sister, appealing to her for reassurance.

'We've probably all been orphans since the night of the bombing. Let's face it. If Vater was still alive then he'd have tried to find us, wouldn't he? So now we're just like thousands of other displaced people but at least we've got each other. Now help me pack.'

Ursula began rifling through blankets and piles of ragged clothes, trying to find the ones that she thought belonged to her little family. As she scrabbled among the heaps of rags, she began to sob. Hermann noticed her tears but, instead of comforting his older sister, he rushed out of the basement with a reddened face, saying he was better off catching rats. Then Ingrid ran after him, with Therese and Stefan scampering close behind her.

Anna put her arms round Ursula, letting her cry against her shoulder. 'I can't do it any more, Etta,' she moaned. 'It's been so hard and we're no better off than we were at the start. And the British haven't helped.'

Anna stayed quiet. Although there had been a sigh of relief within the population when the British first arrived at the very end of the war, there had been rumblings for months that the city was worse off under their control. The previous efficient German authorities had been banished and under the British administration food was less plentiful than before. The occupying force had also ordered the destruction of the docks and closed factories, on the grounds that they had to stop Germany from rearming, so the city's residents felt they hadn't made any progress whatsoever towards restoration.

'Let me help you pack,' Anna said. 'You've been so strong and brave all this time. Life is sure to get better before long, I know it will.'

Ursula sniffed and wiped her nose on her sleeve. 'It will be nice to have a proper bed and hot water. I'm sick of having to wash in cold water from that standpipe and shit in a hole in the ground.' Anna pulled a face at that last remark. The sanitary arrangements were not at all convenient, with all their neighbours vying with them to find a fresh patch of ground in which to dig a hole for their business. The ruins stank not only of hidden corpses but open pits of human waste.

Anna turned to Gertrud. 'Won't you be going off to the Zoo soon as well? It will be so much better for Peter if you are able to keep him properly clean.' The poor child had suffered terribly, his skin sore and red from a lack of washing and clean linen, despite his mother's efforts. In the heat of the summer, flies had tried more than once to investigate his makeshift nappies to lay their eggs.

Gertrud pulled her son from her breast and he wailed and pulled at the fabric as she rebuttoned her blouse. 'We'll manage,' she said, sitting him in the pram and giving him a sweetened twist of cloth to suck and chew. He grew quieter, his large blue eyes following his mother.

Anna longed to hold little Peter, to take him away to the basic resources of the Zoo Camp, where he could be bathed and weaned. His pale skin was so translucent that blue veins were visible on his forehead and on his hollow chest when Gertrud undressed him. She was sure he wouldn't survive another winter if he didn't receive better care. Maybe this was why both his mother's earlier children hadn't lived very long.

Her thoughts were interrupted by Ursula pulling away from her embrace to resume her packing. She wrapped thread-bare clothes in blankets so each of them would have a bundle they could carry. She'd nearly finished when she dragged a small cardboard suitcase tied with string out from behind the mattress where Gertrud had made her bed. 'Is this yours or can I use it?' she said, placing it next to her bundles.

'Leave that alone, don't you dare touch it,' Gertrud shouted.

But Ursula was tugging at the knotted string and opening the case. She stared at the contents. It looked like a charred log wrapped in cloth.

Gertrud snatched the case away from her and the black-ened thing fell out onto the earthen floor of the cellar. She threw a shawl over it, stuffed it back in the case and ran outside howling, hugging the case tight.

'What on earth's the matter with her?' Ursula was open-mouthed with shock.

Anna ran outside too and found Gertrud sitting on the steps to the cellar. She was rocking backwards and forwards, clutching the case to her chest, crooning a soft lullaby under her breath.

Anna sat down next to her, but she didn't seem to notice. She just kept rocking as if she was cradling a baby to sleep. And in that moment, the most awful thought struck Anna. She had never told them what had happened to the children she'd had before Peter.

'You can tell me about it,' she said, rubbing Gertrud's back. 'You can tell me what happened, if you want.'

Gertrud took a deep breath, as if gathering her strength. In a voice devoid of emotion, staring straight ahead and not at Anna, she said, 'It's my Peter, my last Peter, my second child. My first died early on in the war from measles but this one died the night of the bombing. He was only a few weeks old. I couldn't do anything to help him. He was in his cot, asleep. He wouldn't have known a thing.'

'That's terrible. Have you had him here all this time?' Anna was trying to reconcile the incinerated thing that had fallen from the case with the image of a tiny baby. She had not seen any discernible features, no ears, nose or limbs; it was fused, like a lump of charcoal.

Gertrud nodded. 'I couldn't get back into the house that night. Everything was on fire, but I went back for him when it was over. I'd only gone out for a moment, just to find out what was happening. I would have taken him with me to the shelter if I'd known. I was just about to, but boof! In seconds it was like a flame-thrower hit the building. Every living thing inside was consumed, only charred bodies remained. Even grown men and women were burned to death on the spot.'

She continued her hypnotic rocking, cradling the little scuffed suitcase. 'I couldn't leave him there. And I couldn't bury him. I didn't know what to do. I just knew he had to stay with me. I did the right thing, didn't I, Etta?'

Anna put her arm round her. 'Of course you did. You did what any good mother would have done. You kept him close by you. You did your best to keep him safe.' She wished she could have kept her own child safe too and never signed away his life.

Anna kissed the top of Gertrud's head and the crooning resumed. But Anna knew Gertrud would never forgive herself, because she had, however briefly, abandoned her baby on that terrifying night of fire, with the most dreadful consequences.

THIRTY-FIVE

HAMBURG, OCTOBER 1946

Anna returned to the basement later that evening after a brief meeting with Reg, who'd loaded her arms with eggs and bread. 'Where's Gertrud?' she asked, on hearing Peter's grizzling.

'We haven't seen her for hours,' Ingrid said, jiggling Peter on her hip. 'Thank goodness you're here now, Etta, this one's been screaming for his mama and we've had to try and keep him quiet with whatever we can.'

'Poor baby, he's hungry, isn't he?' Anna gave Ursula her packages and took the distressed child in her arms. His sour urine-soaked smell wasn't pleasant, but she told herself she could wash and change him once he was fed. 'We don't have milk, but we could try giving him eggy bread. Mash it up and feed it to him.'

Ursula set to work to prepare his food before making supper for the rest of them. 'It's not like her,' she said, crumbling the bread into the beaten egg and heating it on the stove. 'She never stays out this long. She's usually here all day with him and doesn't go out till the evening for a few hours' work. But today she'd already gone by the afternoon, when I came back from the Zoo Camp.'

'I thought you were hoping to move in there right away?'

'I was, but they're overflowing. They said we can go every day to wash and eat, but they've no spare beds at present. The rebuilding work all over the city is driving people out of their shelters, just like it's going to push us out of this cellar. It's all very well, but there's nowhere for everyone to go.'

Anna thought it sounded like rats were streaming from the sewers. She blew on the hot mash and held a small spoonful to her lips before she offered it to Peter, sitting on her lap. He tried to grab the spoon, but she held it tight as she couldn't afford to waste any of the precious food. Ursula began boiling potatoes for them all to eat that evening. There was little else. No butter, no cheese, just potatoes; but they would be hot and filling.

Once she had finished feeding Peter, Anna laid him down on a blanket and removed the rags swaddling his lower half. His buttocks were painfully red and she knew that despite her cleaning him, the minute his urine touched his skin he'd be in agony. 'You poor little boy,' she said, dabbing him gently with a rag soaked in clean water. 'What can we do to make it better?'

'He's going to scream all night, Etta, if we don't protect his skin,' Ursula said. 'Here, take a little of the oil.' She gestured towards the cooking oil they used sparingly.

Peter kicked his legs and tried to roll over onto his stomach. Anna finished cleaning him and lubricated him with the greasy oil. 'You're going to smell like fried potatoes,' she laughed as he giggled at her touch.

Once he was freshly wrapped and comfortable, Anna dressed him and laid him in the pram under a blanket. He was warm and his belly was full. She'd had her share of the sparse supper and the others were quietly talking, settling for the night. 'I think I should try to find Gertrud,' she said. 'You're right, it isn't like her to stay away from him for so long.'

'I know,' Ursula said. 'And I felt dreadful when I realised

what was in her case and why she was so upset. Poor Gertrud, she must have taken it with her.'

'I'd like to check she hasn't met with trouble out there. She was very distressed this morning.'

'Would you like me to come with you, Etta?' Hermann stood up and she noticed he was almost taller than her now. His deepening voice was uneven and if he'd been dark-haired, she'd have expected to see a shadow of down on his upper lip.

Anna hesitated. She knew he longed to help, to provide for his family and to protect them, yet she wasn't sure she wanted him to see the degrading life on the streets at night. But maybe now he was growing up he should understand what the women in the group had faced in providing for them all.

'You can come with me if you stay right by my side,' she said. 'If some of the men out there think you are going to cause trouble, you won't be safe.'

She tucked the blanket around Peter. His eyes were already drooping and he was sucking his thumb. Hopefully he'd sleep until she returned, giving the others some peace and maybe a chance to rest too.

As they began walking the unlit streets, Hermann said, 'You don't have to hide things from me, Etta. I'm not a child. I do know what you and Gertrud have to go out and do each night. I understand that you had to do it to help all of us.'

Anna grasped his arm and pulled him close to her side. 'You've seen a lot of things a boy of your age shouldn't have to see, I know that. It's not normal, it's just because of the times we've had to live through.'

'And it's not only girls and women who are selling themselves either.'

'What do you mean?'

'There are young men and boys as well, especially down by

the docks. And I've been asked more than once by soldiers and other men if I'd like to earn some extra money or cigarettes.'

'But you haven't accepted, have you?'

'No, I don't want to.' His voice croaked. 'But I'd do it if I had to. If it was the only way we could buy enough food for all of us.'

She squeezed his arm tight. 'But you don't have to do it. Please promise me you won't ever stoop to that.'

He hugged her back. 'Don't worry. As long as you and Gertrud can keep providing for us and while the Zoo Camp can help feed us as well, I shan't have to.'

They were nearing the army barracks and, as usual at this time of night, she could hear the scattered sounds of men and women laughing, talking and occasionally shouting. The combined odours of cheap tobacco and even cheaper scent welcomed them. She held Hermann's arm tight as they drew near. 'If we're lucky we might get you some chocolate, but you stay close to me.'

She hoped that Reg had gone straight back to his billet and that there was no chance of him finding her here. She had never told him about her past life or that one of the occupants of the cellar was a prostitute. Up ahead of them she thought she could see her old friend Lili, leaning against the wire fence and smoking as if she was resting between jobs. Anna called out to her and Lili turned round. Her face was as hollow as many of the city's hungry residents, but in the glare of the camp's lights, Anna could see that she also bore bruises.

'What's happened to you?'

Lili took a drag on her cigarette. 'Punter thought I was asking too much. It's got worse since you first turned up. Too many girls around these days. Now the punters think we should drop our prices as well as our pants.' She noticed Anna's companion. 'Who's this then? You going for the younger ones now, Etta?'

'No, this is Hermann. He lives with us. We've come out to look for Gertrud. She hasn't been seen since early this afternoon.'

'Not seen anything of her in a long time but then she's always favoured the docks. I know it's a mess down there since the stupid Brits blew it all sky-high, but that might still be the best place to go looking.' She then began to cough, a hacking, rasping sound of alarm, warning that she probably wouldn't last through the winter.

'We'll try down there then.' Anna turned to leave, then said, 'Is there any news of Rita?'

Lili shook her head. 'She's gone, poor girl. Her chest got bad last winter. Shame. I miss her. These new ones aren't half as lively.'

'I'm sorry to hear that. You were both very kind to me back then. I'm very grateful. Please take care of yourself now.'

'I'll do my best, darling. And bring that boy of yours back when he's a bit older. I'll give him a lesson he won't forget.'

Anna pulled Hermann away. 'Pretend you didn't hear that,' she said. 'We've got a job to do. We've got to find Peter's mother.'

They made their way down to the docks, where the wind was picking up, bringing with it the scents of seaweed, fish and motor oil. Against the background of boarded-up warehouses, they looked out across the water, bobbing with the remains of shattered fishing craft.

'I don't understand why they had to scupper the boats, Etta,' Hermann said. 'We're surrounded by water full of fish and we can't even catch them now. We'd all be far less hungry if they'd let us go out to catch them for ourselves.'

Anna sighed. 'I know. It doesn't seem to make any sense but we can't worry about that now. Come on, we've got to see if

Gertrud's down here anywhere.' She took his hand to keep him close and they walked around the harbour's edge.

Although no fish had been landed there for some time, she thought she could still detect the smell of hefty catches of cod and herring, tipped out of nets and then gutted and scaled on the quayside. Despite the dark, she was aware of figures skulking in corners, sometimes singly, sometimes in pairs and groups. Now and then she called out Gertrud's name but the only answers she received were crude jeers from men hidden in the gloom, inviting her and her companion to join them. 'Herkommen. Wir haben Schnapps.' Their voices were carried away on the wind as it whistled, whipping the waves splashing the harbour walls.

When they had almost finished their tour of the harbour, Hermann said, 'Something seems to be happening over there. I think one of the fishing boats must still be seaworthy. It looks like they're unloading their catch right now.' They walked across to the little group of three men, lit only by the moon, to see them lifting a bulky net, which they laid down on the quayside.

'What have you caught?' Anna called out as they grew closer, and the men turned to look at her. 'We didn't think anyone was still going out fishing.'

One of the men shook his head. 'The sea's full of fish, but they want to starve us.'

His companion said, 'It's not fish. But you don't want to go looking at this.' He held up a warning hand.

But Anna could already tell what they had caught. It was a body, a body with long hair, the body of a woman. She drew closer to take a proper look, praying it wasn't Gertrud.

'We are searching for our friend. She is a young mother and her baby still needs her. You must let me see if it's her.'

Even with the bright light of the moon it was hard to see clearly, so one of the men lit a match and held it close. Anna leant down and brushed the wet strands of hair from the woman's face. It was indeed Gertrud. She did not appear to be injured and her expression was peaceful, as if she was sleeping.

'Oh, Gertrud, dear, what has happened to you?' Anna looked up at the men, gulping back her sobs and tears. 'It's her. Did you see her falling in?'

'She didn't fall,' said the man who'd produced the light. 'We saw her jump in. She'd been wandering around here most of the day, looking lost and carrying a little suitcase, but I think she only jumped about an hour ago.'

'Oh, poor Gertrud. Her little boy is only just learning to walk.'

'We could never have stopped her. It keeps on happening. We can't go fishing to keep us all fed, we can only catch fallen souls, like this one.'

'What will happen to her now?'

'We report it to the authorities and they deal with it all. There'll be another one tomorrow, for sure.'

Anna knelt beside the body, feeling in Gertrud's pockets and checking she wasn't wearing any jewellery. 'She has nothing of value on her, not that she ever had anything anyway. Did you find her suitcase?'

He shook his head, 'I saw she had it with her when she jumped, but we couldn't see it when we fished her out. Probably sunk by now. Can you give us a name for her?'

'We only knew her as Gertrud. I don't think any of us knew her last name.'

'I know it,' Hermann said, his voice strangely twisted as he tried not to cry. 'We were with her when she registered at the Zoo Camp. I heard her say her name was Petersen.'

Anna bit her lip to stop herself crying at Gertrud's pitiful reference to her children, those alive and those dead. 'Then put that on your report. Now that we know her fate, we must return to her son. We are all he has now.'

She grabbed Hermann's hand and pulled him away, her tears coursing down her cheeks without the aid of sobs, flowing salty tears like the salt water that had taken Gertrud and her dead child, giving her son's remains a proper burial after all, a burial at sea.

THIRTY-SIX

HAMBURG, OCTOBER 1946

Sitting side by side on their usual bench in the park as the light faded, holding hands, Anna summoned up the courage to speak to Reg. He might refuse her request, she might even lose her chance to escape and start a new life, but she knew she had to ask him.

'May I ask a favour? A very big favour?'

'Of course, my dear Etta. Go ahead. If it's within my power to help you, I will do my very best.'

She took a deep breath. 'How would you feel if I asked you to let me bring a very young child to England with me?'

She felt the shock of his reaction in the stiffening of his fingertips as he slipped his hand away from hers. 'Etta, my dear, are you trying to tell me you have a child? That you are already a mother? You've never mentioned this before.'

'No, he's not my son, I swear to you. I've just been helping to care for him. But his real mother died yesterday. She was desperately sad after all the hard times she's experienced and she drowned herself in the harbour. We went searching for her last night and saw her being dragged out of the water.'

'How perfectly dreadful. And where is her husband? The child's father? Doesn't he want to look after his child?'

How could she explain? Had Gertrud even known who was the father of her son? It could have been any one of the many clients to whom she had given her body for money or cigarettes. Anna couldn't bring herself to tell Reg that Gertrud had been a woman of the streets. And she didn't dare let him begin to suspect that she too had followed her example for a while. He believed she was unfortunate and respectable, not disreputable and shameful.

'She never told us who the father was. I think he was long gone. Either as a casualty of the war or disappeared. She was all alone, poor girl. I think that must be why she was so desperate and couldn't face life on her own any more.'

'But your friends? The people you've been living with? Can't they look after this boy now instead of you?'

'They're trying to, we all are. But they're much younger than me and can barely manage for themselves, let alone one as vulnerable as him. You don't realise how incredibly difficult living conditions are here day to day. Trying to stay healthy and well fed is such a challenge for all of us. If I leave, they will find it very hard to stop him becoming ill again, especially if there is an exceptionally harsh winter. The place we're living in is far from ideal for a baby. Please let me give him a chance.'

'It's not what I'd imagined, Etta, it really isn't. I want children, really I do, if that is our destiny, but I hadn't ever imagined giving a home to another man's child.'

Anna began to feel desperate, picturing little Peter's blue eyes staring at her, the faint purple veins on his temples pulsing. 'I was very concerned for Peter's health even before Gertrud died, but at least he had a mother to care for him then. Now she's gone, I'm really worried about him.'

'Peter? Did you say his name was Peter?' Reg's voice softened and he sighed. 'I had a younger brother named Peter once.

It was a long time ago. We lost him just after the Great War. Spanish flu. He was such a funny little chap.' He shook his head to chase away the dark thoughts and said, 'The young can so easily fall prey to childhood diseases.'

'I'm so sorry to hear that. It's so tragic when a very young child dies.' She squeezed his hand, hoping that she was transmitting her desire to care for Peter through their touch.

'But I know I said I hadn't imagined caring for another man's child, but I care deeply about you, Etta and will do anything to make you happy. So, if you really feel that you must take responsibility for this boy, then I'm prepared to take both him and you. But I must say, I'd really like to think we'd also have our own children one day.'

'Of course we will. I want that too, very much so. I want us to be a real family.' She kissed his cheek, breathing in the clean smell of soap. Perhaps she should ask Reg for more soap another time.

'Well then, we must make arrangements. I'll be off to Blighty next month. So, what is the little lad's full name?'

'His mother said her surname was Petersen, though I don't think she ever registered his birth with the authorities. She may have put his name down for a ration card at the Zoo Camp, but I don't think there's any other paperwork.'

'Then why don't we register him in your name? Look, I know that's not really how it is, but I think it might be the most straightforward route for dealing with this. Then, when I complete your details, we'll say you're a widow and your son was born soon after you lost your husband. I think that would cover everything and in due course I'll adopt him officially so he can take my surname.'

Anna thought of all the layers of deception she had employed to get this far. Her choice of name for herself, the scar on her arm and now widowhood. 'That's a good idea,' she said. 'You're so clever, Reg. I knew you'd understand.'

'My dear, I desperately want to give you a fresh start. You and the child, if that is what you want. And I've been thinking,' he said, pausing to light another cigarette, 'I hope it won't be too difficult for you to settle into a new life, but you may find that not everyone is that welcoming to people from your country, particularly since seeing the newsreels of those dreadful camps. I know that doesn't apply to you, but people can lack under-standing. So, I suggest it might be better for you if your name sounded a little less foreign. Margarete is very like Margaret in English, so that is how I would formally introduce you. But it's often shortened, to Maggie or Margie. Which of those do you like? Are you a Maggie or a Margie?'

'Margie,' Anna said, trying it on for size. 'I like the sound of Margie.'

'Then Margie it is, my dear Margie,' he said, kissing her lightly on the lips to christen her with her new name.

Another name. The third name in her life, Anna thought. Her original name would still exist somewhere in records compiled by those who had required order and had a reputation for horrifying efficiency, but once she was in England and married, using her new husband's surname and her anglicised first name, her transformation would be complete. At last she'd escape to safety, away from suspicion and away from The Others, but never from her memories.

When Anna returned to the cellar that evening, once more laden with the fresh food Reg had provided, she decided she should share her decision with the group. 'I won't be staying with you for much longer, so I think you must try really hard to leave here before winter sets in properly. I am expecting to go to England in the next few weeks, to marry a very kind man I have got to know recently. And I'm going to take Peter with me. I'm worried he'll get seriously ill if he has to stay here for another winter. And you will all find it easier to manage if you don't have him to worry about as well as yourselves.'

The Ausgebombten Gang was stunned. They looked at her with open mouths. 'You're going to leave all of us?' Ursula looked annoyed, but Hermann seemed sad.

'Can't you take us too, Etta?' Stefan and Therese rushed to her side, throwing their arms round her.

'No, she can't take all of us,' Ingrid said. 'You've got to stay here. Etta's going to get married.'

'Of course you must go,' Ursula said. 'You've got a chance of a better life, so you must take it. And if you are taking that whining brat with you, it will be much easier for the rest of us.' She still looked cross, but she wiped away a tear with her sleeve. 'We'd never be able to look after him properly all through the winter. We'd have to leave him behind at the Zoo Camp.'

'Then it's definitely better that I take him with me,' Anna said. 'He already knows me. He'll soon come to think of me as his real mother.' She had already bathed him and fed him that day and he hadn't once asked for Mama.

'And does this man of yours know who Gertrud really was?' Hermann stared at her with mournful eyes in which she saw reflections of the tragic scene he had witnessed the previous night at the harbour.

'He knows only that she was Peter's mother and that she died. He doesn't need to know any more than that. As far as he is concerned, Peter is an innocent child in need of loving care and he is prepared to raise him as his own son.'

'Are you going to be Peter's mutti now?' Therese looked up at Anna with a pleading smile and went on, 'Can't you be our mutti too?'

Anna bent down to the level of Therese and her brother. 'I can't be a mummy to all of you and it wouldn't be fair to take you away from Ursula. She's been like a mother to you ever since you were left on your own in the park. She has cared for you for more than three years now.' She wished she could take them and the older members of the gang too. In the time she'd lived with them she'd grown fond of all of them and knew she would always think of them and wonder what had happened to them.

She hugged both the children, then stood to address Ursula and Hermann. 'But if I can, if I can spare it, I will send back money for all of you to help you cope. I will send you my new address once I am settled.'

Once I am settled, she thought. Once I find out where we are going to live, how we shall manage and whether I will be accepted by the people of Britain. Talking with Reg is helping my English, but they will still realise that I am a foreigner and will they ever want a German as a neighbour? I will have to try to lose my accent, learn to be as British as I can possibly be, and forget my past as much as I can. And that means Peter will grow up not knowing anything about his origins. He will be British from the beginning. But this Peter will be safe and will be 'special' because he is loved, not because he is not good enough to live.

THIRTY-SEVEN

LONDON, FEBRUARY 2017

I've left it far too late, Anna thinks. I should have gone when I was much younger. But as long as Reg was still alive, how could I have left him? He was the kindest, sweetest man I've ever known. I couldn't have gone while he still needed me to cook and clean and care for him. It was my way of repaying him for his decency, for saving me from a life of slow starvation and degradation.

She sits on her sofa staring at the hissing gas fire, her hand protecting her scarred arm. The clock on the mantelpiece has a steady tick; late, late, too late, it says, again and again. But when could she have gone? Not while the children were young, that's for sure. They had to be fed, kept clean, taken to school, encouraged to be good citizens.

You foolish old woman, she says to herself. What on earth made you think you could leave with your pathetic little case? How far did you think you'd get? The case had gone back under her bed soon after Lauren and Freddie brought her home that night in November. She's only looked in it once since then. There's no point in checking the contents every day now. She

knows she's never going to leave. She will only leave when she is
dead.

How could you ever have thought you could leave the country? She berates herself silently. You're too old, too unused to
travelling anywhere now. A walk to the corner shop or the
church is about all you can manage these days. You know
nothing about modern travel, you don't have a credit card, you
even find it difficult remembering the number you have to use
for your bank card. You're a stupid, useless old woman and
you'll have to stay put until one of these days they come and
get you.

Maybe she should have taken off the year after Reg died.
But where? And why? Peter and Susan had come back the year
of his funeral. 'This is the last time we can afford to do this,' her
daughter had said. 'My doctor says flying's not good for my
blood pressure and my heart,' added her son. His health never
was good and she knows that's a legacy of his early years, in that
cold, smoky basement, without the benefit of National Health
Service cod liver oil and orange juice.

Peter knows he wasn't born in the UK and that he was
adopted by Reg, but she's never told him she wasn't his birth
mother. He didn't really need to know, did he? If she'd told him
that, he'd have wanted to know more, wanted to know who his
real mother was. And what could she have said then? Your
mother was a whore. She started out in a brothel and worked
the streets. Your mother had no idea which of the many men
she'd slept with was your real father. Nor who sired the so-
called Peters she gave birth to before you either.

Poor Gertrud. Anna feels sad at the thought of all the lost
children, both Gertrud's, and her own. She wouldn't have ever
wanted to tell Peter about the fate of his mother and his older
brothers. Her own child was 'special' but not considered good
enough to live, Gertrud's earlier children perished through fate
and fire. And she knows that Gertrud might not have lived to

see Peter grow up. She would probably have perished in the big freeze of the winter of 1947, or eventually succumbed to tuberculosis, like many of the street girls.

If I had left, I'd never have wanted to return to Hamburg, Anna thinks. Going back, even though the city has been rebuilt and is prosperous again, I'd still see the street names and remember when they were piles of blackened, broken rubble. Still see the smoke curling from the cellars and those pitiful messages of hope chalked on the walls. In fact, I don't think I would want to go anywhere in Germany. I'd find myself looking at all the older people and trying to guess what they had done in their youth, wanting to ask them what they did in the war. Were you one of the boys who casually passed around the basket of free cyanide pills at that concert? Did you bully a child in your school or smash a shopfront window, because of who their owners were? Or did you do things even worse than that?

No, there's too much history for me ever to go back there. Maybe Spain would suit me. A warm country that's welcomed so many from the UK. Or what about South America? Yes, why did so many of the guilty Nazi hierarchy hide away there? They slipped in easily and must have already set up their escape routes years before because they anticipated losing the war, knowing that the thousand-year Reich was a fabled myth that could never be sustained, I suppose.

Maybe I shouldn't worry any more. They can't find everyone. What clues are there, after all? Annaliese Kohlmann transformed into Margarete Löwenthal, then she became Etta Eckstein, who is now Margie Wilson. There is no trail, no paperwork, no one left alive to point a finger and say she is not who she says she is. No photos either, probably, though maybe the job application for that secretarial position survived. All the childhood pictures went up in a puff of smoke when my parents' home was bombed. No pictures at all, until in preparation for my marriage to Reg I had to have a passport and entry visa.

Anna laughs to herself. It's quite clever really. During that time of chaos and confusion at the end of the war anyone could escape if they thought about it, and the crafty ones did. And many of those who were caught were so arrogant, they just went back to their old lives after serving a minimal sentence and picked up where they'd left off before the start of the war. Like Dr Franz Lucas, convicted for gas chamber selection, and the dentist, Willi Schatz, who didn't even go to prison because the prosecutors couldn't make the charges stick. And even if they were charged and sentenced, what did they have to serve? Karl-Friedrich Höcker, sentenced to seven years' imprisonment for aiding 1,000 murders in Auschwitz, was freed after only five years. Virtually a slap on the wrist, by claiming he was just following orders. They and the ones charged since have paid very little for their crimes.

There are many who are more guilty than she. Many who should have been imprisoned long ago. She knows, because every time there is a report in the paper she adds it to her pile, growing more slowly as more years pass. She spreads her collection of press cuttings out on her lap. Some were guards, some were office staff; all of them claimed they were only doing their duty.

The ticking clock chimes four and Anna is startled from her drifting thoughts. It's late afternoon; the streets will soon be lit and Freddie might be here any moment. He will be hungry. She must be ready for him, with tea or coffee, a glass of healthy milk to help him grow tall, present him with one of her fresh wholesome cakes and speak with him in the language of her birth. Before his enquiring gaze, she will hide her fears and escape in the pleasure of his company.

THIRTY-EIGHT

HAMBURG, DECEMBER 1946

Reg was so generous before he left to return to England, pressing both money and cigarettes into Anna's hands. 'My dear Margie, I want you and Peter to have warm clothes for your journey. Buy whatever you think you might need,' he said. 'It will be a cold voyage across the North Sea this late in the year. We don't want you both catching your deaths here or on your travels.' He called her Margie all the time now, helping her get used to her new name and the new identity that awaited her in his homeland.

The cigarettes were more use than the currency and once Anna had bought what she and Peter would wear to travel, she thought that she should share her good fortune. If she purchased more clothes, she'd never be able to pack them all in her little case, which was all she could manage at the same time as carrying a child on her hip.

She decided she should give some of this bonus to the Ausgebombten Gang, but she also wanted to thank Lili, if she could find her. Thanks to her and Rita's sound advice in directing her to the relative safety of Rolf's house, she knew she had been given a better chance of survival during those first few months back in Hamburg. Girls on the street were always at risk of abuse and disease, but the rooming house had been a secure refuge for her at a time when she desperately needed to provide an income for both herself and the younger members of the Gang.

Anna didn't know where Lili lived, so she had to face walking the streets again in her search for the girl. 'I have to go out tonight,' she said to Ursula. 'Peter is clean and has eaten well. He shouldn't disturb you once I've settled him down.' She warmed his bed with a brick heated on the top of the stove and wrapped in cloth, then tucked him up in the pram with an extra blanket, for the nights were already very cold.

'You've not started work again, have you, Etta?' Ursula looked anxious. 'I thought you weren't doing that any more, now that you're leaving us soon. If you need this money, I can give it back to you. We're very grateful for your help, but I don't want you taking risks, now you have the chance of a better life.'

'There's someone I need to thank before I finally leave. Someone who helped me early on in my time in the city. She may be in need of help herself now. I promise I'll be careful and I will come back very soon.'

Anna wrapped herself in the thick coat she had bought with Reg's money and tied a woollen scarf over her head. She had new fur-lined boots too, thanks to his generosity, keeping her feet warm as she walked the streets, which were already slick with an icy sheen of sleet.

Anna headed for the British barracks, where she had met Lili and Rita when she first decided to try her chances on the streets in the early summer of 1945. Now that Reg had left Hamburg, she was no longer afraid that he would associate her with the girls still touting for business among the remaining troops stationed there.

In spite of the cold, a few girls were huddled near the wire fences, pulling their unfastened coats over their breasts so they could quickly reveal their charms the minute a soldier showed the slightest hint of interest. They glanced at Anna in her tightly buttoned coat and recognised that she was no threat to them. 'I'm looking for a girl called Lili,' Anna shouted out. 'Have any of you seen her recently?'

A couple of them shook their heads, but one of the girls said, 'Is that the Lili who used to hang around with Rita? The pair who started out in Tante Kitty's?'

'Yes, that's her. Do you know where I might find her?'

'She's not been up here in quite a while.' The girl shivered and pulled her coat closer.

Anna noticed her legs were bare and she wore laced shoes, not warm boots, and wasn't even wearing socks. It made her think how all these girls were going to suffer if they continued trying to work outside in the wintry weather. And how grateful she was that Reg's generosity had dressed her in suitable warm clothes. She could feel the bitterness of the night piercing her legs and feet in spite of her thick boots and woollen stockings.

'You could try the docks,' another girl said, pulling up the collar of her thin coat.

'No, I think she's started hanging around the station more often these days,' said the first. 'Try there before you go down the docks. It's a bit safer and there's more lights.'

Anna shuddered, remembering her desperate search for Gertrude that night at the docks. Even though she'd had Hermann by her side, the jeers from the dark warehouses and hidden alleys had been unnerving. 'Thank you, I'll go there right now,' she said. 'Here, take these for your trouble.' She gave the girl a pack of cigarettes. 'And I really hope you won't have to stay out here all winter.'

'Thanks. But a girl's got to go where the work is, if she wants to eat. And I hope you find Lili. Tell her Rosa sends her regards, won't you?'

Anna waved at the pathetic girls, then strode off into the

night. They too would be dead before spring, killed by disease, malnutrition or the freezing cold of a long Hamburg winter. So many more people were going to die over the next few months.

The area around the main station was dimly lit, but she could see men here and there, smoking in doorways, collars pulled up to their ears, hands in pockets. She could sense their eyes following her with interest as she walked around, trying to see if Lili was slouched against a wall or sheltering in a porch. The whole area stank of urine, like a latrine. Now and then a match flared or a cigarette tip glowed red in the dim recesses, revealing a brief glimpse of a girl's or a man's face, white in the darkness.

A man slipped out of an alleyway and sidled up to her, trying to put his arm round her waist. 'How much?' he said in a low voice.

'Go away. I'm not working tonight. I'm only here because I'm looking for my friend.'

'How much for the two of you then? I can pay well and I have a room.'

'I just want to find my friend, Lili. Now clear off.' She shoved him with her elbow and walked away smartish.

'Stuck-up bitch,' he shouted after her. 'Bet you're not worth it anyway.'

A moment later, Anna saw a woman sitting in a doorway, her knees bent up to her chest, as if she was trying to keep warm by wrapping her legs in her coat. 'Lili? Is that you?'

The head lifted slowly and Anna gasped. Lili's face was drawn, with dark circles under her eyes. Her cheeks were bruised and her left eye was swollen closed. 'It's me, Lili. It's Etta. I've been looking everywhere for you.' Anna knelt down beside her. 'You shouldn't be out here in the cold on a night like this.' The sleet was turning into flakes of snow and the temperature was dropping even further. 'Why don't you go home? I'll walk there with you, if you like.'

'No home.' Lili's voice was faint and rasping. 'Nowhere to go.' She coughed several times into a bloodstained rag of a handkerchief. 'Need a man and a room.'

Anna knew that Lili would have no chance of surviving if she stayed outside for many more nights. Her only hope was a customer prepared to pay the extra for a room somewhere, so she'd have warmth and shelter after she'd conducted her business. But what chance did she have of attracting men in her sorry state? She was a sick woman whose looks had been worn away by poor nutrition and disease. Her large, luminous eyes were the only attractive feature she had left and they were but a side effect of the tuberculosis that was gradually eating her lungs, just as it had taken Rita before her.

'What you want, anyway, Etta? You working tonight?'

'No, Lili, I'm here because I came to find you. I'm going to be leaving Hamburg soon, for good. But first, I wanted to thank you for helping me early on, when I first came back here.'

'It's all right. Us girls got to look out for each other.' Lili's hand clawed Anna's sleeve. 'No one else looks out for us, only us and Auntie. But Auntie's long gone.' She began to cry.

'Listen Lili. You can't stay out here, it's freezing and it's started snowing. I'm going to help you up and walk you over to Rolf's place. We'll see if he has a spare bed for tonight.' Anna put her arms round Lili and hauled her up. She was hardly any weight. Her loose coat disguised how thin she'd become beneath its light folds, which offered little protection in the bitter cold.

Together they shuffled at a painfully slow pace through the streets, to the rooming house where Anna had once worked. She knocked at the door and a burly man answered, taking a quick look at the two of them. 'You can come in, but not her,' he said, pointing at Lili, drooping at Anna's side.

'Where's Rolf?' Anna tried to look over his shoulder, into the downstairs rooms Rolf used for himself. She desperately hoped his premises hadn't been taken over by less scrupulous, unsympathetic operators, fleecing the girls as well as the punters.

'He's busy. Who's asking?'

'Tell him Etta's here. He'll remember me.' Anna knew that the night of Ribbentrop's arrest, indelibly imprinted on her memory, was sure to be unforgettable for Rolf too. The man hesitated, so she didn't bother to wait any longer and shouted out, 'Rolf! Are you there? It's me, Etta!'

A door nearby opened and Rolf looked out. He was older and thinner, but he smiled when he saw her. 'Let them in, Franz. I know both of them.' He winked at Anna with his good eye and opened the door wide to welcome them.

Franz stepped aside and the girls slipped past him and into the warmth of Rolf's sitting room. It was cosier than Anna remembered, so perhaps business was going well.

'Since when did you employ a bouncer?' she asked, after kissing him on his scented cheek.

'I'm not as young as I was,' he said, sizing up Lili, who was clinging to Anna's arm. 'The shortages and the black market have made Hamburg a more dangerous place these days. I decided I needed protection. He's harmless really, but looks the part. So, what can I do for you, ladies? A room together, or one each?'

'We're not going to be working tonight,' Anna said. 'But my friend Lili needs somewhere to stay. Have you got a room to spare?'

'How long for, are you thinking? If you don't mind me saying so, Etta, Lili looks as if she might not be getting much work these days.'

'Exactly. She's not too well right now. It was Lili and her friend Rita who told me to come to you in the first place but now I'm going to be leaving Hamburg very soon. I've had a bit of luck and I wanted to thank Lili and make sure she would be able to cope through the winter. I think this one's going to be a particularly hard one. So, I'll pay for her room for as long as she wants it.'

'She's not going to need it for very long, is she?' Rolf's voice had dropped to a whisper as he continued to assess Lili. 'Bring the poor girl through and let her rest in here for a while.'

Anna half-carried Lili into the room and laid her on the patched couch, its arms and back shiny with years of hair oil. She removed Lili's coat and laid it across her, like a blanket, wincing at the sight of the bruises and sores on her friend's arms and legs. She could detect a trace of the cheap scent that Lili still used, but now it was blended with a sour odour that meant poverty and imminent death.

'I can't give her a room upstairs,' Rolf said, pouring them both a small cup of coffee from the pot on the glowing stove that warmed the room. 'They're only for working girls. But I can let her sleep in my quarters, if that's acceptable. I've got another bed as well as the couch.'

Anna glanced at Lili, who had fallen asleep with her mouth open. She was struck by how young Lili looked as she slept. She couldn't be much older than Anna herself, twenty-five, maybe thirty years old at very most. What had set her on this destructive path? A man perhaps – or a degenerate mother in the same profession, more like.

'I don't really think she's going to be working any more. She won't be able to pay you for her keep, but I'm going to leave you money. I doubt she'll eat much, the way she is. Are you sure she can stay here?'

Rolf nodded, then looked over at the snoring girl. 'I've got a soft spot for you ladies. So yes, she can stay. And what about you? A bit of luck, you say?'

'I'm going to England. I'm going to marry a very nice British soldier.' Anna smiled and held out her hand with the simple ring, set with three small diamonds, that Reg had slipped onto her finger.

'Congratulations. I'm very happy for you, Etta,' Rolf said as he held her hand to examine the modest ring. 'Is he handsome? Film-star looks?'

'Hardly.' Anna laughed, thinking of solid, decent Reg with his combed hair and neat little moustache. 'But what matters is that he's kind and generous. And it will be a whole new start for me and the little boy I'm taking with me.'

Rolf squeezed her hand. 'I wish you all the best, Etta darling. At least someone is going to have a happy-ever-after ending.'

And Anna looked into his moistly glistening eyes and saw loneliness there, but kindness too. 'Thank you,' she said. 'You are a very dear man.'

THIRTY-NINE

TILBURY DOCKS, DECEMBER 1946

The ship that brought Anna from Hamburg was little more than a ferry. Cold, uncomfortable and full of seasick passengers, battling its way across the North Sea, where ice floes had formed early that year, signalling that a harsher winter than usual was threatening the northern towns of Germany.

She too was sick on the voyage, shivering despite her thick, warm coat. She had to ask another passenger to mind Peter for a moment, so she could step out onto the slippery deck, hoping the icy air would quell her nausea. But as the ship rocked on the waves, she heaved her stomach over the rails and the fierce wind whipped some vomit back into her hair and face. Anna tried to wipe herself clean in the toilet, which was overflowing with paper and puddles of every kind of human waste. Sleep was almost impossible, but every time Peter dozed off, she closed her eyes and told herself this journey was not as bad as that endured by The Others.

She still felt queasy in the morning, as she finally walked down the gangplank onto dry British soil. She clutched the little case she had been able to buy second-hand with the money Reg had left her, carrying a tired and grizzly Peter on her hip.

'Margie, I'm sorry I can't stay here and look after you,' Reg had said before he left, 'but there are matters I have to deal with back in England before I can arrange for you to join me. And I want to find a place for us to live first too.'

She'd felt nervous when he first left, handing her as he did plenty of cash, cigarettes and an English phrasebook so she could begin learning his language. He had already taught her a few phrases that he said she would need for her journey. 'I want to take a train to Fenchurch Street station' was the most important one for when her boat docked at Tilbury.

'Your boat should reach England early in the morning,' he wrote to her, confirming her travel arrangements. 'And you should be able to get the ten o'clock train into London, which will arrive around eleven. I'll be waiting at the station for you and will wait there for every train until you finally arrive. I am so looking forward to seeing you again.'

At first, after his departure, she had worried that he would forget her once he was home and that he wouldn't keep his word. His friends and colleagues might be horrified at his decision to marry a woman from the enemy country. But his regular letters reassured her, always signed, 'Your future husband, Reg, xx'. That signature was so comforting and she wrote back to him often in a positive tone, albeit in German, saying, 'Peter and I are so looking forward to our new life in England and send you our best wishes.'

She mentioned Peter often, to remind him that he was providing a new life not only for her as his wife, but also for Peter, who would in time become his adopted son. She hoped so much that Reg would learn to love the little boy as much as she had come to. He was learning to talk, picking up more words every day, and she thought how quickly he would learn this new language and be far more proficient than her in no time.

Clutching the rail ticket Reg had sent, she followed signs from the dock to the station and asked where to find the right train. A porter pointed to the large clock hanging over the station platforms and she saw that it wasn't due for another hour. Peter was unhappy and needed food as well as a change of nappy, so she looked around to see if she could work out where there was a toilet. Seeing 'Ladies Waiting Room' in large letters, she thought that must have facilities.

The empty room was furnished with hard benches, but the clean toilets were a relief after the cesspit on the ferry; they were sparkling, with a strong smell of bleach. However, she didn't like to lay Peter down on the cold, tiled floor next to the lavatories, where there was little space, so she laid him on a bench while she opened her case for a fresh nappy. She had just removed the soiled napkin when a well-dressed woman entered and made no effort to disguise her distaste at the sight of Anna attempting to clean Peter's buttocks with a dampened handkerchief. The woman visited the toilet, then washed her hands, and as she left, Anna heard her loud voice saying, 'Disgusting foreigners. No manners.' In her haste to leave, as she barged through the waiting room door she bumped into a young nurse.

Anna couldn't fully understand the words, but she could tell from the woman's sneer and her tone of voice that she disapproved of her and her half-naked child. She tried to concentrate on cleaning Peter, but she felt her lips trembling and tears welling. Then she heard another female voice, but a kind one this time. 'Stuck-up old cow. She's obviously never had to deal with small children on a long journey.'

Again, Anna couldn't understand all that was said, but she could tell that, unlike the previous voice, which had been arrogant and mean, this one was sympathetic and friendly.

'He's a dear little chap,' the nurse said and Anna knew that she was admiring the baby boy she had managed to keep clean and in fairly good health ever since Gertrud's sad death. 'Have you just got here?'

'Aus Hamburg,' Anna said, guessing that was the correct answer to the question.

'Oh, you lot had it bad there, I've heard.' The nurse bent down to let Peter hold her fingers, which he tried to pull towards his mouth. 'He must be hungry. Have you got any food and milk for him?'

Anna understood the word milk. 'Keine milk,' she said shaking her head. 'We go London.'

'Well, that's my train too, so there's enough time to get something for him to eat before we leave. Look, you finish cleaning him up and I'll dash into the station café and see what I can find.'

By the time the nurse returned, Anna was pulling up Peter's trousers and wondering how to dispose of the soiled nappy. 'We can go into the café,' the girl said. 'They're warming some bread and milk for him and there's a cup of tea and a bun for you too. And while I was there, I grabbed a bit of old newspaper to deal with this.' She laid the paper on the bench so Anna could dump the dirty cloth there, then wrapped it up and stuffed it into the toilet's bin. 'Sorry, I haven't introduced myself. Nancy, pleased to meet you,' she said, holding out her hand.

'Margie and Peter,' Anna said.

Nancy looked surprised, but smiled. 'You two sound English already.'

Inside the warm steamy café, Anna felt she could relax a little. She spooned the mushy, milky bread into Peter's mouth, despite his wriggling and attempts to grab the spoon. Her tea was dark, strong and sweet and the nausea she had been feeling since she boarded the ferry had disappeared. She nibbled her currant bun, giving Peter a little piece and keeping an eye on the clock, while the helpful nurse chattered.

'I was home for the weekend seeing my parents and I'm on my way back to St Thomas's Hospital, where I work. Is someone meeting you at Fenchurch Street?'

Anna could hardly understand anything that was being said. The chatter, the hissing of the tea urn, the opening and shutting of the café door, the harsh tannoy of the station announcements, made it hard to distinguish words, let alone know what they meant. She caught the name of her destination and said, 'Ich heirate hier,' pointing to her finger, bearing the modest ring that Reg had given her before his departure. 'Don't ask how I found it,' he'd said. 'Just let me reassure you that it didn't come from a hoard of stolen goods, it was bought honestly, but maybe not for cash.'

'You're getting married?' Curiosity crossed the nurse's face as she looked at Peter and then Anna. 'Is he the father?' she asked, pointing at the little boy on Anna's knee.

That was a word Anna knew. She thought she should at least try to give Peter a respectable heritage and said, 'Vater, tot,' pulling a sad face and shaking her head a little.

'Oh, you poor things. Poor little boy.' She smiled at Peter. 'So, Mummy's found you a new daddy, has she? Clever Mummy.'

Anna glanced at the clock. Their train should be here in ten minutes. She drank the last of her bitter tea and shifted Peter onto her hip as she stood up.

'Let me,' Nancy said, picking up her case. 'You've got enough to carry already, with your little boy.'

Anna thought she understood, but felt a little nervous being escorted by this bright, bubbling girl, who seemed to want to know all about her. She knew she couldn't answer probing questions with her inadequate English and she didn't want to attract stares from other passengers. Would they realise she was German? Would they be hostile if they knew her country of origin? And would they be curious about her reason for coming to England?

As the train rattled away from the station, Anna attempted to keep Peter occupied by pointing out sights through the window. The greyish-green waters around the docks widened into a broad river, then the railway line turned towards brown fields and dark trees, which she guessed would turn leafy green in spring. And when the train left the countryside, the landscape became more industrial and suburban, with rows of houses, side by side, so different to the apartment buildings of her home city. But here there was also damage, not as bad as Hamburg, but still clearly the work of bombs dropped from the sky.

'You're going to see a lot of bombed-out places,' Nancy said with a sigh. 'There's loads of places worse than this round here. The East End's simply awful.'

Her words were almost meaningless to Anna, but she caught the word 'bombed', which seemed recognisable. 'Wir wurden ausgebombt,' she said, hugging Peter and reaching for the handkerchief tucked into the sleeve of her sweater to wipe his runny nose, while he slept.

'You were bombed too. Awful, wasn't it?' Nancy's widened as Anna's cuff slid up her arm, revealing her livid scar. 'Thank God it's all over at last.'

Anna nodded and let the sleeping child lean back in her arms, knowing that her disguise was already gaining her sympathy and acceptance and perhaps a safe haven.

True to his word, Reg was waiting by the platform entrance for the arrival of her train. He greeted her with a dry peck on the cheek and took her case. 'I expect you've had an awfully tiring journey, my dear Etta. Would you like a cup of tea before we continue?'

The last thing she wanted was another cup of the station café's stewed tea, but she did want to find a toilet for herself. 'Toilette?' she said, looking around the huge, busy station concourse.

He looked a little embarrassed, coughed, then pointed to a sign in the far corner. 'Etta, you'll need one of these,' he said, finding a penny in his pocket.

Anna pushed Peter into his arms and marched across to the entrance marked Ladies. It smelt more of disinfectant than urine and she was glad to see the cubicle had a roll of toilet paper. In Hamburg when they dug their latrine holes in the ruins, they had used scraps of rag, or newspaper if they were lucky. After washing her hands and trying to dry them on a rather damp roller towel, she left to rejoin her new family and was pleased to see that Reg was sitting on a bench with Peter on his knee, laughing as the little boy brushed his fingers across his moustache. At least Peter liked the bristles, even if Anna found them itchy.

'I've found a room for you in Bayswater,' he said, standing up and handing Peter back to her.

'With you?'

'No, just for you and the boy until we're married. We should be able to do that in about a month's time. There's paperwork to be sorted now you're here, you see, so we can't get married until that's all completed and approved.'

She felt nervous, realising she wouldn't have him by her side to interpret and explain all the time, but he noticed her expression and said, 'I'll come to see you each day after work and we'll be together every day when term ends for Christmas. I've found a flat for us near Paddington station and I hope you'll be able to come and see it very soon, when the present tenant leaves.'

Anna was too tired to respond, other than to nod her head. She let him take her arm and guide her, with Peter on her hip, towards a line of people standing outside the station in the street. Within minutes, a big red bus arrived and Peter's eyes fixed on this impressive vehicle. So far in his short life, he had travelled on trains and a ship and now he was going to ride on a real red bus.

'The view is best from the top deck,' Reg said. 'I always used to run up the stairs when I was a boy, but you're a bit laden, so we'll save that treat for another day.' However, they were able to take a double seat at the very front of the bus, next to the driver's cabin.

'Look, Peter,' Anna said in German, knowing that soon she would always have to converse with her adopted son in English, 'we are here now in London on a London bus. What a grand treat for you!'

Reg frowned at the way she spoke to the child he was going to raise as his son, and spoke in English, saying, 'Peter, this is a bus. A big red bus. Say bus, Peter.'

The little boy immediately picked up some of his words, bouncing on Anna's lap and repeating, 'bus, bus, bus,' with great excitement. She hugged him tight, knowing that with his rapid grasp of English and the name he would acquire once his adoption was complete, his past would never be questioned, even if hers was. He would have no memory of his real mother, his birthplace or any of his life before this time; but she would always have The Others lurking in her thoughts, reminding her that she had never done enough to help them.

FORTY

LONDON, MARCH 2017

Anna likes Freddie very much. She sips her fresh morning coffee and thinks how much he sometimes reminds her of Hermann, Ursula's earnest rat-catching younger brother of seventy years ago. She often wonders what happened to all of them after she left. They still hadn't managed to move out of the cellar by the time she was ready to leave the city. She hopes the gang lived on, but she is sure that if she hadn't brought Peter with her from Hamburg that December in 1946, he would never have survived. He was already sickly and that last winter in Germany was harder than ever.

When their ship finally left the port of Cuxhaven for the voyage to Tilbury, she could see the ice floes forming in the North Sea. The ice that year had eventually made it nearly impossible for ships to enter the harbours in the Elbe estuary, so if she hadn't left when she did, they would have been holed up there the whole of that long, bitter, deadly winter. In early January, the temperature dropped to minus twenty-eight degrees and remained below minus ten degrees for several weeks, not rising above zero until March. Many of the residents in the city, already weakened by years of poor food and insanitary living conditions, died during those months, adding to the toll of bodies caused by the war and its aftermath.

How could the Ausgebombten Gang have coped in their cold, cramped cellar? She was sure that they and the other wild children, used to living on the streets, would have plundered the goods trains for coal to give themselves a chance of surviving those freezing months. But did they manage to survive? In the early days after her marriage she had sent money, as she had arranged with them, via the refugee agency based at the Zoo Camp, which she knew they would regularly visit for supplies. She sent them her London address, but she never heard from them again.

She hoped that Ursula, Ingrid and Hermann had found a new home, even a temporary one, attended school, finished their education and gained employment, so their new lives could begin. She often thought of little Therese and Stefan too and hoped that if they could not stay with the gang members they were perhaps adopted. Maybe they had found a new mother and father to love them and feed them well in a heated house with warm beds. She clung to those thoughts of happy lives, rather than deaths in the icy cold, for all of them.

The winter in London that year was hard too, but at least she had the luxury of hot water, electric fires, a warm bed and a loving husband. Anna smiles to herself at the memory of her devoted Reg, so reserved on the surface, so attentive to the woman he loved. His love meant she was soon pregnant, and she was delivered of a healthy girl in October 1947. A little sister for Peter, a daughter for Reg.

At first, when she realised she had become pregnant so quickly, she was not only nauseous with morning sickness, but fearful as well. Her first child, her first Peter, hadn't been considered fit to survive. She'd never known what was wrong with him, but what if this second baby wasn't perfect either?

At one of her early prenatal checks, the nurse asked a question she found it hard to answer: 'Is this your first pregnancy?'

She couldn't bring herself to say, 'No, it's my second.' She'd have been asked if the baby had survived and if not, what had been wrong. So, all she could say was, 'Yes, it's my first,' and hope none of the medical staff would ever detect signs that she was lying to them.

But all was well. From the start, Susan was a strong baby with lusty lungs. Certainly stronger than Peter, who was always prone to winter coughs and colds, earaches, tonsilitis and stomach upsets, perhaps because of his poor diet and unhygienic living conditions in the first year of his life. But at least she was sure she had saved him by taking him away from Hamburg and that cold, damp cellar.

But what of Ursula, Hermann, Ingrid, Therese and Stefan? If they'd moved out of that cellar, as planned, before that harsh winter froze the streets as well as the seas, perhaps they were even now gathering together from time to time to recount tales of when they'd discovered the grocery shop's hoard of hidden staples, or laughing over the mystery ingredients in their *eintopf* stew. She imagined them meeting up every year for a merry reunion in a bierkeller, to clink great steins of beer and eat huge dishes of *schweinbrot mit kartoffeln*. They'd joke it wasn't nearly as tasty as the Hamburg rats, nor the liver-like placenta, nor the concoctions of tinned fish and vegetables thrown together out of necessity. She liked to think they'd all be rosy-cheeked, plump and jolly, toasting their good fortune at still being alive and maybe drinking a toast to her and Peter too.

How Freddie would love to hear these stories, Anna thought. What boy wouldn't enjoy tales of war, a life lived underground, an existence based on foraging and crafty scavenging? He'd admire the spirit and fearlessness of the Ausgebombten Gang, imagine hiding from officious authorities and outwitting all the other rats of the city, as well as trapping and cooking the furry vermin that swarmed in the ruins. But she couldn't tell him all about it, could she? He'd ask how she'd come to be there and how she'd earned money and cigarettes. There was so much she couldn't share with a thirteen-year-old boy, even if he was sensible and mature and pushing fourteen.

And besides, Anna knows that he really wants to know about the war and her experience of it. She stirs her coffee slowly, thinking all the while. Could she tell him about her Peter, born to an unmarried mother? She was reluctant to talk about the discarding of imperfect babies when she knew that Freddie had been born with displaced hips. Maybe his life would not have been considered worth saving either.

But what has he learnt about her so far? He has discovered that German is her native language and he knows that she came to England as a war bride. She has often said that her husband rescued her, but she has never said from what. Freddie probably imagines extreme poverty, a shattered bombscape and starvation; he'd never think she was really escaping from the truth of her previous life.

The other week, he had tried so hard to encourage her to talk openly to him, showing her that poignant girl's face on the postcard. Of course she knew who Anne Frank was, but if she'd acknowledged that she knew the name and her fate, he would have wanted to ask her more questions about the persecution during those times. Did she know that the lives of Jews were being restricted, did she know about the camps, did she know about the slow deaths from starvation and the more deliberate killings in the factories of death?

It is all far too dangerous, she thinks. She cannot answer his questions, much as she cares for him and understands why he has to ask. But why can't it be forgotten? Why must he study the horrors of that time in school? And it hurts her too, remembering those times, and the probability that her best friend Margarete and her family didn't enjoy their supposed life of luxury in Paris for long. It was all too likely that a few years after their departure from Hamburg, they were confined in that terrible transit camp Drancy on the outskirts of the city, then deported to their final destination – Auschwitz.

Anna feels that she has tried her best to escape and yet she never will. She swills the coffee pot and strains off the grains, which she throws into the pedal bin, where that stained face had stared at her accusingly from the postcard Freddie gave her. When he comes again, she hopes he will see that she has not thrown it out but displays it proudly on her kitchen worktop, next to the calendar of Australian birds, which Peter sends her every year with his Christmas card.

DER FROSCHKÖNIG

THE FROG KING

The princess began to cry because she was scared
of the cold frog. She did not even want
to touch him and she certainly didn't
want him sleeping in her royal bed.

FORTY-ONE

LONDON, JANUARY 1947

It could never have been the wedding Anna had once imagined, when she was young and in love with Günther. No white dress, veil or circlet of flowers; but she could take comfort in the fact that her marriage had the advantage of ensuring she was now safe and her past was well hidden.

Her lips met Reg's in a chaste kiss, when invited to do so by the officer at the Westminster Register Office in Marylebone, before they emerged into the cold grey January day as man and wife. The two teachers from Reg's school, who had attended as witnesses, both had to return to classes, so the newly-weds scurried along the bleak streets to a nearby Italian restaurant, before spending their first night together in the rooms that would now be their home.

Reg had arranged that for the day of their marriage and their honeymoon night, Peter would stay in the care of the school nurse. Anna was worried that he wouldn't settle, but Reg said, 'Now, don't you go upsetting yourself, Margie. Matron is very kind. She's more used to older boys of course, so she'll probably spoil Peter rotten. She's so looking forward to having your little chap to look after.' Anna told herself he would be safe and it was only for one night. She was also relieved that Reg appeared to be taking to the little boy, tickling him under his arms and playing peek-a-boo games with him.

The Italian restaurant Reg had chosen for their celebratory lunch was quite a cheerful haven in the greyness of ravaged London. Raffia-wrapped bottles with candles on the red and white checked cloths on each table, soft lighting and a glass of red wine soon helped her to feel it was a special lunch and she began to relax and enjoy herself.

'Here's to us, my dear,' Reg said, holding up his wine glass so they could toast their marriage. 'May we have a long and happy future together.'

'Prosit,' she said, then frowned as she recollected that she was meant to avoid using her native language now.

'Good health, Margie,' Reg corrected, clinking her glass with his again, so the candlelight shone through the ruby-red wine.

When their meals arrived, Anna thought her cotoletta alla Milanese was more likely thinly sliced pork than veal and Reg's beef steak was possibly horse. But they were both very hungry, and enjoyed the food, with another glass of wine. 'Margie, you must try the zabaglione to finish,' Reg said. 'They always do it very well here.' And Anna realised he had probably dined here before, with the girl who had left him for another, earlier in the war.

It was the best meal they'd had since Christmas, when Reg had taken her and Peter to the Lancaster Hotel near Kensington Gardens so they could dine on smoked salmon, followed by roast chicken. It was very different to the Christmas dishes she had eaten in Hamburg years before, when Mama had made roast goose with apple and pork stuffing, served with red cabbage flavoured with cinnamon and caraway seeds. Anna thought the dark steamed pudding that followed would be too rich for Peter, so Reg ordered a dish of custard for him, which he greatly enjoyed.

After lunch, which Reg referred to as 'the wedding break-fast', the term greatly confusing Anna, he announced that they would take a taxi to their new home, as it was a special day and they should treat themselves. Anna held her breath for the whole of the short journey, hoping she would be pleased with the rooms he had rented for them. But then, she thought, how could she complain at anything he had managed to find in this war-damaged city when a little over a month previously she had still been living in a damp, smoky cellar, with the Ausge-bombten Gang of five young people and children? And although the people of London were still shaken and subdued by the terrors of the Blitz, they had not seen or been involved in the horrors that assailed her nightmares.

When the cab drew to a halt and Reg said this was it, she thought it didn't look so very bad after all. The row of tall creamy-white houses was less handsome than it had once been; patches of stucco had fallen away, making the walls look as if they were suffering from a disfiguring disease. Steps curved down to a basement, which she hoped wasn't where they'd be living, and more steps, set between large pillars painted with the house number, went straight up to a large black front door. To one side there was a list of all the tenants and their flat numbers, alongside a row of doorbells. Many of the names were handwritten and stuck down with yellowing sticky tape. The name 'Wilson' was right at the top and had been typed, which pleased her.

Reg unlocked the door, flung it wide open, then swung her into his arms to carry her inside. His impetuous gesture caught her by surprise, but made her laugh. He set her down on the cracked black and white tiled floor at the bottom of the wide curving staircase and said, 'It's a British tradition to carry a bride into the marital home for the first time, Margie, but I don't think

I can manage to carry you all the way up four flights of stairs. I'm afraid we're right at the top of the house. I know it's a long way up, but it means we have the whole of the top floor to ourselves.'

Reg led the way up the uncarpeted stairs, their steps echoing in the stairwell. He carried the same little case Anna had brought with her from Hamburg. She had already disposed of some of the shabbiest items that had travelled with her, but she had bought a silky nightdress for her wedding night with money Reg had kindly given her. Remembering how her frugal mother had improved garments with trimmings, she had visited Whiteleys department store to buy lace for her nightwear and underwear. She'd also added a froth of black spotted net to the little black hat that had once belonged to Gertrud, to complement her plain grey dress and coat for the wedding.

Once they had climbed all the stairs, they reached a landing where a glass fanlight above them illuminated the floor, covered in greasy brown linoleum. The door to the apartment was brown too, but when Reg unlocked it and the door swung open, Anna's initial impression was of a light, airy space and a smell of furniture polish. They stepped into a hall area with a tall, mahogany stand for hats and coats, incorporating a blotched mirror. That led into a sitting room, which also had a dining table standing next to the window with a view over a garden square.

'We can sit out there in fine weather, Margie,' Reg said, pointing to the trellised summerhouse she could glimpse through the bare trees. She could see benches and paths that criss-crossed the grass, and thought it would be like their trysts in the park back in Hamburg.

The kitchen was not as well equipped as Mama's had been, but Anna thought that in time she could manage reasonably well. The small sink was large enough for her washing and for bathing Peter. There was a small gas oven with a two-ring hob and although there were no cupboards, there were shelves stacked with crockery, and pans behind the blue and white checked curtains that hung below the countertop.

Reg took her hand and led her to the next two rooms. 'Our bedrooms are here, Margie,' he said, pointing out a large room with a double bed and a smaller one with a single bed. Anna immediately decided that her little suitcase should live under the bed, in case she suddenly had need of it. She noted that the bed was made with clean sheets, topped with blankets and a padded eiderdown in paisley fabric.

'Do you think Peter is ready to sleep on his own or would you prefer him to stay with you in the big bed for now? I can sleep in the little room until you both feel at home, my dear.'

She was deeply touched by how restrained and considerate he was being. He was such a very decent man. Wouldn't any other man have immediately assumed that now they were legally married, he could exercise his conjugal rights immediately? She stroked his dear, kind face. 'You are my husband now, Reg. We will share a bed together. I'm sure Peter will settle happily once he sees how well you have provided for us all.'

And he had provided for them. He had thought of just about everything. A tray was set with a teapot, milk jug, sugar bowl and two cups. There was a fruit cake studded with almonds in a tin, a fresh loaf, butter, eggs and bacon for their breakfast and a bottle of milk, stood on the outside windowsill to keep it cool. The windows sparkled, the floors were clean and a fresh tea towel hung from a hook near the sink.

'Badezimmer?' Anna said, looking around. 'Wo...?'

'Aah, I'm afraid we have to share the bathroom on the floor below. We could have been nearer, but I thought it was worth the sacrifice to have the extra space up here. But there are clean towels in a chest in the bedroom. I knew you wouldn't want to share towels, Margie.'

Anna went across to where he'd indicated and fetched a towel and a flannel. 'I will not be long,' she said, kissing him on the lips. She noticed how his freshly shaved cheeks blushed a little, and reminded herself she shouldn't be too forward. She couldn't let him suspect that she might have ever employed seductive techniques with anyone before. But as she went down the stairs to the bathroom, she couldn't help wondering: was he going to be surprised that she wasn't a virgin? She'd never told him about Günther nor any of the details of her past occupation in Hamburg, and she hoped he would never question her about her intimate history.

Locking the bathroom door, she thought that next time she washed in here she should bring her own soap. The sliver on the side of the sink was cracked and grey, but when she held it under the running water it didn't smell too bad. Not strongly carbolic, at least. There was also very little toilet paper provided, so she made a mental note to add that to her list too. She couldn't understand the workings of the strange contraption that hung with a spout over the sink and the bath, so she washed in cold but soapy water, once she had rinsed the basin and flushed away the dark, curled hair that clung to the porcelain. As she washed between her legs, she was reminded of Gertrud's crude advice early on in her former profession, when she was unsure she would be able to attract clients: 'As long as you offer them a freshly washed fanny, they'll love you forever! Add a stein of beer and any man will come back for more!'

Once she felt clean and fragrant, she returned to their rooms, to find Reg had another surprise for her. He had poured two glasses of champagne. 'I thought we couldn't celebrate our marriage without a special drink,' he said, clinking glasses with her. 'A toast to my beautiful bride. To Mrs Margie Wilson.'

'A toast to my dear, kind husband,' she said, taking a sip.

They sat down on the lumpy brown moquette sofa cushions in front of the hissing gas fire. Anna could feel the heat toasting her shins, while her neck was cold. She turned to look at the window, thinking perhaps it was letting in a draught, and saw the sky was streaked with pink. Her first day of marriage had nearly ended.

'If you are hungry later, I can rustle up some supper for us,' Reg said.

'Perhaps,' she said. 'But for now, I think we should enjoy our champagne and then go to bed together.'

Later, much later, they sat by the fire again, wrapped in dressing gowns, eating scrambled eggs and buttered toast on their laps. Anna felt warm and satisfied. Reg really was a man of surprises, she thought. He may have seemed dry and reserved on the surface, but she had just experienced the most wonderful love-making of her life. Günther's quick fumblings, her clients' urgent heavings, Herr Reiser's silent, miserable pokings had never brought her joy. Those couplings had only resulted in her lost child and then the cash and cigarettes necessary for survival. But Reg had transported her to the heights of delight. How he knew what would give her such pleasure she was too shy to ask, but she was thrilled and overwhelmed that some woman before her had taught him so well. She guessed he had possibly learnt to make love in Paris, where he had perfected the French that he was still teaching.

Anna turned to look at him, bent over his supper, his little moustache twitching like a curious rabbit. Maybe she could really love this man after all, she thought. She'd never imagined before that she could, she'd only ever been able to think of him as her rescuer, her saviour, but now he was more than that. Dear, decent Reg had been transformed and was now her lover.

He noticed her looking at him. 'Is something the matter, Margie? Why are you staring at me like that?'

'I was just thinking how lovely it is here. Thank you for

doing all this for me and Peter.' And then she noticed the window. It was now dark and large flakes of snow were falling like white feathers. 'Oh, and look outside!'

He turned to look, then chuckled. 'As we didn't have confetti for our wedding, shall we make do with snow?'

They both stood up and went to look out. It was falling softly, caught by the light of the street lamps, spreading over the street and the garden square. Anna put her arm round her husband and laid her head on his shoulder. 'It's a fresh start,' she said.

FORTY-TWO

LONDON, MARCH 2017

'But Mum, if Mrs Wilson won't help me, I won't be able to do a really good project about the war, will I?' Term has ended for the Easter holidays and Freddie is gloomy about the prospect of completing the work that's been set. As well as finishing *The Diary of Anne Frank*, he and his classmates have to write an essay about the causes of the Second World War and what it would have been like to have lived then.

Lauren puts her arm round her son. How much longer will he tolerate her hugs and her help? He is growing taller by the day and some of his friends are already showing signs of rapid maturing, with shadowy upper lips and creaking voices. 'Don't worry, love. I'm sure we'll think of something. There's lots of information on the internet, isn't there?'

'It's not the same as talking to a real live person though. If I could ask her questions, I could record her. Or do a video even. Or I could see if my teacher would let her come into school with me to talk to everyone next term.'

She doesn't want to dampen his enthusiasm, but that's not going to happen, Lauren thinks. Margie has so far resisted all their attempts to encourage her to open up. And if at some point she did decide to talk honestly, and revealed that she'd had truly horrific experiences, then what would the school think? The kids might be open-minded, but the teachers? The parents? And they don't know if she'd agree to do it or even how she'd react if she confronted her past. Would she lapse into German again if she was pushed to recall memories she has obviously tried hard to forget? Or she might completely crumble and fall into the clutches of dementia or a fatal stroke.

'Why don't we just wait and see what she says next time you try to talk to her, Freddie? Maybe she'll change her mind and want to tell you everything she can. She loves seeing you still, so that's good, and she enjoys helping you with your German.'

'Yeah, I'll still go round and visit her. She makes awesome cakes too. And it's cool talking to someone that old who was really there when the war happened. Charlie's been talking to his granddad, but it's not the same because he's not as old as her and he didn't even fight in the war. He was sent away from London to live in Somerset.'

'Evacuation. That's what it was called.' She gives him another hug. 'I don't think I could ever have done it. Send my kids off to stay with some strangers the far side of the country? No, I'd have had a problem with that. I don't think people even knew at first who their children were going to be living with and in some cases the hosts could choose who they would take into their homes.'

'But you wouldn't have wanted us to be bombed to bits, would you?'

'Course not, silly.' She ruffles his hair. 'I'd have wanted to keep you safe. You and your annoying sister!' Amy was meant to be coming home for the Easter break but now seemed to think she would have a more exciting time with her friends in France, justifying her absence with an excuse about improving her French. Lauren wasn't looking forward to spending the holiday without her as it made her feel more alone, even though Freddie was still there with his limitless insatiable appetite.

'Mum! Stop it!' He pulls away from her as she goes to give him another big hug topped off with a kiss.

And at that moment, there is a light knock on the front door. Lauren can see a small shape through the frosted glass. Not the postman; too late for him, and too short for him too.

She opens the door. Margie stands on the doorstep, holding a plate draped with a tea towel. 'Is Freddie home from school already?'

'Yes, it's the end of term. They only went in for the morning. He's just come back.' Lauren holds the door open wide. 'Do come in, please. We were just talking about you.'

Margie follows her through to the kitchen, where Freddie is filling the kettle. 'Guten Nachmittag,' she says to him.

'Oh yeah, I mean Guten Tag,' he laughs as he switches the kettle on. 'Are we having a lesson today? I thought I was coming round to yours tomorrow.'

'Any day is good for a German lesson, nein?' She puts the plate on the table and whips away the cloth. There in front of them is a golden sponge cake, dusted with icing sugar. It looks like a sheep.

'I have made *lammkuchen* for you, Freddie. I have never made it in this country before, but my mother always baked it for us every *Oster* and showed me how to make it. It is a traditional cake in my family.'

'It's beautiful,' Lauren says, thinking Maggie has never mentioned any family traditions before. Is this a sign she is willing to start talking? She peers at the sculpted shape standing upright, perfectly in proportion. 'How ever did you manage to make it?'

'I found the tin in the church spring jumble sale. As soon as I saw it, I said to myself, that is what I must have and then I can make *lammkuchen* for Freddie for Easter, just as ve used to do in the old days.'

Lauren and her son study the unusual cake, with its dusting of fine, white sugar. 'It looks almost too good to eat,' Lauren says.

'What kind of cake is it?' Freddie asks. 'Does it have a filling?'

'No, it is a plain sponge made with butter but I must say I never thought I would find a tin to make it in this country. My mother had such a tin and promised to pass it on to me, but that never happened, sadly.'

'Did you make this cake in the war?' Freddie asks her.

'Nein, we did not have luxuries like this then. Times were hard. And the baking tin was lost.' She shrugs and gives a long sigh.

Lauren senses that Margie is hovering on the verge of saying more about her wartime experiences, but is hesitating because she isn't sure she can bear to reveal all about her past. 'Come on, Margie, sit down. I was going to make toasted sandwiches for lunch. Would you like one?'

'Yes, thank you, that is very kind.' Margie lowers herself shakily to a chair and sits with her hands clasped, staring at her creation.

Lauren butters the bread, thinking how thin Margie looks these days. Her delicate bony wrists poke from her cardigan, her hands have prominent blue veins and her cheeks are more hollow than ever. She may do a lot of baking, but she clearly doesn't do much eating and in fact, thinking about it, Lauren realises she never sees her eat a complete slice of cake herself. She glances over her shoulder and wonders if Margie will be able to eat a whole toasted sandwich; she looks as if she can only nibble, like a little squirrel with a habit of hoarding for when food is in short supply.

'Didn't you have much food in the war then?' Freddie persists. 'Were you hungry every day?'

'Freddie,' Lauren snaps at him, 'Margie might not want to think about when times were hard. I'm doing you cheese and ham.' She places it in the sandwich toaster and clips it shut.

But Freddie isn't listening to his mother. He sits next to Margie and says, 'I've got to get a good mark for my project, you see. It's about the war. We could talk about what food you had then, if you like. And I could record you talking or film you.'

Margie is staring at him with a blank look. She is silent for a moment, then in a slow, deliberate tone, says, 'My child, you cannot possibly imagine what real hunger is like. You think you are hungry now and you often say you are starving, but you had breakfast this morning, you had your dinner last night. That is not hunger. You have no idea. You do not know the lengths to which a man will go to get a crust of bread.'

She stands up suddenly, the chair falling backwards with a loud clatter as she steps round the table and leaves the house by the back door.

They watch her go in shocked silence. 'Oh my goodness,' Lauren says, 'I've never seen her behave like that before. I think you've really upset her.' She watches Margie walk round to the back of her own house and let herself in by the kitchen door.

'I didn't mean to, Mum. Honest I didn't. I was only asking a question,' Freddie pleads with her, his face reddening. 'Should I go round and apologise to her right away?'

'No, leave her for a bit. Let her calm down. Maybe I'll pop in later on and thank her for the cake. Or, better still, ask her back here for tea so she can cut it for us and then we can all eat a piece together and see what she says then.'

'Yes, please. I really didn't mean to upset her. I just thought I could ask a couple of questions. I was only trying to do my schoolwork properly.'

'Quite blunt questions though, if you think about it. Here,

eat your sandwich. And mind, it's red-hot.' Lauren places the toastie in front of him, cheese oozing between the crusts. 'You never said what you wanted, so you've got cheese and ham, like it or not.'

She drapes the tea towel over the cake again. 'And don't you dare touch a crumb of this cake before Margie comes back this afternoon, you hear me?'

His answer is muffled as he tries to speak with his mouth full. 'It's too hot,' he says.

FORTY-THREE

LONDON, MARCH 2017

Perhaps I shouldn't have made that cake, Anna thinks as she sweeps the aisle in the church. Easter isn't until the middle of April this year, so she shouldn't even be thinking of eating sweet things in Lent; the lamb cake isn't meant to be brought out until Easter. Is that why she feels so conflicted?

There is very little debris for her to sweep up in the empty church today; as the church flower arrangements are absent in Lent, there are few leaves and petals to clear away. That is another reason she doesn't like this time of year. Ever since the children were settled at school, she has been one of the flower ladies. She's always enjoyed pushing the rigid stems of chrysanthemums and dahlias into the blocks of stiff green foam, adding seasonal sprays of foliage from her own garden or that of the vicarage. But at present the church, without its floral decorations, feels austere and bare. It smells only of dust, Pledge polish and old prayers, and she longs for it to be scented with lilies.

She hears her cleaning partner, Doreen, hoovering the carpet near the altar, and knows she'll soon turn her attention to the steps where the congregation kneels for Communion. Usually, Anna finds cleaning the church a soothing activity.

She's very good at such a domestic chore because of her horror of filth and although the church has never offered her the most satisfying of cleaning jobs, being always so well kept in itself, it has always calmed her: the rhythmic action of her broom and the circular polishing of her duster. What she really needs is the challenge of a neglected house with muddy floors and cobwebbed cupboards, so she can bring order out of chaos. How often she had seen it, the desire to make all things right with a neatly folded blanket, however dirty, and the addition of a frayed ribbon to lice-rich hair.

And sweeping away dirt in the House of God has also often felt like a small act of atonement. It is not the church of her childhood, but she has grown used to its rituals. But today she cannot forget the cake and Freddie. How could she have been so hard on the boy? How could she have said such harsh words?

Dear Freddie. He is just a curious boy, keen to do well at school. Maybe his teachers will be greatly impressed if he finds a living witness to the war and its horrors. There can't be many pupils in his school with a relative or neighbour who had been alive during that long war. Some would have been children at the time, others might have fought but not be capable of telling a coherent story now. And Anna knows it is most unlikely that there is anyone like her.

The hoovering stops suddenly and she hears Doreen muttering words that sound like curses. 'Ruddy thing's blocked again. I'm going to stop for a bit now, Margie. You got time for a cup of tea?'

Anna accepts and they sit in the tiny kitchen off the vestry with their mismatched cups and saucers, and a pack of rich tea biscuits. 'That's all I could find,' Doreen says. 'Lucky to have biscuits at all, with the mice they've had in here recently.' She points to the humane trap in the corner. 'I ask you, Margie, what's the point of catching them and letting them go?'

'If you don't kill them, they always come back,' Anna says,

thinking, and if you don't hang them or lock them away for life, they return to their pre-war lives as if nothing had ever happened. And then she suddenly pictures the time Reg laid a traditional spring trap in their first flat. She was the one who had found the mouse the next morning, snared across its neck, its eyes popping out of its head as if they had grown on stalks overnight like miniature mushrooms. She wouldn't let him use that kind of trap again after that horrific sight. There is never any justification in employing extreme cruelty as punishment or deterrent.

'Too right they keep coming back, little beggars. There's plenty of food for them here, and heating some of the time. I expect there's a nest somewhere hereabouts.' Doreen looks around as if she is expecting to see a cradle of baby mice under the stack of spare chairs.

Anna is reminded of Hermann proudly boasting of his ratting skills, and says, 'We need a rat-catcher. Maybe the church should have a cat. That would be a help.'

'A black and white one, to go with the vicar's dog collar, eh?' Doreen cackles at her own joke but, when she sees Anna isn't laughing, adds, 'You're not yourself today, are you, Margie? Life getting you down, is it?'

Anna sips her tea. She doesn't dunk her biscuit like Doreen does. It always leaves mushy fragments at the bottom of the cup. 'A young friend of mine asked me a difficult question today. It is troubling me. He was asking what I know of the war.'

'Well, he's a one, isn't he? My grandkids never ask me anything like that. Too busy watching telly, they are. Not that I know about the war, anyway. Too young, though you'd never think it, eh?' She laughs and her wobbling chins and large bosom laugh with her.

Anna has no idea how old Doreen is, but guesses that her large brood of children, her long stint as a school dinner lady and her lazy husband have all taken their toll on her looks and her energy. She wears support stockings, but Anna can see they won't cure the varicose veins that have riddled her legs.

'But I vonder,' Anna says, 'if we all have a duty to tell the young about the mistakes we have made in our lives. Isn't it right to warn them so they don't make the same errors?'

Doreen shrieks with laughter again. 'Oh, Margie, you are a one! If you mean I should tell my grandkids how I was up the duff before me and Bill got married, I think I'll give that one a miss! I'll leave them to work it out for themselves one day.'

But Anna can't help pondering as she returns to her polishing in the stalls, working her duster around the intricacies of the carved patterns. If she and her friends had known what their education was leading to, was it possible they could have anticipated the consequences? They might have walked away, if they had known how it would all turn out. Their parents might have been too burdened with the aftermath of the first war to see where the new regime was heading, but maybe the younger generation should have had a clearer idea. But the trouble was, none of them was encouraged to think for themselves, none of them was allowed to question the order of things.

That's it, she thinks. If Freddie wants to ask questions, she must allow him to ask them. She must encourage him and others like him to be determined to uncover the truth. The witnesses to the true horror have mostly died and she is one of the few left. But will she feel like answering him honestly or will she persuade him to find out for himself? He may find the facts unacceptable, he may not wish to hear everything she could tell him. He is still so young, so unaware of how callous mankind can be. But she is no longer afraid. She is not going to run away again. Her case will stay under her bed.

Lauren waits a few days before facing Margie after that scene in the kitchen. It is time to confirm her supermarket delivery, so she thinks that is a valid excuse for knocking on her neighbour's door.

Margie never came back later that upsetting day to eat the lamb cake. By the time Lauren had called next door, the old lady had gone out. She didn't often leave the house, but it was a fine day and she sometimes popped to the corner shop or the church, so there was no need for concern. She hadn't lapsed into another language again, since that incident at the bus stop months before, so Lauren tried to convince herself that all would be well.

She sees Margie is in her kitchen, washing up at the sink. She knocks on the back door and, once she is sure Margie has heard, opens it a crack. 'Good morning. Just checking whether you want anything added to my delivery order,' she says. 'It's coming tomorrow afternoon.'

'Come in, please. I have a list here.' Margie removes her rubber gloves and wipes her hands on her gingham apron. 'I have need of more sugar and also flour.'

'Again? I suppose you've been making more cakes,' Lauren says, although she then notices that the kitchen is not filled with the warmth and scent of fresh baking today.

'Not so far this week, but I will make another *lammkuchen* for when Freddie comes here for our conversation lesson.'

Margie opens her kitchen cupboards to check her supplies, counting under her breath. And Lauren is reminded that she always counts in her own language – ein, zwei, drei – as she ticks off the well-stocked shelves with their rows of tins, packets and jars. This is a woman who is never going to run short. If Lauren needs to borrow the proverbial cup of sugar, she knows where to come.

'Oh, he'd love to have that cake again. We both enjoyed the last one you made. I'm afraid it was all gone in no time. It was delicious.'

'I am glad you liked it.'

Lauren thinks Margie looks tired. Maybe her great age and frequent baking is finally catching up with her. 'But we don't want you putting yourself out for us. You should take it easy sometimes.'

'I like to be occupied. Sit, my dear. You will stay and take a cup of coffee?'

'I'd love to, if you're having one as well, Margie.' Lauren watches as she busies herself with cups, tipping heaped scoops of ground coffee into a large pot. Cream is poured into a dainty cut-glass jug and set on the table, along with sugar in a matching bowl. Coffee at home is never served like this, just instant in a mug.

'I vish to apologise to you and Freddie,' Margie says. 'I am sorry I was not at all patient with him the other day.'

'Oh, you mustn't worry about him. He wasn't thinking, when he came out with those questions. It's his age, you know. And he's really keen to do well at school.'

'But he is right to ask questions. How will he discover the

truth for himself if he does not seek it out? And I am sorry I wasn't willing to answer him that day.'

'You'd make him very happy, Margie, if you were able to tell him about your experiences in the war. He's very keen to get a good mark for this project.' Lauren doesn't voice the thought that she also thinks it would be good for her neighbour to talk about her life. She wants to help her son with his schoolwork, of course, but it's this elderly lady she is more concerned about, feeling as she does that she is burdened with the sad weight of her hidden past.

Margie strains the coffee as she pours a cup for Lauren, then sits down at the table opposite her, after fetching a plate of thin chocolate biscuits. 'I am very fond of dear Freddie. He reminds me very much of a boy I once knew a long time ago in Hamburg.' She looks wistful and distant, staring into her cup.

'Oh, is that where you were born? We've always wondered where you came from. So that's why you can speak German.'

'Yes, it is the language of my homeland and of my birth. I am glad to be able to help Freddie learn to speak it. He is doing it really good, I think.'

'Oh, he's been getting such good marks in German at school. That's all down to you, Margie. His teacher said he's really come on in the last couple of months. He might even take it further and go on to do it at university.'

'That would make me very proud indeed. I'd like to think that our friendship is helping him in his studies. But perhaps he should also take history as well at university, as he has such an interest in the past. I think he should study German history and concern himself with vhy such terrible things happened there and across the rest of Europe.'

'I'll tell him that. He's very fond of you too, you know.' Lauren looks at her watch. She ought to finish her coffee and get back to finishing that order before Freddie comes back from visiting his best friend Charlie. He's been spending more time socialising than studying this Easter holiday. 'So, is it all right if I tell Freddie that you're happy to answer all his questions, then? I hope he won't get too nosey and ask anything personal.'

'He can ask me whatever he likes. And I vill try to reply as truthfully as I can. I may not know the answer to everything he is curious about, but I can tell him about my experiences of that time.' Margie's hand hovers over her arm and then she strokes her skin through the wool of her cardigan.

Lauren notices the familiar action and wonders if she dares voice her suspicions. She is hesitant, but she knows she must ask. She feels she has to prepare Freddie for what he might learn, as a result of his questioning.

'Margie, I really don't like to pry. And please tell me if you think this is out of order but before I get Freddie to come round here and start pestering you with questions, is there anything you want to tell me? I mean, do you think is there something I should know, so I can warn him about what you might be going to say?'

'I was too hard on him the other day, when he asked if I'd been hungry. I've seen dreadful hunger, my dear, far too much hunger. I can never forget it. But it was not my fault.'

Lauren lays her hand over Margie's to stop the rubbing. She hesitates and wonders if she dares ask the question that is at the forefront of her mind. She feels certain that the reason Margie cannot forget is because of this scar, the mark that she is always touching, scratching, rubbing. It can never be erased or scraped off, like an indelible stain on a white shirt or burnt custard in a saucepan.

'You can tell me, Margie. You don't have to, but if you have something to say that might upset him – and you as well – it might be better if I warn him first. He is still young and maybe it's best if I know what he can expect to hear from you.'

'It is so very hard to talk of it, after all this time. Not even Reg, my dear, kind husband, knew everything.'

'But he was aware of some of what happened?'

'He knew that I was one of the many thousands struggling to stay alive in Hamburg after the war. We didn't have a proper home after all the bombing. All of us lived in a cellar, like many in Hamburg at that time. Like the rats we sometimes ate, we were. We barely had enough to eat. Day after day we had to search or beg for the little to make a meal of sorts. And ve had to fetch and boil water to keep ourselves clean. Life was very hard then.'

'Is that all you told him, Margie? Did Reg never suspect there was more to tell?' Lauren feels as if she is holding her breath, bracing herself for the truth that must come.

'I think he did, but he always said that he would never make me tell him everything. He said if it would upset me to speak of it, then it was enough for him just to know that he had rescued me. Which he did. He saved me and Peter, before the terribly hard vinter of 1947 when many hundreds died in Hamburg from the cold and starvation.'

'Oh, do you mean you had Peter before you met your husband?'

'Yes, but Peter is not my son. I did not give birth to him, he just thinks I am his mother.' Margie clutches Lauren's arm. 'But you must never tell him. He was the child of a friend. A friend who sadly died. I saved his life by bringing him to England with me. He was little more than a baby and he could never have lived through that last freezing vinter in a cellar.'

'What a wonderful thing to do, Margie. Freddie would love to hear all about that. And you mustn't worry, he'd never mention it to Peter either.' Not that your son or your daughter are ever going to show any interest in what Freddie finds out from you, Lauren thinks.

'But there is more, so much more...' Margie lets go of Lauren's arm and slumps in her chair.

And Lauren decides she must jump in and take the chance

to help Margie to unburden herself of these memories. 'I think I understand, Margie. Do you want to tell me or shall I make a guess?'

Margie nods, looking down at her hands, clasped in her aproned lap, so Lauren assumes she has given her assent. 'I'm guessing, then, that you had a really terrible time in the war. So terrible you have never wanted to talk about it.

'But if you can bear to, Margie, it might ease your mind. Give you what's nowadays called closure. You might find that facing your darkest memories could take a huge weight off your shoulders. And knowing that you are helping today's generation understand the past might make the experience less painful for you.'

She waits a moment, to be sure, then plunges ahead. 'So, I'm guessing, Margie, that you were held in one of those awful camps. Am I right?'

Margie nods again and Lauren thinks she can see a tear trembling, on the brink of falling. She clasps both of Margie's hands and says, 'I'm so sorry. You poor thing. It must have been absolutely dreadful.'

'No, you don't understand,' Margie whispers. 'I wasn't a prisoner, I worked there.' She lifts her head and looks straight at Lauren with shimmering eyes. 'I worked in a concentration camp for almost two years, until just before the end of the war.'

HÄNSEL UND GRETEL

HANSEL AND GRETEL

The witch had built the house of
gingerbread to catch children, so she could kill
them and cook them in her oven, once they
were fat enough to eat.

FORTY-FIVE

THE CAMP, APRIL 1943

Anna fingered the silver trim on her jacket collar. That and the eagle insignia on the left upper sleeve instantly reminded her of Günther. How she had admired him when he'd posed, surrounded by all the local girls, in his smart uniform. She could still remember thinking how handsome he was and how much she had wanted him to notice her. She turned this way and that in front of the mirror in the bedroom allocated to her at the camp; the tailoring gave her an air of authority and made her feel she would perform her duties well.

She hadn't realised when she'd applied for the post that she too would be expected to wear a uniform. As it was not an enlisted position within any of the armed forces, she had assumed she would continue to wear a modest office suit, as most secretaries did, but as soon as she arrived she was issued with the grey-green jacket and pleated skirt that all the camp's Kriegshelferinnen wore with a white blouse. They weren't adorned with the same badges as the SS Helferinnen guarding the prisoners, but they were cut from the same cloth.

Anna hung the jacket, skirt, blouse and coat from her previous life in the wardrobe in her new room. No longer was she the same as every other office girl or factory worker; she was now an important employee of the Reich, essential to the efficient operation of the state. Only a few hours after leaving Hamburg, travelling eastwards by train with a package of food pressed into her hands by Mama, she felt as if a whole new life was about to begin.

At home she had still been a child, subjected to her parents' rules and questions, but now she suddenly felt very grown up, moving away to this life where she had her own accommodation in a block with the other female members of staff. Her very own bedroom and living room, with fitted cupboards and a washbasin. Each floor of the two-storey block had a small kitchen and a bathroom that she shared with only five other female employees. The best she could have managed if she'd stayed in Hamburg would have been a small three-bedroomed flat, shared with at least five other girls.

And here she and other members of staff did not have to concern themselves with any cooking, cleaning or laundry, as all the domestic chores were performed by selected prisoners under their supervision. For camp personnel, it was not a bad place to work at all; there were leisure facilities on site as well. 'We have a cinema for our sole use,' Birgit, one of the prison guards, told her as she showed Anna around the comfortable areas reserved exclusively for the camp's staff. 'And when we get extended leave a group of us is taken away to a special resort for some rest and recreation.'

Anna had imagined she might have to travel back to Hamburg and face her dreary parents when it was time to take leave, so the thought of a leisure facility where Birgit said they could 'sunbathe and swim in the summer, hike in the winter' sounded much more to her liking. In time she might even meet another handsome officer who would help her to forget the feelings she still harboured for Günther.

At first, Anna could not believe her luck in finding a job

with such good working and living conditions. Although she was aware it was a prison, her office and accommodation were separate from the prisoners and she was never close to them or their huts, although from her office window she could see distant groups marching out on work details, accompanied by guards. She had no reason to ask why the inmates were here. Like the vast majority of Germans, she believed that the camps that had sprung up all over her country and the occupied territories were legitimate places for the detention of political opponents and anyone considered to be antisocial.

She kept telling herself this even when it began to dawn on her that this was not like a normal prison. But I'm not doing any harm, she told herself. I don't have contact with the prisoners, I'm here just to type up orders, record instructions, file the information efficiently. So, she kept her eyes on the lists she was typing, on the messages she had to send, and didn't look around the site when she walked from her accommodation to the office. If she didn't know what was happening elsewhere, maybe she could persuade herself it wasn't her responsibility.

So, when was it that she began to feel unsettled? Did it begin with noticing the transformation of new recruits, particularly the SS Helferinnen, the female guards, who had daily contact with the prisoners, like the day after Herte arrived? 'Please can you polish the shoes I've left out in my room?' Herte asked the thin prisoner in a striped dress, assigned to Anna's floor. 'You don't have to say please,' roared Birgit. 'Just chuck your shoes at her. Then she won't forget to clean them.' The timid woman avoided their eyes and continued to sweep the floor, but hefty Birgit slapped her round the head as she passed her.

Herte's eyes widened in surprise at her colleague's behaviour, but she grew more confident from then on. Not only did she throw back her shoulders in her new uniform but, once she'd cocked her field cap at a jaunty angle and pointed her toes in her smart new high boots, she acquired a swagger. After a few days she was pushing and shoving the servants as much as the other guards, while Anna stayed silent, grateful for the comforts this life provided and thankful that her role didn't require her to have close contact with the prisoners.

But Anna quickly became aware that the health of the women assigned to clean their quarters was deteriorating. They were getting noticeably thinner and weaker. She was aware of one in particular because she looked so like her friend Etta from years before, although her lank hair was mostly hidden under a scarf and her cheeks were hollow. One day, instead of going straight to the office, Anna returned to her room after breakfast to fetch a clean handkerchief and found this particular maid stripping her bed. As she bent to fold the sheets, she crumpled and had to steady herself on the bedstead.

'Are you feeling faint?' Anna asked, trying to peer at the woman's face, noticing she had a black eye and a bruised cheek. The woman shook her head, took a moment to collect herself and continued folding the bedclothes.

Anna found her hankie and was about to leave when she heard the woman murmur a few words. 'What did you say?' she asked, turning to look at this sad figure properly. Her clothes were shabby and dirty, the sourness of poor hygiene hovered around her like a cloud of scent sprayed from an atomiser, her skin was sallow and she was very thin.

'We are all very hungry,' she whispered. 'Everyone is ill.'

And in that moment, Anna understood, and she saw clearly that this was not a prison for temporary punishment and rehabilitation. If this prisoner was a typical example of the inmates, then the camp was a place with no regard at all for the value of human life.

'Are you all starving? Tell me your name.'

'Margarete. I am Jewish.'

Anna felt a stab in her heart. This couldn't possibly be her old friend but it was someone like her. Was this what was happening to her childhood friend and the Löwenthal family too? 'Margarete, I once had a very good friend with the same name as you. For her sake I will try to help you, but my ability to do anything about your situation may be limited.'

Margarete looked at her with appealing eyes that seemed to shimmer with unshed tears. 'Food,' she said. 'We need food to survive. We must stay alive.'

'I will try to take bread from breakfast every day and hide it under my pillow. Then when you make the bed you will find it easily and no one will ever see you take it. Do you think that will be enough to help?'

'Thank you. It will make all the difference.' Margarete's voice quivered, but she didn't cry. And at that point, they both heard Birgit shouting: 'Hurry up, you lazy bitches!' Margarete's eyes were wide with fear and Anna knew then that Birgit must have slapped and punched her in the face, causing her injuries.

As she slipped out of her room and into the corridor, she heard a muffled groan and saw Birgit thumping the back of another prisoner's head in a nearby room. 'Shouldn't you be at your desk by now?' the broad-shouldered guard said as she caught sight of Anna.

'Just going. I needed something from my room.'

'All right in there is it, or do I need to go in and tell her to get a move on as well?' Birgit's eyes narrowed and Anna noticed her fists clenching as if she was ready to exercise her authority with force.

'No, she's doing a good job. She's nearly finished.' Anna hoped this would satisfy Birgit and let Margarete escape further punishment. The guard's brutality sickened her, but she guessed that an obvious show of distaste might encourage Birgit to launch a further attack.

'Good, they've got another whole block to do after this.'

Anna didn't look back as she quickly walked along the

passageway and down the stairs. She didn't want to see any more of Birgit's harsh supervision and she was thinking about how much food she might be able to slip into her room without being noticed.

When she returned at the end of the day, her head full of the long lists of figures she had typed, she was followed by Birgit, marching upstairs after her. At first, she thought the woman might be suspicious of the rolls she had stuffed in her pockets, but when she called good night, Birgit said, 'Look, how my best boots are almost ruined.' Anna glanced down and saw that the shining leather was scuffed and sticky with something dark and tufted.

Mud and grass perhaps? No, blood and hair.

FORTY-SIX

LONDON, APRIL 2017

Lauren feels so cold. It's as if her body has frozen. Her hand is over her mouth and she can't speak. Margie is still talking, but she can't seem to make sense of the words, because her mind is stuck in a loop, repeating the phrase over and over again, *I worked in a concentration camp.*

She cannot shake the images that are reeling through her mind, of bodies carelessly discarded, piled up and left to rot, of hollow cheeks and dark, desperate eyes, of stick-like limbs and concertina ribs. And Margie was a small but vital part of that vile system.

'I can't believe it,' she hears herself whispering, as if her voice is coming from someone else, far away. 'This can't be true.' She is hearing Margie's voice through a fog of confusion, accompanied by the ticking of the kitchen clock and the dripping of the kitchen tap. Drip, tick, drip, tick, true, untrue, drip, tick.

But Margie is sitting in front of her, shoulders back, hands clasped in her lap, still talking, telling her about a lost baby, a dead lover, an attempt to leave and how she tried to atone many times for her part in that foul organisation. Her face is passive, tears no longer tremble, she has stopped scratching her arm, but she grips a twisted tissue in her hands.

'My dear, I can assure you, what I am telling you is all true. You said it might ease my mind to talk about my past and I think perhaps you are right. But I must leave it to you to decide what to make of my confession. I am no longer afraid of being judged. I have hidden the truth for so many years, but I have little time left to me now, so facing judgement or even a prison sentence would not be so very hard for me to bear.'

Lauren takes a breath and tries to speak. Her throat feels parched and she takes a sip of the coffee, which has grown cold during their conversation. It suddenly tastes bitter and she adds another spoonful of sugar, which she stirs into her cup, stirring, stirring, as if she will be able to summon up the words with her pirouetting teaspoon. Staring into the whirlpool of liquid, she coughs and says, 'I'm not sure what to think. It's such a shock, hearing all this. Did you know what was really going on there? Did you see people dying all around you?' She feels herself trembling as she asks the questions and has to put her shaking cup down on the saucer.

'Of course I did. Death was commonplace during that time and even once the war was over. But the full extent of what had been done in the name of the Reich was not known to us at the time I worked there. We were members of the Party but we didn't know that these terrible acts were deliberately planned and authorised by those above us.'

You may not have known then, Lauren thinks, but you knew later. You knew and you wouldn't face it. And we all know what you and your kind did. We've seen the news footage, read the horror stories, we know and we despise everyone who had a hand in those crimes.

Lauren is trembling too much to drink the coffee. She suddenly stands, knocking the edge of the table in her haste, so a little of the liquid spills into the saucer. 'I've got to go,' she says.

'I must get on.' She heads for the back door, desperate to escape the thoughts crowding her head.

'You will tell Freddie I'll talk to him, won't you?' Margie is still sitting, her face blank and calm. 'I will look forward to his visit later on.'

Lauren hears her, but doesn't look back. She must go home. She has to think.

Lauren is shaking and can't concentrate. She stares at the supermarket order on her laptop screen but can't find the will to add Margie's items to the list. All around her there is silence, apart from the squawk of a blackbird in the garden, the screech of a motorbike on the road and the screaming, nagging thoughts in her head. These humdrum sounds, the normal accompaniment to her everyday routine, the banal background to ordinary life, cannot erase the images that are flashing through her mind of mass burials of starved human beings, thrown like rubbish into pits scattered with lime. She hears snatches of Richard Dimbleby's sonorous tones, as he related the horrors of the liberation of Belsen, echoing in her memory.

What she has just been told is reverberating in her mind. The words *I worked there* repeat themselves again and again. Margie worked in a concentration camp as a secretary. She wasn't a guard, she didn't injure anyone, she didn't fire a gun or operate a gas oven, but she was still a vital cog in the machine.

But she's also a dear little old lady, who keeps her house spotless, bakes wonderful cakes and babysat my children many times. She cleans in the church and arranges the flowers, she's been a good neighbour all these years, and now she tells me this. How am I meant to react?

We've all seen photos of those camps in articles and programmes. And I've been to Anne Frank's house. I've been encouraging Freddie to ask questions about the war, and now she tells me this. She tells me she was one of the people we've been taught to hate. I can't get my head around it.

She can't shake the image of Margie sitting beside her at the table in her neat, well-ordered, well-stocked kitchen, telling her about her past. 'We were all so stupid,' she said. 'But we didn't know any better. I was only eighteen. I thought it was a good job in a proper prison for people who were not suitable to mix in our society. But it wasn't long before I realised what it really was.'

Lauren had sat there, barely able to react, let alone speak. She was open-mouthed, aghast at what she was hearing. 'I never wanted to talk about it because I was afraid. When all the others, the guards and the commanders, faced charges after the war, I thought it would be me next. And soon after I left the camp there were prisoners, slave labourers and others all roaming the countryside, trying to find their way home but also ready to punish those they thought were guilty. So, I hid and I have stayed hidden, until now.'

So why has she finally decided to speak out? Lauren thinks if she hadn't pressed her, on Freddie's behalf, Margie would probably have kept quiet. But maybe it isn't just her prompts that have caused this revelation, she thinks, as she recalls Margie's voice. 'I always knew it would come out one day. They are finding everyone who has stayed hidden. They would have come to me in the end.'

There was something in the papers a few months ago, wasn't there? A man who'd been a bookkeeper at one of the camps. He hadn't harmed anyone, he hadn't been one of the vicious guards, yet he was still charged. But was he sentenced? Lauren wonders. She can't remember, but isn't that sort of administrative job on a par with being a secretary?

Lauren tries to concentrate again on completing the order. She adds sugar and flour to the list of groceries. She switches on the kettle. She needs a strong coffee. She never finished the cup Margie poured for her; she was so agitated, she let it go cold.

She adds an extra spoonful of sugar to her mug and stands while the water boils, staring out of the window, wondering what she should do next.

Freddie will ask her if she's spoken to Margie yet. He will want to continue his German lessons with her and he will still be keen to ask questions about her past. Lauren wants to protect him from the unpleasant truth, but isn't sure that is the right course of action. Maybe she should tell him a little of what she knows and see if he wishes to continue. Or perhaps she should let him proceed and find out whether Margie will be as truthful with him as she was this morning. He would then have to assess the facts he is given and decide how to present them. Perhaps that is the best way to handle this.

But he is only a boy, Lauren reminds herself. I can't leave it to him to decide what to do next. The fact is that people in similar positions have been charged. And now I know what she did I have to decide whether she should be reported. I know she is very old and has lived a blameless life for many years, but it's not up to me to judge whether or not she is innocent; she was still a part of the whole awful process.

Lauren abandons her supermarket order and googles 'prosecution of war crimes'. And there she finds link upon link to the organisation still pursuing those who were involved in the concentration camp system. But time is running out and the Central Office for the Investigation of National Socialist Crimes may not operate for many more years. And slowly Lauren's conviction grows as she reads that, despite their great age, individuals are still being investigated as 'accessories to murder'. They may be old, but there are also aging victims, who witnessed dreadful events and have been hoping for years that they would see justice for themselves and their families before they finally died.

She was running away, Lauren thinks. That night we found her at the bus stop. She hadn't gone out shopping at all. That was a suitcase she was carrying. She was trying to escape before they could come for her.

She slumps in her seat, wondering what she should do now she is in possession of this devastating information. She reflects on how long she has known Margie, all the years of cakes, the shared cups of coffee, the funerals of their husbands, the babysitting and Margie's fondness for Freddie.

Think woman, think. Stop being hysterical, just deal with it. What would Colin say if he was here? He always said you go by the book, inform the appropriate authorities. He'd have known what to do.

But how can I shop a 92-year-old granny? Do I call the police, contact these German investigators or do nothing? If I wait too long, she might not be fit enough to answer any charges, she might even die before anything could happen. Or she might decide to take off again and maybe this time she'd get away for good.

And now that she's talking about her past, isn't it better to encourage her to keep doing so? She may never be charged, but surely it's better to have a witness presenting the true facts than let the deniers have their say? But is it really up to me to decide whether I should report my elderly neighbour to the appropriate authorities?

Lauren breathes unsteadily. She cannot shake the thought repetitively pounding in her brain. Your neighbour is a Nazi. She's the Nazi next door.

Every day, Anna managed to leave a small amount of food underneath her pillow for Margarete. Sometimes it was no more than a crust from the bread served with her soup, if she couldn't help herself to another whole slice. Other times she left a boiled potato, a chunk of cheese or an apple. It was so very little, so insignificant, that she knew it would never be missed from the meals prepared for the staff. Yet such tiny scraps could mean so much to those who had almost nothing to eat but a crust and watery soup. It really was enough to make the difference between life and death.

Was it her imagination, she asked herself, or had Margarete started to look slightly better? Her hair was still lank, mostly hidden beneath her scarf, and she was still very thin, but she was alive and had not yet succumbed to one of the illnesses that were reportedly infecting other prisoners. She didn't always see her in the mornings as the cleaning of the rooms began while the staff had their breakfast. But if she made an excuse to run back upstairs after she'd eaten, she could hide the stolen food and sometimes catch a glimpse of the women sweeping and making the beds.

One time she dashed back to her room and Margarete was just straightening her sheets, but jumped back, as if she'd been caught in the act. Anna assumed she had already checked beneath the pillow, which had covered a roll from the night before. She pressed into the trembling woman's hand a piece of sausage that she had saved from her own plate that morning. 'I hope it is helping you,' she said.

Tears welled in Margarete's eyes as she said, 'It helps all of us.'

'You mean you don't eat it yourself? You have to share this out?'

Margarete nodded. 'We all have to survive to help each other.'

'Then I must bring more. This will barely feed you, let alone more of your friends as well.'

'No, please,' she said, shaking her head, 'too much is dangerous. You will cause trouble.'

'I will see what I can do. You mustn't starve.'

At that point they both heard the stamping on the stairs and the bellowing shouts from Birgit. 'Lazy bitches. Aren't you finished up here yet?'

Margarete bent her head to sweep up a last speck of lint from the floor, then scuttled away into the corridor. Anna followed her and caught sight of Birgit thwacking another prisoner on the back with her cane. Birgit saw her watching and grinned, saying, 'Fancy having a turn, do you, before you go off to your nice quiet office?' Anna ran down the stairs, trying to forget the look of pleasure she had seen in her colleague's eyes.

All that day, as she typed names and numbers, reports on supplies and conditions, duplicated orders for the movement of prisoners, she tried to tell herself that this was a place of correction and that all prisons often employed punishment as a way of improving antisocial behaviour. But day by day it was dawning on her that this was no ordinary prison. She was faced with the truth. The inmates would not eventually be released to serve society for the good of the nation, they would not be improved by their time here, but would be worn down, ill-treated and starved, until they died. And their bodies would be disposed of in the crematorium, which she had never seen, apart from the chimney above the far side of the camp, but had been told operated regularly.

Anna looked around her warm, well-organised office. When a timid woman in her striped dress brought her and the other administrative staff their mid-morning coffee, she began to look more closely. Was she thinner than the previous week? Was she bruised? Were her clothes more ragged, less clean than before? And the smell, she couldn't help noticing the smell. It reminded her of the garbage bins outside her childhood home, a smell of rotten cabbage, old peelings and dirt, overlaid with the pee of stray cats and dogs. She held her breath as the woman came near with her cup. It wasn't the prisoner's fault, she knew. How could anyone manage to be clean and healthy in the insanitary quarters she now realised they were living in? But she couldn't stop herself from wrinkling her nose.

Birgit noticed her doing it. 'Filthy Jews. You should see what it's like in their disgusting huts. Lucky you don't have to go near them like I do.'

'Can't we give them better living conditions? Surely it would be better if they weren't dirty like this?'

Birgit shrugged. 'Who cares? They're not worth it. This lot'll be gone soon and then we'll get more. I'm hoping we get a trainload from Italy bringing us decent salami and mortadella.'

Anna felt sick inside. Her skin felt cold and clammy. 'I don't know how you can be like that. They are still human beings.'

'Not for long. If you don't like it, don't look at them.'

So, Anna tried not to. Walking between her accommodation, the staff quarters and her office, she didn't have to go near the prisoners' huts or work areas. She didn't have to see the majority of them, but she couldn't avoid those who had been selected for domestic duties. And if those prisoners were considered to be sufficiently acceptable to be near the camp staff, how on earth were the others faring? Were they thinner, frailer, sicker, filthier?

One day a week or so later, Anna found that her hidden stash of food had not been taken. She left it untouched, thinking maybe Margarete had been moved to other duties or was ill that morning. But it was still there at the end of the next day. And the following morning, when she dashed back to her room with a fresh bread roll, a different woman was sweeping the floor.

'Where's Margarete?' Anna said, wondering if the new woman had already taken the stale bread left under her pillow from the previous day.

'She's in trouble,' the woman whispered. 'They think she was stealing.'

'Stealing? What had she taken?'

'Bread,' was the faint, barely audible answer. 'She was searched.'

'And where is she now?'

'Outside. She and those from her hut are all outside.'

Anna looked out of the window. The spring day was not so springlike. There was a cold wind and rain was pouring down. She pulled on her overcoat and cap and dashed down the stairs, telling herself that, for once, she had to go and see what was happening. This time, she could not look away. She began walking towards the female prisoners' compound.

A line of women stood in the mud, in the heavy rain, their heads bowed, their shoulders sagging. One of them was Margarete. Her eyes slid towards Anna and she gave the slightest of nods. The prisoners were dressed only in their thin regulation dresses, with bare feet and bare heads. Some were recently shaven-headed, some had thin strands of wet hair plastered to their scalps.

As Anna watched, feeling herself chilling in the cold rain despite her protective coat, one of the women fell to her knees. The two either side bent to begin lifting her up, but then she heard the awful, screeching, commanding voice of Birgit. 'Leave her! Let her drown!' They left her lying in a puddle in the mud, straightened their shoulders and continued to stare straight ahead.

Anna thought she couldn't bear to wait to see what the guard might do next, but Birgit noticed her and marched across to where she was standing near the fence. 'See what happens when they get too much to eat? They get careless.' The smirk on her face told Anna that Birgit knew about the hidden food and was enjoying the pain and humiliation she was inflicting on these weak, sickly women, as well as provoking her colleague.

'How long are you going to make them stand out here?'

'Till one of them confesses. I've got all day.'

'They're all going to get very sick out here in the cold.'

'Want to look after them, do you? Want to go in their stinking hut and feed them up?' She grasped Anna's shoulder, her strong meaty hand heavy with meaning, her fingers digging hard into Anna's flesh, despite her coat. 'I think a certain someone has been giving out extra rations, don't you? And maybe that someone needs to see what happens when they get found out.'

Anna pulled away. 'I don't know what you're talking about. If I were you, I'd get them all inside. You won't have anyone to boss around if you let them all die off.'

Birgit removed her hand, her eyes narrowed and her lips set in a thin, tight line. She marched across to the row of shivering women. She made sure Anna was still watching, then swung her foot in its steel-tipped boot to give the fallen one a vicious kick.

Anna turned away, ashamed and angry. She walked off quickly, back to her office, back to typing lists of the dead and the living and wondering whether, by the simple act of leaving bread under her pillow, she had helped or harmed.

Flies and biting insects from the marshland that surrounded the camp swarmed and stung in the hot weather. There was no escape from the pests, nor the smell that floated over the whole camp from the wooden barracks housing the prisoners.

Anna tried to stop herself thinking about how much the inmates must be suffering in their work, mending roads in the heat. They were unlikely to have fresh water and she knew they had little food. Guilt bit hard when she found she felt relieved to take up the invitation to escape for a short while to the leisure facility designated for the exclusive use of the staff.

'Lucky you,' Birgit sniped at her. 'Bet you're glad to get away from the stink here while the sun's out. I'm not due a break till October.'

'I was told I could go early on compassionate grounds,' Anna said. 'I haven't been able to contact my family since Hamburg was badly bombed. I've been so worried about them, it's been affecting my ability to concentrate on my work. I begged Kommandant Eisfeld to let me go back home, but he thinks it's not advisable at present. He said a trip to Solahütte would do me good.'

Birgit sniffed. 'I bet. Is he going too, sly old dog? He always picks his favourites. Can't wait to see them strip off in the sun, the men as well as the women. You'd better watch it. Or maybe you want to encourage him and earn a few special favours, eh?' She added this last comment with a sly grin as she poked Anna in the ribs.

On the coach taking the small group away from the camp she sat next to Johann, a quiet man with round wire glasses that made him look serious. Like her, he was an administrator, an accountant, totting up the possessions that came into the camp with each batch of newcomers. Gold, jewels and furs were snatched away and entered into his books in efficient columns of numbers. He added up the figures, kept the records and organised the dispatch of valuables. He didn't have daily contact with the prisoners or mete out punishment, he just applied his brain to keeping count.

'You're very quiet,' he said on the journey. 'Are you not feeling well?'

'I'm worried about my parents,' Anna said. 'My family home is in Hamburg but I've not heard from them since the city was bombed.'

'Oh, I see. That's awful. But they may have got out in time. You'll hear from them soon, I'm sure.'

She nodded and looked out of the window at the farmland they passed on their way to the resort. Beyond the fields she could glimpse the sea and the sand dunes. If it hadn't been wartime their destination would have been the white sandy beaches, where they could have swum in the cool, clean sea and lain in the sun, fanned by the breeze. But in the middle of war they had to hide away in a Tyrolean-style chalet in a forest.

When they arrived, she was reminded of the maternity home where she had given birth to Peter. She had long resigned herself to the fact that he had not lived for many hours after he'd entered this world, but she still thought of how he could have grown into a handsome boy like his father. He'd be blond and blue-eyed, smiling as she tickled his tummy, bathed him and held him to her breast. In a year he'd be learning to walk, maybe even trying to speak as well, calling her Mutti as she kissed him.

But here there were no babies lined up in cots in a crèche. Rows of reclining chairs were turned to face the sun on a deck to one side of the chalet. A pool beckoned swimmers and a prisoner was employed to fish leaves and insects from the water every morning with a long-handled net. Other detainees cooked and cleaned the accommodation, so the camp staff had only to think about playing tennis, swimming, eating good food and resting in the sun. In the evenings various members of staff took it in turn to perform their party pieces, songs and musical numbers. Kommandant Eisfeld's speciality was a song popularised by the movie star Zarah Leander, which he emphasised with fluttering hands and eyelashes as he warbled, 'Ich Weiss, es wird einmal ein Wunder geschehen.' Anna felt uneasy as he sang these words, wondering if by miracle he meant winning the war. And she also had a sneaking suspicion that he had a hankering to dress like the famous Zarah, as well as sing and act like her.

The day after they arrived at the resort, Johann asked Anna if she'd like to take a walk through the forest. He wasn't like the camp's *kommandant*, who winked at her whenever he spoke, nor was he insincerely charming like the handsome Günther, so she felt it would be safe to join him on a stroll. They walked around the shores of the resort's lake, sparkling in the sun. Other staff members were fishing or paddling in boats.

'I'm sorry you haven't heard anything from your parents,' Johann said. 'It's very difficult for all of us being far away from family for so long. But is there anything else troubling you?'

She couldn't tell him about her grief for Günther, nor about Peter, but she felt she could trust him, so she said, 'I never realised when I accepted this job that the prisoners would be so badly treated. I feel very uncomfortable whenever I see what is happening to them.'

He offered her a cigarette and she accepted, although she rarely smoked, just to calm her nerves. 'I feel the same way,' he said. 'A few of the guards here enjoy the work, even joke about it. Have you heard them saying they're looking forward to the next consignment of Hungarians, because of the hams they bring with them? But for the rest of us it's a case of shutting our eyes and trying not to think, isn't it?'

'Ones like Birgit, back at the camp, you mean?' Anna couldn't even bear to think that the ham she'd been eating so far had been ripped from the hands of desperate new arrivals.

'She's pretty bad, but the dog handlers are the worst. You haven't seen what they can do, have you?'

Anna shuddered to think how much worse a dog's bite might be than a steel-tipped boot. 'I've been feeling I can't take much more of it. I know I don't see the worst of it, day in day out, but I know what is happening to them and it makes me feel sick. And I know that what you and I are doing, even though we have little contact with the prisoners, is helping this cruel system to function efficiently.'

'Are you thinking of leaving? Where would you go?'

'That's just the trouble.' She sighed and tapped the lengthening cigarette ash. 'I would have gone home, but now I don't know whether I still have a home. I feel completely trapped.'

'They wouldn't be keen to let you go anyway. We all have to maintain the illusion that this is a normal prison. They don't want us talking about our work to the outside world. And our camp's not the worst of them either, by a long stretch. There are rumours that others, further east, are no better than death factories. They ship them in, sort them out, gas them and then burn the bodies. Jews, Romanies, homosexuals, all for the chop. No pretence there that they've been brought in to work.'

'And they're killing most of them at our camp too, aren't they?'

'Some straight away, the rest they work to death. Even this place,' he jerked his head towards the centre of the resort, 'was built by slave labour. The road here, the whole structure. Who knows how many died in the process, dragging great bags of cement and heavy beams for the buildings?'

'So how do you cope? How do you make yourself work back at the camp day after day, knowing that you are tallying stolen possessions and depriving honest people of their lives and livelihoods?'

Johann took a long drag on his cigarette and let the smoke spiral in the fresh air. The sun was hot in the open glades around the lake, but underneath the trees there was cool shade and the smell of leafy mulch on the woodland floor. 'I have to tell myself I am following orders. I don't make the decisions, I just follow orders. You'd do well to do the same.'

'I suppose I'm in a similar position. We didn't create the place where we work. We didn't make the rules. We aren't the ones ill-treating and punishing them.'

'You know most of those who do the dirty work drink heavily to blot out the sights and sounds?'

'But I thought you said many of them enjoy being cruel?'

'Some do. But they have to work so closely with those unfortunate creatures that they see things no one wants to remember. They drink to forget. I don't drink. I just close my eyes and concentrate on the paperwork.'

'I suppose I do the same.' Anna thought about the columns of figures she typed, the names with numbers, the transport details to other camps further away. If she knew the consequences of her efficient typing, knew more of the reality of the horrors, would she too drink to excess? Would she too, in the quiet of the night, wake with her heart pounding, remembering a beaten woman, cowering in the mud because she had shared a forbidden crust of bread?

She leant back against the tree trunk, wondering how long she could maintain her composure. As both of them smoked and gazed across the lake, a fish leapt in an arc from the cool mirrored water, leaving ever-widening ripples.

FORTY-NINE

THE CAMP, SEPTEMBER 1943

Lagerkommandant Hans Eisfeld's eyes narrowed as he answered Anna's timid request. 'You realise you signed an oath not to reveal the nature of the operations undertaken here?'

'Yes, I know,' she whispered. 'I understand that, of course. None of us can ever speak of our work. I never would and really, I know very little of the details of the camp's function. But that's not why—'

She stopped because of the look on his face as he stood up to reveal his full height. He was not a big man, but he had a huge presence. Maybe it was in part due to the accoutrements that enhanced his position: his tailored uniform, always freshly brushed and pressed, and his boots, always highly polished – with their inner lift, a secret that Margarete had told her after another prisoner had cleaned them.

Eisfeld strode about the camp, a pair of black gloves held in one hand, delighting in slapping the faces of prisoners and staff alike with the studded leather. If he was feeling particularly impatient, he snapped his short-handled whip or commanded one of his lackeys to deal with a situation. He didn't undertake the worst punishments himself, but he liked to watch the humiliation, pain and agony. Everywhere he went he floated on a trail of musky cologne, perhaps to foil the stench of the camp's inmates.

Anna tried to speak again in the face of this intimidating man. 'I'm not sure I'm well suited to the work here...'

'Your work is perfectly satisfactory,' he barked. 'I have no complaints.'

'But the circumstances are not...'

'Not what? Not to your liking? Were you expecting the luxuries of the Grand Hotel in Baden-Baden perhaps? Your colleagues don't seem to have any complaints and find their quarters are to their liking.' His left eyebrow lifted in a quizzical expression as he paused to fit the monocle that she heard he wore more for effect than for practical purposes. He stared at her as if he was waiting for her response.

'It's just that it's the purpose, I mean the function of the camp, that I find difficult to accept.' She finally managed to deliver the words she found so hard to say. 'When I applied for the position, I thought it was just a prison.'

He smiled and his tone softened. 'But it is, little one, it is a prison. And sometimes measures have to be taken to ensure discipline is upheld. Is that a problem for you?'

'No, I understand there must be rules...'

'Of course there must.' He sat down again and swivelled his large leather chair to one side, then patted his knee. 'Come here.' He beckoned.

She couldn't refuse. He was the *kommandant*, after all. He had supreme authority in this realm of his. He could make life very unpleasant for anyone under his command, as well as for the prisoners. She took a couple of steps to stand by his side.

He patted his knee again. 'Sit down on my lap and let me reassure you that you are a valuable member of our team here. I wouldn't like anything unpleasant to happen to you. And I don't want you upsetting yourself so you can't continue to do your work to the highest possible standard.'

Anna had heard about the games he liked to play with both male and female staff. She hoped he wasn't going to play one with her but she felt she had to do what he asked, so she sat down on his knee, her toes touching the floor.

He put his arms round her waist and laid his scented head against her breast. 'There now, don't you feel better already?'

She couldn't find the words to respond, so she just nodded and murmured assent without opening her lips.

'You see, if you are friendly, friendlier than you have been so far, you might find your time here much more tolerable. Do you know what I mean? I know you don't spend much of your spare time with your colleagues, but maybe if you did you'd enjoy yourself more, don't you think?' The arm across her waist was lowered to her lap.

She could feel herself stiffening at what she thought might be coming. Hoping that what she had heard was simply malicious gossip and wasn't true.

'Now, if you try a little harder to be a bit more sociable, having fun with your friends and workmates, you might feel much more comfortable with your role here.'

She could feel his fingers crawling towards the hem of her skirt and gradually, slowly, they shifted the fabric higher up her thigh, an inch at a time. Holding her breath, she didn't dare say a thing, and eventually his hand met its destination and she felt her stocking garter being pulled and stretched and then, PING! It snapped sharply against her thigh with a resounding snap, stinging her flesh.

He laughed and pushed her off his lap, slapping her bottom as she stood before him. 'If you don't like what you see, you don't have to look,' he said. 'Ignore everything but the work on your desk. You don't have to directly concern yourself with the prisoners, just keep on top of the typing and the filing. Efficiency is everything here.'

'Yes sir,' she replied, saluting in the approved manner, to which he responded in kind.

'You can come and see me for another private talk any time you are feeling anxious.' He winked and dismissed her with a wave.

Anna turned to leave his office, knowing her cheeks were burning. Her thigh was smarting and her buttocks still felt the weight of his hefty slap. As she emerged into the general office area, she was aware of the looks and the smirks of other staff as she returned to her desk. She bit her lip, sat down and began to type out a long list of names, numbers and dates. She knew she was typing out the names of prisoners that might result in punishment, execution or deportation to other camps, but what could she do? If she couldn't leave the camp, then she too was a prisoner.

DER SINGENDE KNOCHEN

THE SINGING BONE

The king found the skeleton of the murdered
man under the bridge. So he ordered that the
wicked brother be sewn up in a sack and drowned.

FIFTY

THE CAMP, APRIL 1945

The place had begun emptying out in late January. It was now spring and if Anna waited any longer she'd be risking rape and retribution from the Russians, who were closing in from the east. She knew she had to leave soon too.

She'd seen the prisoners go, forced into lines with blows and shouts, shuffling along the road, poorly dressed for the winter cold, slithering in the freezing snow. Some wore thick socks and shoes or clogs, but many only had rags tied round their feet. All wore every item of clothing they could find, their skeletal figures padded out with coats, woollens and blankets, tied with rope and string. How long they'd last on the march, no one knew, but the order was sent to take them all away, to leave no evidence of the camp's hellish work. No more guards, no more prisoners, no more files. She didn't know where they were going, but suspected few would reach their destination.

All this time Anna had been steeling herself to leave. Even the most loyal staff said it would be better to slip away now. Two years she'd been there, struggling to keep her eyes on the paperwork and not on the grim reality around her. If she lifted her head from her desk, from the forms, from the hand holding the pen, the typewriter tapping the keys, there was a danger that she'd go mad and never stop screaming. So, she never questioned the purpose of the camp and the way it was run; but she knew that when the Allies came here, with eyes freshly open to the horror, they would seek to blame and punish those responsible. And although she hated seeing what was happening, she made sure she knew about the selections, the executions, the rapid disposal of newborns and little ones, so it could never be denied.

When she had first accepted the job, it had seemed as if her dreams of an independent life had come true. The pay was three times better than she could have earned anywhere in Hamburg, such as the munitions factory. Besides, with her secretarial qualifications, she could by rights expect to work in a good position. And despite deductions for board and lodging, she was still left with more money than she could ever have had in the city.

Early in her time here, she had clung to the official definition of the place – prison camp – as stated in the job advertisement. She told herself there were legitimate reasons for the incarceration of the inmates, that they were a danger to decent society. As a member of the Helferinnenkorps, she was there to assist in the smooth administration of the place and although she was not obliged, like her male counterparts, to be a member of the Party, she had already joined some time before, so that confirmed her status.

She had watched other members of staff come and go and knew that if she'd insisted, she could have left earlier and not stayed for the two years she'd served. But she guessed the family home was no more, maybe her parents too; Hamburg was said to be in ruins, and where else would she find a well-paid job in the war? So she stayed and tried not to see what was all around her. When the new guards arrived, she watched their nervousness with curiosity. Unlike her, they could not hide behind a desk and a typewriter; they had to face the prisoners and their appalling conditions every single day.

These new Aufseherin were shy for a day or so, teased by their colleagues for saying 'please' and 'would you mind' and 'excuse me', when the more experienced ones knew that a slap or a punch would achieve a quicker result. But the power of their uniforms soon transformed them, especially the jaunty cap and the steel-tipped leather boots, capable of delivering a lethal kick to the ribs and stomach. One of these girls soon developed a taste for kicking and earned herself the nickname 'the Mare', because she was like a high-spirited horse ready to use her heels and toes whenever she was disgruntled.

But despite the protection of her office and her form-filling, Anna could not pretend she wasn't aware of the true nature of the camp. However much she tried not to look, the prisoners' quarters were near enough for her to see the filth and degradation, the work details filing past her window, the obsessive roll-calls taking place in the quadrangle within earshot, to the accompaniment of shouts, barks and savage blows. She knew that the punishment meted out to the prisoners was inhuman, she knew the death toll was calculated, she was fully aware of the nature of the camp and feared retribution when the Allies discovered its true purpose and how many had died there.

Anna threw the last of the paperwork onto the fire outside the *kommandant's* empty headquarters. They can't think this will be enough to cover up their crimes, she thought. There will be witnesses, no matter how many die on that final march of death. There will be bodies on the road as well as those buried in woods around the camp.

As she watched the paper curl and blacken, then burst into flames, Johann, one of the few remaining camp staff, came to stand by her side and offered her a cigarette. She rarely smoked, but this time she took it. 'You should go after this,' he said. 'Don't hang around longer. The Russians aren't far away now. It won't be today or next week, but it'll be soon, and you've heard how they treat women. One like you will get even worse treatment.'

Like her, Johann didn't have to exercise violence, just his brain. 'I'm worried about being identified,' Anna said. 'But if I can look more like an inmate or a refugee, I might avoid retaliation.'

'Don't ever let on where you worked,' he said. 'I fear we'll be blamed for war crimes as much as the guards. They'll lump us all together. They'll say our jobs were key to keeping the concentration camps operating.'

'Do you really think that?' Anna paused, wondering when mundane tasks like typing and filing had become defined as war crimes.

'Help yourself to a coat and whatever you like from the store,' he said. 'There's still plenty of good clothing in there. But don't get tempted to grab furs or anything fancy! That will just cause more trouble.'

She laughed at his little joke. 'I promise I'll do my best to look as drab as possible.' She took a drag of the cigarette. It might be her last for quite some time.

'You've got money, haven't you?' When she nodded, he said, 'Stitch it into the hem if you can, like they all did. You don't want it anywhere it can be easily pinched.'

Anna had heard the stories of gold, diamonds and coins tumbling out of the linings of winter coats requisitioned from the new arrivals. She imagined a treasure trove of valuables piled in the store along with the confiscated clothes.

Almost as if he was reading her mind, he said, 'You won't find anything of value in the store. That all went off to some secret mine in Bavaria, I expect. Just piles of clothes and shoes there now.'

She watched the last piece of incriminating paper crumble into charred fragments, then went in search of supplies for her journey and a disguise for her new identity. The storeroom smelt of moth-balls, sweat, sickness and fear. She grabbed the first suitable garment she saw, a slim, black, double-breasted woman's coat that was missing some buttons, with a torn lining and unstitched hem that must once have contained a final life-saving fund of gold or diamonds. She added a warm grey cardigan to wear over a stained blue dress and decided to keep her own sturdy black lace-up shoes, which fitted well and should keep her on the road for long enough.

She stripped out of her official grey-green uniform and blouse and threw them on the pile. Now she no longer looked like an orderly office worker or camp staff member; she'd become a shabby nobody, a displaced person. She rejected a smart green hat with a feather in favour of a squashed brown beret, the kind a child might wear, which fitted her small head perfectly. To vary her appearance if she felt she was being followed, she added a patterned fringed shawl that could cover her head or her shoulders.

Just as she was turning to leave in her new guise, she heard a slight noise. A rat perhaps, making a nest in the warm heaps of wool and furs. She looked around the storeroom and heard it again, but this time she detected rustling accompanied by trembling, terrified breaths. Surely everyone had been rounded up and forced to march away two months previously? She looked hard at the piles of folded clothes, the stacked hats, the piles of shoes, and saw a tiny quivering movement. A hunched man with hollow cheeks and dark eyes was almost completely buried beneath the garments and was shivering with fear.

'Don't worry,' she said. 'I won't tell anyone I've seen you.'

'Food,' his voice rasped. 'We are five. Food, I beg you.'

She thought for a second. She had already packed a small supply for herself in a sack, but she could help herself to more, while the few remaining guards might still take a shot at a fugitive prisoner raiding the camp bins.

'Here, have this,' she said, throwing her sack across to him, knowing it was a pitiful amount to feed five starving human beings desperate to survive until the end of the war. But if the Russians were really coming soon, then the camp would be liberated before long and any remaining prisoners would be helped. And if her small contribution helped the five to stay alive, could that begin to atone for the hundreds of names she had typed on her lists?

'Stay where you are. I don't think anyone knows you are here.' And at that moment she heard fleet footsteps and caught a glimpse of another shadowy figure running from a corner of the storeroom and away into the marshland and scrubby woods around the camp. They were hiding, then fleeing like rats, poor creatures.

Returning to the bonfire later, she found Johann still there, staring at the dying embers. 'I think I'm ready to go now,' she said. 'I've packed some bread and sausage to keep me going, which is more than we ever gave those poor prisoners for their journey. Do you think any of them have survived their long march to tell the tale?'

'Many won't have done but those who do will want the world to know what our country was capable of doing so keep your mouth shut.'

She stared at him, wondering if she was about to launch herself into greater danger beyond the camp's fences than if she stayed here to face the Soviets. But before she could think what to say, he grabbed her hand. She thought he was going to shake it in a gesture of farewell, but he pushed her sleeves out of the way and then she felt a searing pain on the soft skin of her fore-arm, where he had branded her with a hot piece of metal he was holding with tongs. She screamed in horror and pulled away from him, staring at her scorched red flesh. The burning welt was less than the length of her hand.

'You should thank me,' he said. 'That's your passport, if you think about it.'

She stared again at her blistering arm and understood his meaning. It was as if the burn had obliterated a number, the same kind of number that had been inked onto the arms of the prisoners. He had completed her transformation.

FIFTY-ONE

THE ROAD HOME, APRIL 1945

On her long journey back to Hamburg, Anna often felt as if she was acting out the tales of the Brothers Grimm. Witches and robbers peopled the forests, wild creatures fled at her approach and the spectre of starvation walked with her. Each time she broke her journey to rest or buy food in isolated villages and farms, she was haunted by the stories of her childhood, of old women fattening up children to eat and wicked kings imprisoning young women to sacrifice.

Why had she left it so late to leave? Anna fretted as she trudged the roads from the east. How far was it to Hamburg and what would she find if she even managed to get there? It was such a long journey on foot, over seven hundred kilometres by road, hard walking even for a healthy young person, let alone those who were sick and starving. But the weather was mostly fine, so unlike the snows of January when most of the camp inmates had all trooped out under guard. And with the exceptionally mild February, spring had come early to the flat and marshy terrain either side of the highway. Cattle grazed fresh pasture to her left and her right and fields were green with the young shoots of barley, oats and rye. If it was later in the year the potatoes would be ready for harvesting, but this early the new crop would be barely larger than peas.

She lifted her head to the bright spring sky, hearing the swoosh of a stork gliding overhead, its black-tipped, beating wings guiding it to its cartwheel nest of sticks on top of a village house. And then, almost as if it was in competition with the airspace of storks, geese, egrets and dippers, a plane shot past, bearing not life-creating nest-building materials, but more bombs. She sighed; she should have accepted a lift at the beginning of the year, when the camp first began evacuating. But the *kommandant* had wanted the administrative team to stay behind to supervise the clearance of the site and the destruction of the files.

There was never an admission of guilt as such, but it was at that point that she truly understood what was happening. They wanted to destroy the evidence. They were going to dispose of the last of the prisoners and she was left to dispose of the paperwork. And in that moment she could no longer hide from the cold cruel truth of what had really been happening in this so-called prison, where death was the destiny for all of the prisoners and not redemption. Would the Allies understand, or condemn? Would the victors seek revenge and would she be included in their list of the guilty?

Anna bit her lip and shook her head. She could have been back in Hamburg by now. Some of the transports had headed to Neuengamme, the prison camp only a short distance from her home city. She should have gone with them, pleaded that she hadn't seen her parents for more than two years and was desperate to know if they had survived the bombing as she'd not heard from them since the city was devastated. The *kommandant* would have permitted her departure. He obviously had a soft spot for her, had hinted on more than one occasion that she might earn other privileges if she was friendlier, but she had not been able to bring herself to betray Günther's memory, or

Peter's, and had primly answered him by saying she had a fiancé and did not wish to compromise their working relationship.

You can do this, Anna told herself. It's springtime, not the middle of winter. At least you aren't trudging in the snow, like those half-alive prisoners. You are healthy, well shod and have money. She was glad she had taken Johann's advice about hiding her funds in the hems of her clothes. She kept a couple of coins and small notes in her pockets, so when she came across a farmer trundling along with a cart, she could offer to pay for a lift without betraying all of her hidden resources. With the retreat of the German army, farmers were no longer afraid to help, and more than once she was able to stay overnight in a relatively warm and dry hay barn, after paying for a sliver of cheese and dry bread.

Although the farming families were short of strong young men, all ages were helping to milk cows, till fields and sow crops. Women, children and old men alike looked healthy and well fed. They might have had more of their harvest requisitioned than in pre-war years, but they certainly looked as if they had good meals of *bregenwurst*, made from their own home-slaughtered pigs. And being so near the coast, they could probably still obtain the little smoked fish they called *kieler sprotte* too, if their fishing boats could dodge the warships patrolling the seas in the north.

Friendly farmers' wives didn't ask her searching questions, but looked concerned when she tore hungrily into their bread and cheese. One of them noticed her blistered arm and gave her a shocked glance, saying, 'We couldn't help them as they passed by, you know. The guards threatened to shoot anyone who gave those poor souls bread. They were marching them to their deaths. You'll see the bodies by the roadside – if the foxes and crows haven't had them by now.' Anna told herself to keep her burn hidden from then on, fearing its meaning might be mistaken, and she tried to hasten its healing by bathing it in the cold clean dew that lay on the fresh grass each morning.

The people she met looked up at the skies as they heard the roar of passing planes and shook their heads wearily, saying, 'We never wanted this. Those damn Nazis caused all this trouble. Sooner it's over the better.' And in one village an older woman, her face wet with tears, grasped Anna's hand and said, 'They took my sons. Both of them.' Anna nodded in sympathy and thought she would be safer travelling across country, further from the coast, where there might be conflict as the final days of the war played out.

One night Anna crawled into a large hay barn to sleep without seeking the permission of the farmer. She'd bought food in a village earlier in the day and just wanted to rest without having to justify herself. She crept into a corner behind the soft hay, out of sight, to nibble her bread and *ziegenkäse*, the traditional farmhouse cheese made from the milk of goats and cows. As she lay there listening to the rustling of creatures of the dark, her eyes grew heavy. Mice and rats scampered beneath the hay, still sweet with the scent of summer grass, and an owl called to its mate outside. And then she heard voices, deep, male voices, and she was suddenly alert.

She stayed still, hardly breathing, hoping that they too were only sheltering for the night. She didn't dare fall asleep, even though she was exhausted. What if she coughed or sneezed as she breathed in hay dust or mites? What if she snored in her dreams? She felt she had to stay awake as long as they were here.

Peering between the piles of hay, she could see two men in the bright shafts of moonlight beaming through the barn entrance. 'I think we lost them,' one said, standing near the opening and looking out across the yard and the fields.

'They'll be more worried about saving themselves than catching us,' the other said, removing his cap. 'It's the end game now.' At first, she thought they might be deserters, judging by the shape of their greatcoats, silhouetted in the silvery light. But then the moonbeam gleamed on their trousers and she saw that their coats covered the stripes of prison uniform. So, they were fugitives, like her, and yet not like her.

'We'll bed down here tonight,' one said, flinging himself onto a pile of hay. 'This'll do us. Better than those thin straw pallets any day.'

'And cleaner,' his companion said. 'No top bunk shitting over you in the night.' They both laughed and their conversation confirmed her fears. Maybe they hadn't come from her camp, maybe they wouldn't know who she was, but they had escaped from somewhere similar, where three-tiered bunks meant those in the lower levels might be subjected to the uncontrollable filth pouring out of those poor sick creatures above them. No wonder disease spread so easily.

Anna stayed completely still and utterly silent. Even if they accepted her as someone like them, they might still turn on a lone woman. And if they guessed that she was a part of the system that had incarcerated them, starved them and punished them, there was a good chance they'd seek vengeance and she wouldn't live to see her home in Hamburg again.

She watched as they gnawed on something that crunched, raw vegetables pulled from the earth, like turnip or carrot. Anything could fill a belly if you were that hungry. They sipped from a small container passed between them and she guessed they'd found a soldier's hipflask full of schnapps or cognac as well as the coats. Most of the guards at the camp, particularly the men who conducted the main punishments and executions, drank to excess and kept flasks to hand. It was all part of numbing the senses to the horror, of blotting out the grim misery of their actions, day after day.

At last, the two men lay down on the hay, curled their coats around them and began to sleep. After a few minutes she began hearing their snores, like percussion underscoring the melody of the night-time sounds around her. She wondered if she should wait until she was sure they were in a deep slumber and then creep past them. But she was too afraid that one of them might only be in a light sleep, alert to any threat, and he'd jump up and catch her before she could escape. It was too great a risk; she would have to wait until they left.

It was a long night for her, struggling to stay awake. She tried sitting upright, to make it harder to fall asleep, but every now and then her head jerked and she woke, remembering that she had to be as quiet, no quieter, than the mice running around her. Several times she was startled by her body's attempts to persuade her to sleep, and then, the last time it happened, she jolted into wakefulness and realised the men had gone. She couldn't hear their voices outside the barn, so they must have left well before first light. She could see red streaks in the sky through the entrance and hear the distant triumphant cry of a cockerel rousing his harem.

She guessed that before leaving, they must have lit and smoked cigarettes, as she caught a hint of tobacco fumes on the air. But soon she realised it wasn't just the lingering odour of their cigarettes, it was smouldering hay, ignited by a careless match or glowing stub end. She leapt from her hiding place and threw her coat over the charred stems, flecked with red embers, stamping until she was sure it was quite extinguished. How careless of them, risking the farmer's valuable feed store. And if she had fallen into a deep sleep, she might have been caught in the fire herself.

Anna shook the ash from her scorched coat and stood in the barn entrance thinking. *Where there's a cockerel, there's bound to be hens.* So she went in search of breakfast. She had saved the barn; she had earned herself a fresh egg or two.

. . .

As her journey continued, large numbers of planes droned overhead, with increasing frequency. Anna was fairly sure they weren't German aircraft, so maybe this was a sign that the end was coming. Could it really mean this interminable war would soon be over? And would she find a way to live normally again?

Sometimes, when she heard vehicles trundling along the road or saw a group of men ahead of her, she ducked into bushes or under a tree, feeling like the animals she heard scuttling in the dark. She slept in the woods, constantly woken by noises of the night, but then the birdsong each morning made her feel as if each day was fresh and clean and all would be well. But each evening, as starlings formed their swooping murmurations when they flew to their night-time roost, she felt apprehensive, wondering what might befall her in the hours of deepest darkness.

One day she stumbled into the yard of a small farm, where a woman was pegging washing on a line strung between the outhouses. Such a clean, normal activity was a joy to see, the linen bright in the sunlight, billowing in the breeze. There didn't seem to be any men around, so Anna thought it safe to approach her and ask if she might buy an egg or some bread. The woman stared at her, sizing her up. 'You're one of them, aren't you?'

Anna couldn't be sure what she meant by that question and thought it better not to answer. If the woman was a Nazi sympathiser and thought Anna was an escaped prisoner she might pretend to go into the farmhouse for food, but return with a gun or a husband to catch her.

She watched the woman retreat and waited nervously by the edge of the barn, ready to run back into the woods if the situation looked dangerous. But after a minute or so, the woman came back out, followed by a younger woman and two children of about eight and nine. And this time, she thought they all looked scared of her.

'I've hidden them for nearly three years,' the woman said. 'Sometimes in the barn, other times the cellar. But our supplies are running low with these growing mouths to feed. Can you take them with you?'

Anna was not prepared for this development. 'I'm on my way back to my home in Hamburg.'

'If you've still got a home.' The farmer's wife sniffed.

'We fled Dresden,' the young mother said. 'It wasn't safe to stay there.'

Anna gazed at her and the children. Did they know that their home was likely to be in ruins after the bombing of that beautiful city? She'd heard the news on the radio in the camp office. Everyone had been shocked that one of Germany's precious treasures had been devastated and bayed for revenge by destroying Britain's most beautiful cities.

'But you know that the city was almost destroyed?' she said.

The young woman's face fell and she turned to the older farmer's wife, who put her arms round her. 'We don't get much news out here.'

'And that means travelling south anyway. There's no point in you coming with me. I'm headed west. And I don't know what I'm going to find either but the end can't be far off now. You may as well start walking as soon as you can.'

'Here,' said the farmer's wife, passing a small bundle to Anna. 'It's not much, but it will keep you fed for a while. We'll manage here. If it really is nearly over, as you say, then we'll keep going. My sons will be home from the front soon, I hope, and they can help me plough the field. And we've a cow calving soon, so we'll have plenty of milk.'

Anna took the parcel gratefully. Such good people, the ordinary people of Germany, kept in ignorance of what had been done in their name. Out here in the countryside, far away from any camps, they could have no idea of the evils perpetrated by their government. 'Thank you,' she said. 'I'd help if I could, but

I think your lodgers should leave soon. There's not likely to be any risk they will be apprehended on their journey now.' But could she be confident of that? Guards might still be roaming, out to catch stray Jews and escaped prisoners. Or was it more likely now that the jailors themselves were fleeing for their lives?

After accepting a cup of warm herb tea, Anna took her leave of the little group and began walking westwards again. The countryside was mostly flat, pastures and fields of sprouting crops, but where there was woodland she often thought she saw figures disappearing into the trees. From a distance, whether they were army deserters or displaced persons she could not tell, but all seemed anxious to disappear from sight.

One night just when she was thinking she would have to sleep under bushes, she came across a deserted hamlet. It looked as if it had been bombed or shelled, even though it would not have been a principal target. The residents must have been resettled in a safer area. Thinking there might be a quiet corner or a cellar where she could curl up and eat the remains of the bread she'd been given earlier, she began peering into the derelict houses. Fragments of the occupants' lives were scattered within the once-loved homes: a shattered pot, a stein without a handle, a bucket with a hole.

The old inn looked more promising and she pushed open the creaking door to find a room furnished with tables and benches. The floor was littered with leaves and debris, but it was dry and she sat down to rest. She looked around the room draped with cobwebs, sprinkled with dust, and noticed that one table was less dusty than the others. The surface was clear and she realised to her horror that it had been swept. She went to the fireplace and saw that it wasn't filled with leaves and a jack-daw's nest, but with charred wood, recently lit.

It was clear to her that someone was living here, so she

thought better of staying and decided to move on; but just as she was about to leave, the door opened and a man in a faded military uniform entered, carrying dry sticks. His face registered as much surprise as she felt, but he calmly strode to the fireplace and began building a small pyre with the kindling. Looking at her over his shoulder, he said, 'I won't hurt you.'

She relaxed a little and allowed herself to sit down again.

'You can stay if you want. I have supplies here,' he went on.

The thought of a warm meal was tempting, although she still felt wary. 'Have you been living here long?'

'I was a deserter and when the SS caught me they brought me here to guard their secret store. I'll show you.'

Tiredness and curiosity overcame her natural caution and she followed him down some steps into a cellar, where his lamp shone on piles of golden candlesticks, dishes and paintings. The thought of how much more food she could buy with even one of these treasures passed through her mind, but then she felt a sudden shiver of fear at being alone with this man. He bent over one of the crates to pick up an ornate candelabra and while he was admiring its gleam in the light of his lamp, she turned and ran up the stairs and out into the woods. She felt sure she would not have survived the night if she had stayed there. It had felt like Bluebeard's castle and other terrifying stories of murder and sacrifice remembered from her childhood.

Huddling under a low-growing bush, she hoped he would not come searching for her when he collected more kindling for his fire. She eventually fell into a sleep disturbed by dreams of a cooking pot suspended over flames, burning incriminating lists of names and numbers. And she woke in a sweat after dreaming that she was drowning in increasingly hot water from which she could never escape. This was purgatory, she thought. This was her punishment for typing those lists that condemned her and she was on the road to hell and damnation.

FIFTY-TWO

LONDON, APRIL 2017

Lauren sits at her kitchen table, her hands cradling the cooling mug of instant coffee. Margie's words are still circling in her head. And she knows she has to make a decision. Freddie will ask her what happened when she saw Margie today. He might want to go straight there for his German lesson. She has to think clearly.

But before she can decide, before she can make sure she is her usual bright self to greet her curious son, he is home with a slam of the door and calling out to her, 'Mum, Charlie's granddad has given him loads of photos he can use in his war project. I want to go next door now and see Margie.'

'Wait a bit. I need to talk to you first.'

'Why? Did you go round there? Is she still cross with me?' Freddie frowns as he comes into the kitchen and slumps against the countertop.

'No, she's not cross at all. In fact, she said she wanted to apologise for being so hard on you the other day.'

'Really?' Freddie's voice rises and sounds strange.

And in that moment, Lauren hears his voice breaking and knows that he is joining the club of which his faster-maturing friends are already members. She stares at him, realising he has grown taller in just the last couple of weeks. He isn't her little boy any longer. She may still want to protect him and guide him, but she doesn't need to hold his hand all the time any more at every challenging junction.

'Well, what else did she say? Can I talk to her? Is she all right with that?'

'Slow down a minute. We need to have a talk about this.'

'But she will let me ask her questions then? And what about me doing a video of her? That would be great. Way better than Charlie's old photos.'

'I don't know about that. We didn't get that far. Sit down, Freddie.' Lauren takes a deep breath as he pulls out a chair and sits at the kitchen table. 'She told me a lot of things about her past this morning. And... well, it's all really very shocking. I'm hoping you aren't going to find it too upsetting.'

'Why? What did she do? She wasn't a Nazi, was she?'

Now Lauren is shocked by her son's bluntness. She gulps and says, 'Actually, she was. She was a secretary in one of the camps.' And Lauren bows her head and sobs. 'All this time,' she goes on, 'we've been living next door to a Nazi who worked in one of those dreadful concentration camps. And to think, I even let her come here to babysit both of you when you were younger.'

Freddie stands up and puts his arms round his distressed mother. 'It's all right, Mum. Don't get upset. I'm good with it. Well, not good meaning I think it's fine she's a Nazi, but I mean it's okay because I can deal with it so don't worry about me.'

'Oh, Freddie, I feel just awful. She's so old and she's pretended for so long. She told me she changed her name three times. Can you imagine having to do that? And she thinks she might still be charged for what she did back then. I think that's what made her behave so strangely before. I think she was running away, trying to escape because she thinks she could be charged with war crimes.'

'But she didn't actually kill anyone herself, did she?'

'She says she didn't. But she was a vital part of that whole revolting process. I can't tell you how much that disgusts me.'

'I know, Mum. It's awful. But I want to ask her how it could have happened. Like, why did she have to do that job? Did they make her go and work there and then she couldn't get away? I just want to understand. I mean, I know it's all terrible, but I can cope with facing her and asking questions. It'll be like me being like Dad was, when he had to interview suspects, finding the evidence to arrest them and all that.'

And Lauren knows that he will be methodical and dedicated like his father. He will apply himself to uncovering the facts and then assessing the information, however disturbing it might be. She feels so proud of him.

'All right then, I'll let you carry on. But you must tell me right away if she becomes distressed or if you see any sign that she might have a funny turn, like she did that time when we found her at the bus stop.'

'I will, Mum, don't you worry. I'll be patient but thorough, just like Dad was.'

Lauren smiles at this further mention of Colin. He'd have been very proud of his son. 'And you must bear in mind that this might not be the end of it. If she is tracked down, or decides to report herself, she could still be charged and prosecuted for war crimes.'

Freddie hugs her again. 'Like you always say, Mum, we'll cross that bridge when we come to it. I'll see what she says first and if she'll let me record her answers. And I think it's better if I talk to my teacher about it all as well.'

'That might be a good idea,' Lauren says, thinking the involvement of another rational adult in the situation could be helpful. She pulls a tissue from her pocket and blows her nose.

Thank goodness Freddie is so sensible and calm. He really is growing up fast.

He pats her on the back, saying, 'You can stop worrying about it now. I'll make you a cup of tea.'

Lauren nods and stares out of the kitchen window. She sees Margie's back door open, and her diminutive figure comes out and crosses over towards them. 'Oh no, Freddie, look, Margie is coming this way.' She doesn't feel ready to hear more of her stories and can't quite believe that Freddie has fully absorbed the impact of what she has just told him either.

But Freddie doesn't share her fear. He opens the door and smiles at his neighbour. 'Hello, Mrs Wilson. Would you like to have tea with us? Mum says you've said I can ask you some questions now.'

Margie steps inside. She is carrying a black leather case with a shoulder strap, which she puts on the table, along with a large manila envelope. She sits down at the table, clasping her hands in front of her, as she had done earlier in her own kitchen in front of Lauren.

'It is time for me to be truthful with you, my dearest Freddie. I am no longer afraid of being found out. Once upon a time, my name was Annaliese Kohlmann and I had a best friend whose name was Margarete Löwenthal. In memory of her and The Others I was not able to save, I want to tell you what happened and why I ended up having three names throughout my life. I am very ashamed of what I did and the only vay I can atone for my actions, even by the tiniest little bit, is in letting you tell everyone what happened, if you wish to do so. I survived but The Others didn't, so I must speak up now, as soon there will be no one left alive who knows the truth. You must make sure the story I tell you is shared.'

Lauren sees her son nodding at this statement and the huge responsibility it has given him. 'But Mum says if what you did is made public, you might end up being charged. I don't want you to go to prison.'

Margie grasps his hand. 'Dear child, it is very kind of you to be concerned for me. You are a good boy. But I would be grateful if you would tell my story. And if it means that I then have to face charges, then I must do so and I will continue to speak out. And I vill have you to thank for that.'

Freddie sits beside her. 'I don't want you to get in trouble, Margie, but I know how to make sure everyone knows your story. And then, if someone decides you have to be charged, it will be because they already know what happened. It won't be like me or Mum feeling bad because we've reported you.'

'Go on, my dear. I am listening.'

'I know I wanted to talk to you because of my school project, and I still do, but if you let me video you, I can upload it onto YouTube and it can all be seen on the internet. That means it will soon be seen by thousands and thousands of people. Then no one can stop you telling the truth.'

'Such a clever boy, you are.' Margie smiles at him, glowing with admiration. 'I don't fully understand what you are saying, but I will do whatever you wish. You know that there are those who deny the extent of the Holocaust and even that it ever happened at all? I would prefer to speak out and challenge those deniers, even if I am made to testify in a court of law. I know what really happened during that dreadful time. I vant to tell the truth. I have hidden away from it nearly all my life and I must speak out now, before it is too late.'

'If it goes viral, Margie, you'll be famous. We could call it something like *The Survivor*.' Freddie is grinning, eager to take up the challenge, while Lauren is silent, but bursting with pride at his assurance and capability.

'I don't want fame,' Margie says. 'I just want to be free of guilt, though I doubt that I ever will be.'

'Well, all you have to do for now is tell me everything. I'll record it all and work out the best way to make sure it's seen by everyone.'

'My dear boy, I don't really understand what you are saying, but if all I have to do is talk, I will do that with you. I may have only typed and filed during my time at the camp, but I knew that I was typing death warrants day after day. But if it hadn't been me who typed those lists, someone else would still have done the work. Those poor souls were always destined to die, maybe not shot or gassed, but they would have been worked to death or succumbed to disease and starvation. That was how the system worked. They had no value for the state, they were meant to die.'

She hands the stuffed brown envelope to Freddie. 'I have been keeping watch for such a long time. These are newspaper cuttings, printed reports of those who have already been charged for their participation in the system over the years. There can't be many of us left now. Some of them were barbarians, it is true, but some, like me, were fooled because we didn't dare to ask questions and challenge the way things were in those days.'

Then she passes him the leather case. 'My dear husband was a good man, but even he was once tempted to benefit from the misfortune of others. I think it was the only time in his life that he let himself down and I was ashamed for him. He took these binoculars from a hoard of stolen goods he took me to see before I left Hamburg. All of it had once belonged to Jewish businesses and families. My husband said he would use them for birdwatching, but I don't think he ever took them out of their case again. He knew he shouldn't have ever taken them and that I didn't approve, and I think that made him feel uncomfortable.

'Property like this was confiscated and hidden in secret all over my country, while the original owners went to their deaths. I want you to have these binoculars, Freddie. They are stolen goods, but if you use them well, you can make things right. You will be able to see the facts for yourself.'

Freddie opens the case, takes out the gleaming binoculars and holds them up to his eyes to look out of the window and across the neighbouring gardens. He adjusts the focus a little and says, 'Thank you, Margie. I can see clearly with these. I can see for myself.'

And Lauren feels a painful lump in her throat. It's telling her that she must leave this matter to her son and Margie now. The old and the young will speak out. What would Colin say if he was here, she asks herself. He'd say, 'You've done all right, love. You can leave them to it now.'

All she has to do is let them carry on and think how proud Colin would have been of their son. She may no longer have a husband with a strong moral code, but she has a son who clearly knows right from wrong. He may still turn to her for comfort and advice, but he doesn't need her to shield him or hold his hand.

'I'll make that tea,' she says. 'You're both going to need a lot of tea with all this talking.'

A LETTER FROM SUZANNE

Thank you so much for choosing to read *The Woman Outside the Walls*. If you did enjoy it, and want to keep up to date with all my latest releases, just sign up at the following link. Your email address will never be shared and you can unsubscribe at any time.

www.bookouture.com/suzanne-goldring

I hope you enjoyed *The Woman Outside the Walls* and if you did, I would be very grateful if you could write a review. I'd love to hear what you think and it makes such a difference helping new readers to discover one of my books for the first time.

I really appreciate hearing from my readers – you can get in touch through my Facebook page, through Twitter or my Wordpress website.

www.suzannegoldring.wordpress.com

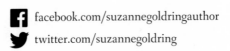

facebook.com/suzannegoldringauthor

twitter.com/suzannegoldring

BACKGROUND TO THE WOMAN
OUTSIDE THE WALLS

On 1 October 2021, I was gripped by the news that a 96-year-old former concentration camp secretary had gone on the run to avoid a war crimes trial. Irmgard Furchner left her nursing home near Hamburg in a taxi and caught a train into the city, where she was found by police a few hours later. Nazi hunter Efraim Zuroff, an American-Israeli who has played an important role in bringing former war criminals to trial, tweeted, 'Healthy enough to flee, healthy enough to go to jail.'

Furchner faced more than 11,000 charges of being an accessory to murder when she was employed as a secretary at Stutthof concentration camp. Christoph Rueckel, a lawyer representing Holocaust survivors, said Furchner typed out deportation and execution orders dictated by the camp commander and initialled each message herself. Yet despite this documentation, she has continued to deny all knowledge of the horrors taking place in the camp.

This case, which at the time of writing has not yet reached a verdict, caused me to set aside the novel I had been planning to write to ask the question – should everyone who played a part in the concentration camp system still be punished, despite their advanced age? And how would any of us react on learning that our docile neighbour might be charged with such crimes? Since I completed *The Woman Outside the Walls*, another case has arisen and has reached its conclusion, with the sentencing of 101-year-old former concentration camp guard Josef Schuetz.

Given the great age of the few surviving Nazi perpetrators, time is running out for the prosecutors. But time is also running out for the remaining survivors of the horrors, who rightly deserve to see the facts recorded and not forgotten in the months or years remaining to them. Christoph Heubner, of the International Auschwitz Committee, which supports camp survivors, said Furchner's escape attempt 'showed contempt for the survivors and also for the rule of law'.

The Woman Outside the Walls is not the story of either of these individuals – my characters are entirely fictional – but it is an exploration of the moral issues surrounding these prosecutions. I wanted to put myself in the place of one who has a close relationship with a person with a past and wrestles with the dilemma of how to respond to the knowledge that they played a part in horrific wartime events.

When I first suggested to my editor that I wanted to develop this theme, I told her that I was going to write about 'the Nazi next-door', for that was how I perceived this story. A kindly old lady who has always seemed to be a good neighbour, trusted to babysit, an inoffensive citizen and a great baker of cakes. I discussed the idea with friends to gauge their reaction and most said they thought that such an elderly person should not be held responsible or punished for the actions of their youth. And given that so much time has passed and some individuals charged with war crimes in earlier trials had served relatively lenient sentences before returning to normal civilian life, can the punishment of the elderly be justified?

This led me to then ask how those facing war crimes

charges had become involved in such terrible deeds in the first place. I saw this process of examination not as condoning their actions in the slightest, but as an attempt to understand. Why did they make the decisions they did? Why did they feel that they were excused because they claimed they were simply 'following orders'?

My research led me to consider the upbringing of the young men and women employed by the state and the persistent moulding of their minds. Education and propaganda cannot excuse brutality, but they are key factors in the shaping of that generation.

As a teenager, studying German at A-level, I travelled from the UK by train to the town of Reutlingen in southern Germany to stay with my penfriend, Lieselotte. She and her family were warm and welcoming and my conversational skills developed rapidly in the two weeks I was there. But subsequently I have often reflected on what her parents might have experienced in the years before, during and after the war. They appeared very traditional in their habits, wearing Tyrolean-style hats, and her father wore lederhosen. Thinking about their ages, they must have been involved with the Hitler Youth, they may have been recruited to fight or they may even have been employed in questionable circumstances. On the surface they were decent citizens and parents of two well-mannered, educated girls, but now I can't help wondering what they had done and what they had seen. However, at the time, at the age of eighteen, I did not have the confidence to challenge them and ask what they had done during the war.

Readers may wonder why I have not identified the camp described in *The Woman Outside the Walls*. Irmgard Furchner worked in Stutthof, which I researched along with other camps. However, I chose not to locate the book in a specific concentration camp, because they were all horrific and all have their own dreadful stories and my story could have occurred in any one of them.

I then had to work out how my character could marry a British soldier and travel to the UK, to eventually be confronted by her sympathetic neighbour. This led me on to Hamburg because the city fell within the British occupied zone at the end of the war. It also allowed me to explore the impact of the war on ordinary Germans and to ask how a returning Nazi who had a conscience might cope in the immediate post-war period.

So, if the characters and the camp depicted in this novel are all fictional, what parts of the story are factual? My research into the devastation of Hamburg is reflected in the sad but true experiences I have woven into the novel. The descriptions of charred bodies, balls of fire, life in cellars and on the streets were all drawn from the reference books listed below, one of which also described the arrest of Ribbentrop in the company of a young woman. All war is terrible, no matter who the instigators may be.

Some readers may question the relevance of the stories collected by the Grimm Brothers, dividing the chapters. But they are far from being 'fairy stories' and as I was writing about the childhood years of Anna and her friend Margarete, referring to the delight they took in the dark theme of Hansel and Gretel, I realised how many traditional German stories contained horrific details. Then, on studying the full Grimm collection of hundreds of tales, I began to feel that these stories expressed a cruel undercurrent to the German psyche.

Finally, in order to give this story some flexibility, I deliberately chose to set it in a time pre-Covid. The characters needed some freedom to tell their tale. I hope you will consider the challenges they faced in the past and more recently and ask yourself, what would I have done, both then and now?

RESEARCH

- *Germany 1945: From War to Peace* – Richard Bessel
- *The Complete Fairy Tales* – The Brothers Grimm
- *Inferno: The Fiery Destruction of Hamburg, 1943* – Keith Lowe
- Auschwitz – Laurence Rees
- *The Last Days of Hitler* – Hugh Trevor-Roper
- *Endgame 1945: Victory, Retribution, Liberation* – David Stafford

BOOK CLUB QUESTIONS

1. Do you think Anna is guilty of a war crime?
2. Is an administrative assistant as guilty as a guard?
3. If Anna is prosecuted, do you think she should be sentenced?
4. Should other members of staff at the camps who were charged and served their time be reinvestigated?
5. Is Lauren right to allow her son to interview Anna?
6. Do you think Lauren should inform the German investigative bureau of Anna's existence?
7. Is the internet the best medium for creating awareness of Anna's past?
8. How do you think Freddie's teachers will react when he tells them about this?

ACKNOWLEDGEMENTS

I am immensely grateful for the support and encouragement of writing friends and colleagues, particularly the Vesta girls, Carol, Denise and Gail. I was also spurred on by the Elstead Writers Group and the Ark Writers, who all commented frankly when we shared our work. I'm particularly grateful to Helen Matthews and Di Stafford, who read an early draft when I was floundering. Special thanks are also due to Tom Searle for his help with Freddie's voice – thank you, Tom.

I feel very fortunate to have the steady support of my editor Lydia Vassar-Smith, who gives me the freedom to embark on challenging journeys of exploration. I am so grateful for her confidence that I will find a story worth telling. I must also thank my agent Heather Holden-Brown for her calming reassurance whenever I think I am getting lost on that journey. And lastly, thanks are due to the entire Bookouture team, who make my books happen and complete the journey from idle thoughts to publication.

Made in United States
North Haven, CT
19 September 2023

41730923R00202